TRIANON

A Novel of Royal France

by Elena Maria Vidal

MAYAPPLE BOOKS   UNIVERSITY PARK, PENNSYLVANIA

First Edition published in 1997 by St. Michaels Press
Second Edition published in 2000 by The Neumann Press

Cover art: "Marie-Antoinette *en gaulle*" by Elisabeth Vigée-Lebrun
Cover design by The Russell Organization
Author's photo by Virginia Crum

ISBN 978-0-557-35171-8

DEDICATED TO THE SACRED HEART OF JESUS

"To glimpse the splendor of supernatural mysteries, reason must have made its sacrifice; it must have renounced seeing by its own light, and must have humbly received the divine light. Similarly, if he is deeply Christian, a deposed king, like Louis XVI, glimpses at the moment of his trial the beauty of the kingdom of God, which is infinitely superior to every earthly kingdom."

—Fr. Reginald Garrigou - LaGrange, O.P. "Effects of the Passive Purification" from *The Three Ages of the Interior Life, Vol. II*

"Never saint more merited to be ranked in the long list of martyrs than Marie Antoinette."

—Catherine Hyde, *Secret Memoirs of Princess Lamballe*

A special thanks to Mrs. Charles Thomas of Lilypons, for her unwavering support and encouragement. I am also grateful to Andrea Vidal Weir and, most especially, to my father, my mother and my husband.

Other Books by Elena Maria Vidal

Madame Royale
The Night's Dark Shade

Visit www.emvidal.com and the *Tea at Trianon* blog,
http://teaattrianon.blogspot.com

TABLE OF CONTENTS

PART I   THE GARDEN

PART II THE CROSS

PREFACE

Trianon is a work of historical fiction. All of the characters were actual people. The incidents, situations and conversations are based on reality. It is the story of the martyred King Louis XVI and his Queen. The fruit of years of research, the book attempts to correct many of the popular misconceptions of the royal couple, which secular and modernist historians have tried so hard to promote. Louis and Antoinette can only be truly understood in view of the Catholic teachings to which they adhered and within the context of the sacrament of matrimony. It was the graces of this sacramental life that gave them the strength to remain loyal to the Church, and to each other, in the face of crushing disappointments, innumerable humiliations, personal and national tragedy, and death itself. Theirs is not a conventional love story; indeed, it is more than a love story. The fortitude they each displayed at the very gates of hell is a source of inspiration for all Christians who live in troubled times. The apocalyptic events through which they lived dealt a serious blow to Christendom from which we have not yet recovered. However, it is necessary to remember that the darkness of the night makes the stars shine with an ever greater resplendence.

LIST OF CHARACTERS

Louis XVI, King of France and Navarre (reigned1774-1793). Born Louis-Auguste, Duc de Berry. Dauphin of France from 1765 to 1774.

Marie-Antoinette, Queen of France. Born Archduchess Maria Antonia Josefa Johanna of Austria, youngest daughter of Holy Roman Emperor Francis Stephen and Empress Maria Theresa.

Louis-Joseph, Dauphin of France. Eldest son of Louis XVI and Marie-Antoinette.

Louis-Charles, Duc de Normandie. Their second son.

Madame Marie-Thérèse-Charlotte of France (Madame Royale). Eldest daughter of Louis XVI and Marie-Antoinette; called *Mousseline la sérieuse.*

Madame Marie-Sophie of France. Their youngest daughter; died in infancy (1787).

Louis XV, King of France and Navarre (reigned 1715-1774). Grandfather of Louis XVI.

Marie Lescinska, Queen of France. Grandmother of Louis XVI. Daughter of Stanislaus Lescinski, King of Poland; died 1768.

Louis the Dauphin. Son of Louis XV; father of Louis XVI; died 1765.

Marie-Josephe de Saxe, Dauphine of France. Mother of Louis XVI; died 1767.

Louis, Duc de Bourgogne. Older brother of Louis XVI; died in childhood.

Louis-Stanislaus-Xavier, Comte de Provence. Brother of Louis XVI; called "Monsieur."

Louis-Charles, Comte d'Artois. Youngest brother of Louis XVI.

Madame Clothilde of France. Sister of Louis XVI; later Queen of Sardinia.

Madame Elisabeth of France (Babette). Youngest sister of Louis XVI.

The Mesdames de France daughters of Louis XV; aunts of Louis XVI. Madame Adelaïde. Madame Victoire. Madame Sophie.

Madame Louise. Mother Thérèse of St. Augustine, Carmelite nun.

Marie-Joséphine, Comtesse de Provence. Born a princess of Savoy. Wife of Provence; called "Madame."

Marie-Thérèse, Comtesse d'Artois. Sister of "Madame"; wife of Artois.

Louis-Antoine, Duc d'Angoulême and Charles-Ferdinand, Duc de Berry. Sons of Comte d'Artois; nephews of Louis XVI.

Louis-Philippe, Duc d'Orléans. Distant cousin of Louis XVI.

Marie-Thérèse-Louise, Princesse de Lamballe. An Italian princess; sister-in-law of Orléans. Widow of the king's cousin. A friend of Marie-Antoinette.

Gabrielle, Duchesse de Polignac. Governess of the Children of France. A friend of Marie-Antoinette.

Madame de Mackau. Subgoverness of the Children of France.

Duc d'Harcourt. Governor of Louis-Joseph, Dauphin of France.

Madame d'Harcourt. His wife.

Joseph II, Emperor of Austria. Marie-Antoinette's eldest brother.

Cardinal de Rohan. Grand Almoner of France.

Madame de Marsan. Governess of Louis XVI.

The Ministers of Louis XVI.
        Maurepas. Calonne. Lomenie de Brienne. Miromesnil.

Marquis de Pezay. Secret Advisor of Louis XVI.

Diane de Polignac. Sister-in-law of Gabrielle de Polignac.

Duc de Vauguyon. Tutor of Louis XVI.

Madame de Noailles. Lady-in-waiting to Marie-Antoinette.

Madame de Pompadour and Madame du Barry. Favorites of Louis XV.

Duc de Choiseul. Prime Minister of Louis XV.

Comte Mercy - Argenteau. The Austrian Ambassador.

Paul, Tsarevitch of Russia. Later Tsar of all the Russias.

Grand Duchess Maria Feodorovna. His wife.

Count Axel von Fersen. A Swedish nobleman.

Abbé Vermond. Reader to Marie-Antoinette.

Abbé Henry Essex Edgeworth de Firmont. A priest for the archdiocese of Paris.

Madame Campan. A maid of Marie-Antoinette.

Cléry. Valet of Louis XVI.

Madame LaMotte. An adventuress.

Cagliostro. An alchemist.

Boehmer. A jeweller.

Madame Vigée-Lebrun. An artist.

Mademoiselle Rose Bertin. A dressmaker.

Robespierre. A Jacobin. Head of the Committee of Public Safety.

Danton. Jacobin leader.

Garat. Minister of Justice in 1793.

Santerre. Head of the National Guard.

Fouquier-Tinville. Public prosecutor.

Pétion. Mayor of Paris.

Hermann. President of the revolutionary tribunal.

Hébèrt. Publisher of the gazette *Père Duchesne.*

Toulan. A guard at the Temple.

Monsieur and Madame Tison. Servants at the Temple.

Sanson. An executioner.

Simon. A cobbler.

Madame Richard. The jailer's wife at the Conciergerie.

Rosalie Lamorlière. A servant at the Conciergerie.

Prologue
Portrait of a Queen

"Favor is deceitful, and beauty is vain: the woman that feareth the Lord, she shall be praised." —Proverbs 31:30

Madame Elisabeth Vigée-Lebrun, autumn, 1787

Madame Vigée-Lebrun dabbed her palette with her paintbrush, tilting her head so that she could see around the edge of her canvas. For the thousandth time, she scrutinized the face of the woman sitting a few yards before her. She reflected and sighed. She began to stroke the surface of the canvas with soft hues of pinks, beiges and whites, in an attempt to capture the silken, translucent quality of the Queen's complexion. Her previous attempts at reproducing on canvas the most radiant skin in all Europe, perhaps in the world, had fallen far short of her own high standards, standards which had won for her positions as a member of the Royal Academy and as court portrait painter. While she was always praised for her magic in making silks and velvets appear as if one's hand could reach into the painting and caress them, as well as for her previous efforts at bringing to life the Queen's famed skin, she, Elisabeth Vigée-Lebrun, was never quite satisfied.

As she delicately applied the paint, she continued to glance at her subject. The eyes, too, were also quite difficult, because of their color, blue—but which blue? Dark blue, of course, a blue which from far away gave the illusion that the eyes themselves were black or slate-colored. But was the dark blue a blueberry-blue or an amethyst blue or a deep sapphire blue? Madame Vigée-Lebrun had a few portraits ago decided upon the sapphire blue, and she hoped that she could once again create just the right hue. With her artist's scrutiny, however, Madame noticed that the Queen's eyes had undergone a transformation over the years. Once they had been rather like the eyes of a doll; large, bright and expressionless. Madame had always wondered about the woman inside. She had wondered, as did many people, whether or not the Queen had a soul. Or whether the cold, gay, but blank expression had been the attempt of a good actress, as Her Majesty was known to be, to protect an exquisitely sensitive psyche from pain and vulnerability. But now, the Queen's eyes had changed. There was a warmth, a light, a genuine amiability, as well as a softness which had not been there before. Madame noted the dilation of the pupils. She could attribute it only to Her Majesty's long-awaited motherhood. Now there was true joy in her laughter. If her eyes were darker and wetter-looking, it was from love, and Elisabeth Vigée-Lebrun knew that Marie Antoinette, Queen of France, did indeed have a soul.

She also had a heart, and a very generous one, as Madame had discovered. All anyone had to do was present oneself before Her Majesty with a tale of financial misfortune or temporal misery in order to receive a pension, a dowry, or whatever else was needed to alleviate one's poverty. The success of the Polignac clan was the consummate example, for which Her Majesty was mercilessly lampooned in the streets of Paris. Madame Vigée-Lebrun had often heard how the Queen would personally collect alms for the poor, going from courtier to courtier with a velvet bag and a dazzling smile. Most people had forgotten how her quip "Belts are no longer worn!" had relieved the populace of a tax known as "the Queen's belt" traditionally levied at the beginning of every new reign. Aside from such obvious instances of largesse, Madame Vigée-Lebrun had her own memory of an incident that went beyond tangible wealth.

She had, several years before, been working on one of her early portraits of the Queen, as well as struggling with the discomforts of an advanced pregnancy. One day she was so ill she was unable to keep an appointment with her august client. The following afternoon, feeling a little better, she hurried (if a woman in her condition can be said to "hurry" at all) to Versailles, by means of a hired carriage, clutching her paint box and easel.

There in the palace courtyard was the Queen about to leave for an afternoon drive. The ostrich plumes and veil of her hat, *à la* Mademoiselle Bertin, were fluttering in the careless breeze. In spite of her agitation, all

Madame Vigée-Lebrun could think of was how the odd greenish-grayish brown color of the Queen's dress so artfully highlighted the auburn tints of her teased and frizzled coiffure. There were those who said that Antoinette of Lorraine-Austria could be cruel and capricious. Madame had never seen such a side of the Queen's personality, if it existed at all. She trembled nevertheless, especially when the Queen, in the midst of extending her gloved hand to a footman in order to climb into the carriage, turned and looked at her. Madame Vigée-Lebrun fell into the deepest curtsey of her life.

"I waited for you all of yesterday morning, Madame," said the Queen, gently. "Whatever happened to you?"

"Oh, Madame, forgive me!" exclaimed the artist. "I was quite sick, and unable to obey Your Majesty's orders." Her heart pounded. "I have come now to receive them, and then I shall go away at once."

"Oh, no, no! Do not go!" The Queen stepped back from her carriage. "I shall not permit you to have made the journey for nothing! Why, I can give you a sitting right now!" With a wave of her hand she dismissed her entourage. The horses clattered away. She directed a young page to take Madame Vigée-Lebrun's cumbersome paint box and easel. "Come," Marie-Antoinette said with a smile.

Breathlessly, with the page at her side, the artist followed the two liveried footmen who walked a slow and respectful distance behind the Lady of Versailles. The courtiers, sightseers and servants in the courtyard parted before her, bowing and curtseying. They entered the palace. The gilded salon was thronging with people. Gentlemen swept off their hats as the Queen passed. The ladies' feathered headdresses trembled as their owners bent like flowers in the wind.

What a crowd it was! In the midst of the aristocrats, Swiss guards, and retainers were foreigners attached to the various embassies, as well as many ordinary French citizens who had come from the provinces in order to catch a glimpse of the King, the Queen, or of any member of the Royal Family. Anyone in proper attire could enter the palace. Men could not be without a hat and a sword, but the latter could be rented from the gatekeeper for a few *sous*. At the foot of the marble staircase and along the galleries, merchants had set up booths and were hawking their wares. Ribbons, jewelry, snuff, silk, perfumes and powder could be purchased by the courtiers without even leaving the palace!

The artist found it rather disconcerting that the Queen's entrance did not stop the tradesmen from their noisy solicitations. Indeed, she noticed that Marie Antoinette's presence elicited not only exterior signs of respect, but some audible hisses and snickers. The throng made the young mother-to-be feel rather faint. She almost swooned from the foul odor which permeated the *château*. It was as bad as the gutters of Paris. Madame Vigée-Lebrun put a perfumed handkerchief over her nose and mouth. She did not know how the Queen, who so loved fresh air and fragrances, could bear to live there. Perhaps that was why she was so often at Trianon.

With great effort, Madame Vigée-Lebrun trailed up the stairs in the Queen's wake. As she watched the woman who glided rather than walked, she could not help wishing for some magical way of capturing Her Majesty's gracefulness on canvas. Unless people with their own eyes actually saw her, they would never understand the liquid, flowing beauty of her every gesture. With a quick, decided gait she floated down the Hall of Mirrors, wide panniers and petticoats billowing around her. The portrait painter was amazed that although the Queen was taller than most French women, even a petite ballerina of the *Comédie Italienne* could not have had a lighter step. She took possession of every room she entered. All eyes were drawn towards her, reflecting either adulation or dislike. Madame knew it was not just because Marie-Antoinette was Queen. She radiated a magnetism; heads would have turned even if she had been an unknown *comtesse* from Languedoc. Whenever she went incognito to the masked balls in Paris, she was recognized within minutes. She had only to take a few steps, make a few gestures, and everyone knew who she was.

They reached the Queen's apartments. Another page emerged out of some corner and opened the door. Bowing, the footmen stood aside, to allow the Queen to enter. Madame Vigée-Lebrun followed, having retrieved her paint box and easel from the attendant. Her Majesty's *femme de chambre*, Madame Campan, and a tiring woman met them inside the door, curtseying deeply. With a nod, she told them they could go. Walking into the Queen's private chambers seemed to be like suddenly finding oneself in a hidden garden. The noise of the merchants, the gossiping of courtiers, even the stench from the antiquated plumbing, all faded away. Bouquets of fresh flowers, mostly roses and blue hyacinths, adorned the rooms of her suite. To Madame Vigée-Lebrun it seemed that the embroidered flowers on the curtains, tapestries, and furniture were also emitting a delicious scent. So skillful was the hand that had executed such needlework that the silken designs appeared to be bursting with life. It was as if one could pick them. Madame was aware that the Queen herself had designed and embroidered some of the work she saw before her.

"Let us go sit in my *méridienne*," said Her Majesty. "Oh, my poor little artist, how weary you must be!"

Going through a small door to the left of the Queen's canopied and beplumed bed, they entered an eight-sided chamber which was more like a jewel-box than a boudoir. A clock cheerfully chimed on the marble mantelpiece. Behind it was a mirror which reflected the golden cherubs, peacocks, dolphins, and garlands of flowers on the walls and ceilings. There were several elegant but sturdy, roomy chairs, all upholstered in an azure silk. Known as "Louis XVI" style, they were the sort of chairs that could hold a hardy, husky, well-built man, the kind of man who liked to hunt all day and make things with his hands. It was the Queen who had encouraged their design. She had a passion for beautiful things but like a typical Austrian, she wanted them to be useful and practical as well.

"The lighting is good here, don't you think? Shall we begin?" The Queen sat in a chair by the window. It reached almost to the ceiling, as did all the windows of the chateau, and allowed a breeze to fan the room. The artist hastily began to set up her easel, carefully putting a cloth under it so as not to get paint on the floor. At that moment the worst happened. She dropped her box of paints. Her little vials of paint, brushes of various widths and lengths, palette and rags, all tumbled in a heap, then scattered on the polished parquet. Madame Vigée-Lebrun gasped and tried to bend down.

"No, no!" exclaimed the Queen. "Not in your condition!" She rose from her chair. "Let me do it for you."

"Oh, no! Your Majesty, please do not!" cried the artist. Blushing, she watched the daughter of the great Empress Maria Theresa get down on her hands and knees to pick up the paints and brushes.

*****

It was something she had never forgotten. Now, several years and several portraits later, while ribald songs and obscene drawings defaming the Queen were boldly circulated throughout Paris, Madame Vigée-Lebrun recognized that they had no connection at all with the serene and lovely woman who delighted in flowers and children. She glanced at the Queen again in her red velvet dress that was somewhere between the

color of garnets and of blood. In many ways, Marie-Antoinette was still the child-bride, separated so prematurely from her mother and her homeland. Her innocence and sincerity made her open prey for devious minds. She had blossomed, with a rich and ripening beauty that came not from midnight dancing at the opera ball, or having Monsieur Léonard dress her hair, but from domestic tranquility and maternal fulfillment. So whenever Madame Vigée-Lebrun heard stories of the Queen's late night card parties, of her appearances at horse races, of her acting in her private theatre at Trianon, of huge sums spent on diamonds, she ignored them, knowing that for the Queen those amusements were things of the past. She was, in the artist's view, the kindly woman who had gotten on her knees to pick up paints for an expectant mother. It was a picture that Madame Elisabeth Vigée-Lebrun
would keep in mind forever.

Part I
The Garden

Chapter One
The Morning Oblation

"My sister, my spouse is a garden enclosed . . . . " —Canticle of Canticles 4:12

Madame Louise of France at early Mass, October 15, 1787

The tower bell at the Carmel of St. Denis announced to the town that Holy Mass was about to begin. The nuns, having just recited the Little Hours, were kneeling by their benches in the monastery choir, clothed in white mantles and long choir veils. Silent and still, the nuns knelt in two lines, one on either side of the choir. In the front, near the grate, were the novices and lay sisters, veiled in white; toward the back were the black-veiled, senior members of the community. There were two stalls on either side of a venerable statue of Our Lady of Mt. Carmel. In front of the stalls knelt the Prioress and the Subprioress. The Subprioress glanced at the Prioress, worried that she had been kneeling far too long for a woman of her age and health. The eyes of the Prioress were fixed on the flickering red of the Presence lamp, discernible in spite of the iron grate that separated the sisters' choir from the outer church. Mother Subprioress knew that Reverend Mother's thoughts were with the Divine Person in the tabernacle, and that if she felt any discomfort in her knees, her heart was momentarily unaware of it, being absorbed into an agony greater than her own.

The bell over the sacristy door could be heard, the signal that the priest was beginning to ascend the altar. The nuns rose and began to chant the *Introit* for the Mass of St. Teresa: *Non turbetur cor vestrum. Creditis in Deum, et in me credite. In domo Patris mei mansiones multae sunt.* (Let not your heart be troubled; you believe in God, believe also in Me. In My Father's house there are many mansions.) The Prioress, Mother Thérèse of St. Augustine, felt tears come to her eyes. How blessed she was to have been called to this holy house, this House of the Blessed Virgin, to spend her days among the Brides of Christ as a daughter of the great Saint Teresa. It was Saint Teresa's Day, a high and holy feast day for all Discalced Carmelite Nuns, and her own name-day feast. It would be a special recreation day for her community, a departure from their rigorous routine. There would be songs and plays in honor of the Holy Mother, the Reformatrix of Carmel. At dinner there would be a suspension of the seven-month Carmelite fast, so that the sisters could enjoy a few treats for dessert. By all worldly standards, the feast-day meals would be simple ones, since the nuns were vowed to poverty, and practiced perpetual abstinence from meat.

Mother Thérèse of Saint Augustine led her daughters in chanting the *Kyrie* and the *Gloria*. How happy she had been ever since she had come to embrace a life of austerity and deprivation! The brown serge habit, and even the prickly hair shirt she insisted on wearing next to her skin, gave her greater joy than any of the silks and brocades she had worn at Court. How much better she slept on the straw tick laid across rough planks than amid the downy coverlets of her bed at Versailles! It was less exhausting to rise at dawn to begin a day of prayerful solitude than to stumble back to her rooms after a midnight supper or dance. At the palace she had always been ailing, but once in the monastery her health improved, as did that of most novices who truly have a vocation to the cloister. Often in her prayers, she savored the verse from Psalm 83: "Better is one day in thy courts above thousands. I have chosen to be an abject in the house of my God than dwell in the tabernacles of sinners."

She had remembered at the beginning of Mass to pray for the soul of her father, King Louis XV. She prayed for him at every Mass, and would continue to do so for the rest of her life. He had mercifully repented and confessed his sins a few days before he died of smallpox, after giving scandal to all Christendom for more than thirty years. She prayed for her mother, Queen Marie Lezcinska, whose heart he had broken. She begged God to have mercy on the soul of Madame la Marquise de Pompadour, who had not only corrupted her father, but had persuaded him to expel the Jesuits.

Mother Thérèse sighed. Where were the Jesuits when they needed them most? With the universities and *philosophes* spewing vile attacks on religion in the most eloquent manner possible, without the learning and logic of the Jesuits the cause of the True Faith in France was as good as lost. Her brother, Louis the Dauphin, had foreseen such a sad state of affairs. He had tried to stop the infamous abolition of the sons of Saint Ignatius from disgracing the house and name of Bourbon. Too wickedly clever, however, had been La Pompadour and her ally, the Duc de Choiseul. The King had listened to them. Her brother had died before he could inherit the throne. The good fathers were gone, their schools taken over by incompetent and often corrupt secular clergy. There remained only the prayers and sacrifices of a few faithful souls, the herculean efforts of her devout nephew King Louis XVI, and the mercy of the Sacred Heart.

Her large, deep-set blue eyes were drawn back to the Presence lamp, glimmering in the candle-lit sanctuary. Sometimes, when she prayed alone at night, the lamps took on the aspect of a heart, throbbing in the darkness. Truly, it was the merciful Heart of God who had led her here!

She remembered the first time she had ever knelt in that choir, still wearing a wide-panniered court dress, the plainest one she had possessed. A voluminous traveling cloak was draped around it and a straw hat with a pretty pink ribbon hid her powdered coiffure; she wept profusely. She had run away from home that very morning. Everyone, including her attendants, had thought she was just going to early Mass at the Carmelite Chapel. The lady-in-waiting became faint when she realized that her mistress planned to stay! Her father the King had not wanted her to go. In many long conversations he had tried to dissuade her. When he saw how determined she was to enter religion, he gave his consent. He knew she planned on slipping away from court in secret. Her confessor had long given his consent, and had helped her to choose the poorest, strictest Carmel in France. Her tears, when she finally found herself in the cloister, were those of supreme exaltation. She begged the nuns not to spare her in their observance of the Rule because of her royal birth.

At the same grate she had had the happiness of receiving the holy habit of Carmel. She willingly changed the cloth of silver bridal array for the brown serge tunic and hemp sandals. Her nephew's new bride, Antoinette of Austria, had assisted the papal nuncio in giving her the veil.

22

On the day of her profession, at the moment she pronounced her vows, the bells of Saint Denis began to peal. The pealing was taken up by churches in other towns and cities, by Notre Dame in Paris, by the Royal Chapel of Versailles, so that soon all the bells of France were announcing the news that the oblation had been made. The King's daughter had offered herself as a holocaust to God for the salvation of France, and of France's king. Madame Louise of France had truly died. She would henceforth be known as Sister Thérèse of St. Augustine, unworthy Carmelite. Morning after morning, she renewed her oblation in union with the Divine Victim of the Eucharistic sacrifice. Moment by moment, she sought to master herself by surrendering her will to God, even through periods of darkness and aridity, when it seemed that all spiritual sweetness had been only a dream. Much against her will, she had been repeatedly elected and reelected to the office of Mother Prioress, a role in which she had to command others and have much contact with the outside world.

At Communion time, she veiled the upper part of her face and led the other sisters to the tiny communion window, where one by one each knelt to receive her Lord. While making her thanksgiving, she tried not to think of the pile of letters on her desk, an assortment of everything from petitions for money to feast-day greetings. One of the letters was a greeting from the Mother Prioress of the Carmel of Compiègne. She could remember the first letter she had received in that handwriting. It had been a plea from the pious but penniless Mademoiselle Lidoine, who without a dowry could not enter Carmel. How odd that it was the lively Antoinette who had happily complied with Mother Thérèse's request, and furnished a dowry for the poor girl. Mademoiselle Lidoine was now the prioress of the Carmel of Compiègne; a monastery whose holiness and austerity evoked the awe and admiration of the other French Carmels. The little Lidoine had been named in honor of the prioress of Saint Denis. She was now a "Mother Thérèse of Saint Augustine," too. Her benefactress had made her promise that she would always pray for Louis and Antoinette, who had helped to make her vocation possible.

After folding up her mantle and choir veil and giving them to a postulant to put away, she processed with the nuns to the room set aside for recreation for some feast day coffee, hot chocolate and pastries. As she received the good wishes and embraces of the sisters, she found her thoughts turning again to Louis and his wife. Whispers of her nephew's deficiencies reached her even behind Carmel's walls. He was said to be dull, stupid and apathetic. She knew only too well that devout people are always thought to be doltish and obtuse by worldly ones. She herself was said to be a dreary spinster who had fled to Carmel to escape the colorless old maidenhood that was the lot of her three older sisters. "If only I were a little more dull!" she sighed. The gossips had no idea of her epic struggles with her temper, her pride, and her quick tongue. And they did not know her love of the chase. It was a great mortification for her to never again gallop through the park of Versailles or the forest of Compiègne. She had delighted in stag hunting with her father and young nephews. She missed the intoxicating fresh air and the exciting illusion of freedom.

After taking some coffee, she returned to her cell for an hour or so of quiet reading and letter writing. Upon entering her cell, her "little heaven," she prostrated and kissed the cold stone floor as a customary act of gratitude to the Mother of God for bringing her to Carmel. The plain, whitewashed walls were adorned by two simple engravings-one of Our Lady of Mt. Carmel holding the Infant, and the other of St. Teresa encountering the seraph with his fiery dart. On the wall over the head of the bed was a bare wooden cross. It had no Corpus. The Carmelite nun was to think of herself as the body on the cross. She remained on her knees for a few minutes, meditating on the naked cross. Every day at three o'clock, all of the nuns would stop whatever they were doing and pray, arms extended, for the conversion of sinners and the salvation of the dying. Mother Thérèse often prayed that way at other times of the day, too, ignoring the pains in her chest and arms. She would think of His pain, of His Heart, His bleeding Heart. She quoted to herself from the prophet Zacharias: "And they shall look upon Him Whom they have pierced: and they shall mourn for Him as one mourneth for an only son, and they shall grieve over Him, as the manner is to grieve for the death of the first born." She prayed for France, the country of the Sacred Heart's special predilection, for her family, and especially for the King.

She recalled the day she had said goodbye to her nieces and nephews before stealing away to Carmel. They had clung to their "Tante Louise," all of them weeping.

"Don't go, don't leave us, Tante Louise!" implored stout Provence, blowing his nose.

"I shall die. I shall die without you!" cried gallant Artois, melodramatically hiding his face in her sleeve.

"Take us with you! Let me follow you!" exclaimed plump Clothilde and little Babette, faces buried in her skirts. Only Berry, the future Louis XVI, was silent. A serious boy of few words, his usual reserve now seemed to build a wall between himself and his siblings. He stood apart for a while, face pale, and then he slowly came to her. Without a word, he put his strong but gangly arms around her. As he kissed her cheeks, he bathed her face in his tears. She knew that he felt the pain of separation much more deeply than the others, but that the piercing of the soul often leaves one speechless. This was the boy whom those who knew no better labeled as phlegmatic and apathetic, but who, at the age of twenty, when his beloved grandfather had died, had fallen to his knees in unison with his wife, both begging God to save them. "We are too young to reign!" they had wept.

She could picture them so clearly, although at the time she had been miles away at Saint Denis. Even so, thirteen years later, her heart still went out to the frightened young couple; she longed to embrace and comfort them. Getting up and going to the little table that served as her desk, she noticed a pile of scapulars and Sacred Heart badges that she kept to send to benefactors. She would send some to Louis and Antoinette with her next letter. Some of the brown scapulars even had the Sacred Hearts of Jesus and Mary embroidered on them, a favored devotion of the royal family. She knew that at Versailles things that ordinary Catholics took for granted were sometimes hard to come by.

She began to read a feast-day greeting from the King. At that moment there was a knock at the door. "*Ave Maria*," said Mother Thérèse. A nun entered the cell. It was the Mistress of Novices. She knelt before the prioress and kissed the superior's scapular.

"How can I help you, my daughter?" asked Mother Thérèse.

"Mother," began the Mistress of Novices, remaining on her knees, according to custom, "*benedicite* to speak with you about one of the novices."

"Let me guess," said Mother. "Is it Sr. Angélique?"

"Why, yes, Mother. How did Your Reverence know?"

"I was watching Her Charity today at Mass, and noticed a rather long tendril escape from beneath her toque. She has not yet cut her hair, has she?"

"No, Your Reverence, she has not."

"Why?" asked the Mother, gently.

"Her Charity is afraid of what will happen if she is sent back home. People in the world would laugh at her if she returned without any hair, or so she says."

"Please bring the novice to me at once," Mother Thérèse commanded.

"Yes, Mother." The nun kissed her superior's scapular again, and withdrew.

Mother Thérèse continued to read the King's letter. He assured her of his love, and then, as he usually did in his letters to her, began to unburden his heart.

> As you know, *ma chère* Tante, the American War left us with quite a deficit. Furthermore, inflation is rising. We cannot borrow any more money, and I do not wish to raise taxes. Instead, it has long been my goal to correct the injustices in our present tax system by not only entirely abolishing the *corvée* and allowing a free corn trade, but also by instituting a land tax. The land tax will cause the nobles and wealthy bourgeois to contribute a larger share to the public well-being; a burden will be lifted off the backs of the poor. In February of this year I summoned the Assembly of Notables to gain their support for my plan. I told them, with Monsieur Calonne's help and theirs, I intended to relieve the people, increase tax revenues, and diminish obstacles to trade, all to build a more prosperous France. Led by the wealthy, higher clergy, the Notables rejected my plan, accusing Calonne my minister of ineptitude. I had to let him go, to be replaced by the Archbishop of Toulouse, whose lack of religious convictions you are well aware.
>
> I dissolved the Assembly of Notables in May and presented the program to the *parlements*. Even though I made it clear that I was willing to share my power with the provincial assemblies, those red-robed lawyers of the *parlements* have refused to register my edicts. They care only for their own bank accounts and popularity!

Pray for me, Tante Louise! So often I am filled with anger at those stubborn judges and politicians—so full of talk about the rights of man. Yet they care for no one's rights but their own. As long as they live in comfort and luxury, the poor can rot. Our Cousin Orléans does much to arouse discontent, especially at his lodge of the Nine Sisters, which is why last August I ordered all the clubs in Paris to be closed. They do nothing at their clubs but foment discord and treason. I do not know where all of this will end. Pray for me. At times my heart is overwhelmed with dread. Louis.

Another knock came at the door. "*Ave Maria*," Mother said. A white veiled novice entered. She kissed Mother Thérèse's scapular. Mother looked with compassion on the kneeling girl. It was never easy for her to administer a correction, even when it was deserved, but it was her duty to admonish when necessary, or else the community would become lax.

"My child," she said, making her voice severe. "We have come to Carmel to die for Christ. There should be no humiliation too great for sinful nothings like ourselves. So what is this I hear, sister, that you are refusing to cut your hair?" As she spoke, the girl kissed the floor, raising her head again only when Mother touched her shoulder.

"Oh, Mother!" Tears streamed down the novice's face. "I am so afraid of being sent home. What a dishonor to my family it would be! And then not to have any hair! I should have to wear a funny old wig. What a disgrace!"

Mother Thérèse put her arms around the nun. "My child, the only true disgrace is sinful pride. It is no disgrace to be sent home if one does not have a Carmelite vocation. As for not having any hair, remember that humiliations are good for the soul—what else do we have to offer to the Good God?"

"Oh, yes, my Mother," the girl sniffingly agreed.

"But you, my child you do have a vocation—or so it has seemed thus far. You must prove to us that you can practice perfect obedience by going to the sister barber today to have your hair cut. Then if you obey in little things, we will know you are prepared to obey in big things, and are ready to make your holy vows. Do you understand, my child?"

"Yes, Mother." No sooner had the girl left, than the Mother Subprioress appeared. She was in her late thirties, young for a subprioress, but wisdom shone in her eyes.

"Come in, Mother Subprioress." She came, giving the customary mark of obeisance. "Sit on the bench, my daughter," said Mother Thérèse. "I do not know what you desired to see me about, but I am glad you came by. There is much on my mind that I wish to discuss with you."

"Mother, I came because I have been concerned about Your Reverence's health. The Mass today was longer than usual and Your Reverence was on your knees through almost all of it. And the physician said...."

Mother Thérèse interrupted her. "Sister, Our Lord will take care of this old nun. I am touched by your concern, but there are far graver matters than my health that I wish to confide."

"What is it, Mother?"

"I have just received a letter from my nephew the King. His Majesty says he is filled with dread at the political and economic situation in the kingdom."

"Truly, Mother?"

"Yes. We must pray very hard. It brought to mind another letter I received yesterday from my sister, Madame Adelaïde. It was full of disturbing rumors about the Queen."

The Subprioress nodded. "I know what you mean, Mother. The letters from my relatives speak of almost nothing but Her Majesty. Apparently the gazettes are full of complaints against her."

"And most of it pure garbage and nonsense, I dare say," said Mother Thérèse. "However, my sister wrote to me that Antoinette entertains quite lavishly at Trianon for a select group of friends. Adelaïde says that by doing so she alienates many influential families."

The Subprioress was silent for a moment, as if searching for words. "Mother," she said at last, "may I ask Your Reverence, since you have known Her Majesty for almost twenty years, what do you think of her? Is she capable of the dissipation of which they accuse her?"

Mother Thérèse searched into the past. "I remember when she first came to visit me here at Carmel. She was not quite fifteen, and talked too much as young girls do, saying whatever came into her head. I must admit I found her frankness to be charming in a rather disconcerting way. I could see that she had many virtues which only wanted cultivation. Her main faults were, and still are, a lack of prudence and discretion. She is quick to like or dislike someone, and once she has chosen a friend, she is intensely loyal, but sometimes to the wrong people."

"I have heard that Her Majesty's education was sadly deficient in many areas. Surely, that does not include her religious upbringing? It is said that the Empress Maria Theresa was very devout."

Mother nodded. "As far as I can deduce Her Majesty's religious training was quite sound. She is naturally vivacious, but has great purity of mind and heart. You must never believe any of the talk about her having lovers. If she is nothing else, she is true to her faith, true to the teachings of her childhood, and true to her husband the King."

"Their Majesties visit Your Reverence three times a year. It has seemed to me the Queen's calm and dignity have increased with age."

"Yes, sister. Motherhood has enriched her character, and sorrow, too. She lost the great Empress, her mother, in 1781, and just last summer, she lost a child."

"It is said that Her Majesty is close to Your Reverence's niece, Madame Elisabeth. She has had a beneficial influence on her, has she not?"

Mother Thérèse smiled. "Babette is high-spirited and fun-loving, like the Queen. They both enjoy dancing and playacting, gardens and children, and caring for the needs of the poor. Babette, however, through her devotional reading and contemplation has acquired a wisdom beyond her twenty-three years that makes her a worthy spiritual guide for the Queen. How Babette longed to be a Carmelite!"

"I know how edified we are all by Madame Elisabeth whenever she comes to stay with us here at Carmel. When she served the community in the refectory, then dropped the tray of food, she kissed the floor like the humblest postulant or novice."

Mother's eyes misted. "It had been her cherished dream to take the Carmelite habit, but her brother, the King, forbade it. 'The day is coming when we will need you here,' he said to her. I do believe that Babette remains in the world for a purpose that has yet to be revealed. Meanwhile, she satisfies her thirst for a life in God's service by reciting the Divine Office with her ladies at her country house at Montreuil, where she operates a dairy farm to provide milk for poor children."

"She is a Carmelite in her own way, Mother," said the Subprioress.

"Yes, she is. But there is another thing that has occurred to me lately. Do you remember when last June in the refectory, we read the writings of the holy Visitandine nun, Sister Marguerite-Marie Alacoque, who died about a century ago?"

"Surely, my Mother."

"Are you aware that those revelations, which she received at Paray-le-Monial from Our Lord Himself, have been the source of the greatest contention and controversy within the Church?"

"I know, Mother, that the Jansenists have opposed the devotion to the Sacred Heart, calling it 'cardiolatry.' They seem to consider it presumptuous to place such emphasis on God's love and infinite mercy. As for the *philosophes*, our enlightened men of science, it is not one more Catholic teaching for them to scoff at, rather they seem to regard the Sacred Heart with a singular malice, ridiculing it whenever possible."

"If you recall, my child, Our Lord told Sister Marguerite Marie that the King of France is the 'eldest son' of His Sacred Heart."

"Oh, yes. Is it not because France was the first western nation to embrace the Christian faith?"

"That is correct. When my ancestor Clovis was baptized at Rheims, and the dove brought the Sacred Ampulla out of Heaven to St. Rémy, he became the first Christian monarch, and in some ways, the First among Christian monarchs, the 'heir to the Tribe of Judah,' as Pope Gregory IX wrote to St. Louis himself. Other nations followed the lead of France in accepting the Faith, but France has always been considered the 'Eldest Daughter of the Church.'"

"Mother, did not Our Lord ask King Louis XIV to consecrate France to His Sacred Heart, in order to triumph over the enemies of the Church?"

"It is that which troubles me, child. My great, great-grandfather the King was charged to perform such a consecration, but he did not, because his spiritual director advised him not to do so. Sometimes, I wonder if the decline in vocations, in clerical fervor, and in religion in general, would be as bad as it is today if the consecration to the Sacred Heart had been made as requested by Heaven?"

"Oh, my Mother, no one but God has the answer to such a question."

"Nevertheless, sister, I think my nephew should make the consecration. If the political situation has not improved by Christmas, I will advise him to do so, asking the Holy Father for permission if necessary. What consequences will come to France, and to the rest of Europe, which so often follows her example, because of the failure to make the consecration, I do not know. But when I hear of riots, of scandals, of nobles openly defying the King's authority, it frightens me."

"Mother, you are right to try to encourage His Majesty to make the consecration."

"I only hope it will not be too late. Well, Mother Subprioress, it is almost time to go down for examen and dinner. *Benedictus Deus in donus suis* for listening to me."

The Subprioress kissed Mother's scapular. "I will pray for the King, my Mother. I will pray without ceasing." She left.

After writing a few letters, Mother Thérèse left her cell. She went out onto the upper gallery which looked down into the quadrangle, where chrysanthemums were still blooming at the foot of a marble crucifix. To her, even the sunlight in Carmel seemed different from light in the outside world; it was brighter, almost tangible. She pondered the fate of France. In some mysterious way it was bound up with devotion to the Sacred Heart. In her cloistered, silent world, God's own garden, she and her nuns were at the pulsating center not only of the kingdom but of the universal Church. Great events were about to unfold and her intuition of them sometimes felt as if it would crush her being.

As she passed the novitiate, she decided to stop in the novices' tiny oratory. On the altar was a statue of the Child Jesus. Like the statue that had once belonged to the Holy Mother St. Teresa, the hands and feet of the Infant bore a bloody stigmata. She paused, as if transfixed. It is always the innocent who suffer for the guilty. Her nephew, King Louis XVI, was such an innocent. She was aware how seriously he took his spiritual duties as Grand Master of the Knights of Saint Lazare of Jerusalem and Our Lady of Mt. Carmel. As sovereign, he was also Grand Master of the Order of the Holy Spirit. He was so like St. Louis, the crusader-king. By all accounts, on that glorious Trinity Sunday in 1774, he had made his coronation oath in a voice that prayed rather than mechanically recited a formula. Before the crown was placed on his head, he was anointed nine times with the sacred chrism, holy oils, and the miraculous unction from the Holy Ampulla of Saint Rémy, conferring upon him the first degree of Holy Orders, although not the priesthood. Henceforth, he alone among laymen would be permitted to drink from the Chalice of the Precious Blood at Mass. As the anointed of the Lord, he had to be ready to shed his own blood for the Church and for his people.

31

The sense of approaching doom oppressed her at times. She spent nights before the Blessed Sacrament as she had when her father was dying. Now it was not her father who was dying, but France, royal France. It was as if the soul of the kingdom were being eaten away. Stories came to her of the Duc d' Orléans and his coterie at the Palais Royal, the site of so many indecencies, masonic cabals and pamphleteering. Poor Louis! One man could not deal with so many demons. She once again made the interior offering of herself. Her family had contributed to the moral decay. Her family would have to pay, but, as always, it is the innocent who paid. She gazed at the Infant Jesus with His plump cheeks, solemn eyes, and mysterious, all-knowing smile. She remembered something. She had forgotten at Mass to pray for her little niece, Louis' daughter, Marie-Thérèse. It was her feast-day, too. Soon it would be time for the midday Mass at Versailles, and the nine-year-old princess would be there. Uniting with the Mass, and with the Masses of all times and places, she knelt before the Infant, and prayed.

Chapter Two
The Angel

"See that you despise not one of these little ones: for I say to you, that their angels in heaven always see the face of my Father Who is in heaven." – *St. Matthew 18:10*

Madame Marie-Thérèse-Charlotte of France, noon Mass, October 15, 1787

A little girl with a white lacy cap, a halo of blonde curls, and ringlets falling down her back, knelt at Mass. The noon October sun illuminated the white and gold Royal Chapel. As the Grand Almoner intoned the *Gloria in Excelsis*, the words mingled with the trembling brightness. The little girl had a very serious expression. Almost nine years old, she was able to follow the Mass in her red, leather-bound missal, stamped with the golden *fleur-de-lys*. Her lowered eyes did not fail to take in the shimmer of the silken, embroidered vestments and altar linens; the flash of jewels on the sacred vessels, the blaze of candles.

Every time her name, or rather, the name of the great *Sancta Teresia* was invoked, she felt a flutter as if a caged bird was about to escape from her chest and fly to the frescoed ceiling. It was grand to have a feast-day that one shared with her sainted, departed Austrian Grandmama-Empress and her equally sainted, still living Tante Louise who, like Saint Teresa herself, was a Carmelite nun. She remembered going to visit her Tante Louise for the first time. Maman had a tiny nun's habit made for a doll, so that she Thérèse could get used to what a nun looked like, and would not be frightened when she saw her aunt. Papa always told her that it was a great honor to have a cloistered religious in the family. Madame Royale, as the little girl was officially called, knew that her patroness Saint Teresa had seen angels many times. A seraph once actually pierced the saint's heart with a fiery dart. She wondered if her aunt in the Carmel had ever seen an angel. Would she, Marie-Thérèse-Charlotte, ever see one, that is, before she went to heaven? She raised her eyes to look at the gilded angels bent in homage on either side of the tabernacle. What did angels really look like? Her catechism said that angels were pure spirits, possessing memory, intellect and will, but no bodies. Nevertheless, saints had often seen them. Her eyes watched the elevation of the Sacred Host in that moment when the seen and Unseen become one, that moment that is beyond the limits of time. She knew that God was there, in the Sacred Host, just as she knew that the angels were there, all around her, adoring the Hidden Deity, although her vision failed to penetrate the veil of eternity.

Madame Royale knelt in the chapel with her family. Out of the corner of her eye, she saw her Papa, the King, strike his breast at the elevation of the chalice containing the Most Precious Blood. Papa loved God very much. His love for God was so immense, so ardent, that she, Thérèse, felt absorbed into it. He did not speak much of it; he did not have to. He demonstrated his faith in every aspect of his life. He was patient, hard-working, generous, and kindly, although sometimes his brusque manner and blunt statements were misunderstood. But Thérèse always understood her Papa; he, too, seemed to have a little window into her heart. Words were usually unnecessary between them. He had only to pat her shoulder, tug on one of her curls, to let her know he sympathized with her completely.

Her Papa was the strongest man at Versailles. With one arm, he could lift a page sitting on the end of a spade. This was because he took after his mighty Saxon grandfather. Also, he worked every morning at his forge in the attic, making locks, and other things from iron, copper, and bronze. He could fix any of their toys that broke. He was as brave as he was strong. He could hold a fierce boar at bay, and slay it with his own hands. In the evenings, before going to his study for more long hours of work, he would come and play with Thérèse and her brothers. He would read to them from his favorite novel, *Robinson Crusoe*; he would ask them riddles and tell them stories of heroes of antiquity, of the great Kings of France, and of lives of the saints, especially French ones. They would all climb onto his lap, where they felt very safe. Such was his strength that he could easily stand up holding all three of them in his arms. The other children who lived at Versailles loved him, too, even though he was not their Papa. Her cousins, Angoulême and Berry; her companions,

Ernestine and Zoë, and even the children of the servants, would run to him to be swung up into the air.

Once in a while, Thérèse would go to her father's apartments. There he kept many fascinating objects. He had scale-models of ships that he wanted to build for the navy, as well as models and blue-prints of the latest inventions. He possessed innumerable, colorful maps, some of which he had drawn himself, in addition to globes, tools and instruments for map-making, charts, clocks and barometers. His library was one of his greatest treasures. He had magnificent atlases, almanacs, dictionaries, the great authors of classical times and all that French literature had to offer. He had a set of Shakespeare's works, and authors of many different countries in languages both ancient and modern. Thérèse was certain that her father was the wisest, strongest, most learned King who had ever lived.

On the other side of her father knelt her mother, the Queen. If Thérèse turned her head slightly she could see the edges of her Maman's black lace mantilla. She could not see her mother's face, but she guessed that her eyes were probably misting, as they often did since Baby Sophie died. Only three months ago, her sister had been toddling about after two year old Charles, laughing like a little bell. She had suddenly gotten very sick, and within a few days she was as cold and still as a wax doll. Her Maman had wept as never before. She had not shed so many tears even during the terrible disturbance over the diamond necklace, an affair which Thérèse had never really understood. She had only gathered that some very wicked people had stolen a very valuable necklace, then had told lies about it. Cardinal de Rohan, who had baptized and christened her, had somehow been involved in it, and was sent away from court. Maman's eyes had been red for months over the diamond trouble. She had stopped rehearsals for the new play she was about to perform at Trianon. She had never again acted in any plays; the little blue and gold *papier-maché* theatre was silent. Dear Baby Sophie! Thérèse had loved having her own baby sister. Princesse de Lamballe and Tante Babette had tried to dry Maman's tears, telling her that baptized children go straight to Heaven.

"Oh, yes," sobbed the Queen. "I firmly believe it. But she might have grown up to be a friend."

"Dear sister," said Tante Babette. "She is now doubly your friend. She is like an angel before the throne of God, and will pray for you, watching over us all." Since Sophie's death, Maman had been much longer at her prayers. The rosary was often seen moving through her fingers. She began to receive Holy Communion more frequently. Today, Maman planned on communicating because it was the feast-day of Empress Maria Theresa, and she wished to pray in a special way for her mother's soul. Thérèse had not yet made her first Holy Communion, but she would make an act of spiritual Communion, as her parents had taught her.

Next to Thérèse's mother knelt her brother, Louis-Joseph, Dauphin of France. In exactly one week he would turn six, but he seemed much older. For one thing, he could already read, and amazed his governor, Monsieur d'Harcourt, with his retentive memory. He was a very truthful boy, who never defended himself when corrected. He was a handsome boy, particularly in his blue velvet sailor suit. Louis-Joseph had his own little garden, outside of his apartments, near the parterre. Every morning in good weather, he and Papa would work in the garden together. Papa said that not only was gardening beneficial for one's constitution, but also it was important for a future King of France to learn agriculture, since that was how the majority of his subjects made their living. In the last few months, Louis-Joseph had not been well and complained of pains in his back. The doctors were often examining him, their faces grave. Thérèse once overheard Madame d'Harcourt whisper to Madame de Mackau, the sub-governess: "I doubt that he will ever be king." They had thought Thérèse was playing with her dolls and had not heard them. But she had.

Charles, the little Duc de Normandie, was too young to come to Mass every day. He was in the nursery with Madame de Polignac, where he could run, climb, laugh, and ride his rocking-horse. She would see him that afternoon, when they would all go to Trianon together. Thérèse knew that she must not give into distractions at Mass, but it took quite an effort not to think of Trianon. There were no crowds there, no gossiping courtiers. She and her brothers could run and play on the lawn, feed the hens, stroke the cows and watch them being milked; take turns churning the butter. It was always so jolly there. And today, her special day, she was going to spend the entire afternoon at Trianon.

She pushed the thoughts of Trianon from her mind and applied herself to her prayers. It was communion time. She saw her Maman rise and approach the altar. Thérèse knew Maman had been fasting all day, which was difficult for the Queen to do; it made her feel faint and a bit dizzy. It was not difficult for Papa, however. He rigorously fasted every day of Lent, taking only his usual bread and lemon juice for breakfast and a meatless repast in the evening. It was a sacrifice for him, because she knew how at other times of the year he enjoyed a hearty supper, especially after a day of hunting.

The Grand Almoner gave the final blessing, and Mass ended. After praying quietly a few minutes, the Royal Family rose and left the chapel. They went to dinner. Thérèse could hardly eat for excitement. Finally the meal was over, and she was in her *petits cabinets* being changed into an afternoon dress of silk with yellow and blue stripes; muslin fichu around the neck and shoulders; a straw hat on her head. It was so difficult for her to keep from running down the rose-colored marble stairs to the carriage. It was a fine day, quite warm for October, and the sun was bright upon the open carriages, which took them off in the direction of Trianon. Maman and Princesse de Lamballe, the Superintendent of the Queen's Household, sat in the same carriage with Thérèse, Ernestine and Zoë. In the other carriage were her brothers with Madame de Polignac, Governess of the Children of France and Madame de Mackau the subgoverness. They laughed and were very gay.

Before long, they were driving through the black, golden-tipped gates of the Little Trianon. The carriages were reined in in front of the classically simple, square house, brownish-beige in color, with large, rectangular windows, a flat roof, and welcoming verandas on either side. It was so plain and small compared to Versailles, but to Thérèse it was home. The footmen, who had been standing at the back of the carriages, helped them to dismount. The Queen climbed out first. She wore a white muslin dress and a wide-brimmed straw hat with a single ostrich plume and a gauzy veil. There was an exquisite portrait of Maman by Madame Vigée-Lebrun in just such a costume. Maman had shed tears over it, because people had not liked it.

"They accuse me of trying to ruin the French silk merchants by wearing simple attire," Maman had complained to Madame de Polignac. "Yet they accuse me of extravagance when I wear one of Mademoiselle Bertin's silk creations. Can I do nothing right in the eyes of my husband's subjects? The King has been adamant in cutting our expenses, but when I obey, it nearly provokes a riot!" Henceforth, she never appeared in public in her white muslin dresses, but saved them for Trianon.

Madame Royale was helped out of the carriage, followed by the Princesse de Lamballe. Madame de Lamballe looked lovely in a lavender-blue, cotton voile gown, with a white muslin scarf about her shoulders. Her luxuriant hair was tucked into a white gauzy cap; a few golden brown ringlets escaped it, hanging down around her neck and shoulders. Thérèse hoped that the princess would not faint today, as she was known to do. Maman said they must always be gentle with "dear Lamballe," since as a young girl she had experienced a terrible shock. She was easily upset, and had been known to faint at the sight of a dead bird or a bunch of wilted violets. Thérèse could not imagine what had caused the princess to behave that way. Madame de Lamballe was always loving and attentive to herself and her brothers. She helped many poor people and anyone in trouble could go to her for succor and consolation. Princesse de Lamballe's baptismal name was "Marie-Thérèse-Louise." Today was her feast-day, too. Although the princess loved children, she did not have any of her own. Her husband had died many years ago, and Madame de Lamballe, being an Italian princess closely related to the King of Sardinia, had not been able to marry anyone else, because all of the princes of high enough rank were already married. Thérèse pitied her. It was sad not to have any children. Perhaps this was why she fainted so much, and her doe-like eyes tinged with sorrow.

Lastly, Ernestine and Zoë, Thérèse's adopted sisters, jumped out. They were lively and pretty little girls, about her own age, whom Maman and Papa had adopted. They were treated exactly like Thérèse herself, even though they were not princesses, but children of palace servants. They were with her at her lessons, her play; they were given nice clothes and dolls, as well as hugs, kisses, and corrections from Maman, Papa, and Madame de Polignac. Maman had grown up in a family of sixteen children. Besides her own brothers and sisters, young girls from noble families had been brought to the palace to be raised with her. Grandmama Empress believed that it was important for royal children to learn to share with others, so that they would not grow up thinking they were the center of the universe. Maman shared this belief. Also, she thought it made for a happier childhood to be surrounded by many siblings, as she herself had been. It was better than being alone and coddled. She liked to speak of the days she had spent scampering through the gardens of Schönbrunn with her sisters Amalia and Carolina, her younger brother Max, and all of their dogs combined. Papa and his brothers, on the other hand, had been raised practically isolated from those their own age.

They were joined by Madame de Polignac and Thérèse's broth-ers, who had just been helped out of their carriage, too. "La Belle Gabrielle," as Madame was called, had on a muslin dress similar to Maman's, with a purple sash and a black lace shawl. A nosegay of asters was jauntily stuck into her wide straw hat. La Belle Gabrielle with her white skin, dark curly hair and blue eyes, exquisite features, was an angel of loveliness. Her warm smile and easy charm drew the children to her. She never raised her voice, but as Governess of the Children of France she was loving but firm. Maman had chosen Madame de Polignac because of those qualities, but also because any other governess would have wanted to have complete control of the nursery. Because Madame de Polignac was a close friend, Maman was able to oversee the rearing of her own children without any interference. Thérèse was aware that most royal children hardly saw their mothers, as Maman had hardly ever seen Grandmama Empress. With Madame de Polignac as governess, Maman was able to personally supervise her children's education; correcting their faults, choosing their clothes, planning their menus, taking them for walks. Other governesses would have been offended by this, but La Belle Gabrielle was not. Maman felt that she herself had been rather spoiled by her own governess in Vienna; her education neglected. She often spoke of it.

"My governess would write out my lessons for me in pencil. I would merely go over her work in ink. She did not realize it, but she was doing me a grave disservice, by not demanding I learn to concentrate, and seriously apply myself." This was not to be the case with Thérèse. Her mother daily asked her to recite everything she had learned the day before. She insisted on the careful molding of her character. After the duties of her religion, Maman wanted her to learn the duties of her rank.

"We are not on earth for ourselves, but for others," was her constant adage. "Privilege entails heavy obligations. You have serious obligations to the people of France, especially to the poor."

In addition to Ernestine and Zoë, there were several orphans for whom Maman provided. Although they could not all live at the palace, they sometimes came to play. They were children from destitute families whose education Maman supervised, paying for art and music lessons if they showed any inclination in that direction. She would take Thérèse to visit infirm servants who lived in retirement, bringing them fruit, bread, and flowers. Her Papa, devoted to all of his subjects, also had a special love for the needy. He would go in disguise to villages, hospitals, prisons, and factories so that he could gain a first hand knowledge of the conditions of his people. He would right wrongs, give alms, and dismiss those in charge if they were not doing their duty. Papa and Maman were Patron and Patroness of the *Maison Philanthropique*, a society which helped the aged, the blind, and widows. The simple folk loved their King and Queen.

Having arrived at Trianon, her little brothers were anxious to play.

"May we feed the swans on the lake, Maman?" asked Thérèse.

"May I feed the chickens?" begged the Dauphin.

"Chickens! Chickens!" cried Charles, jumping up and down.

"Now, my darlings, you know you must first have a little rest," said the Queen. "You have a long afternoon ahead, and soon your cousins will be here. Before they arrive, you must all have naps."

Charles burst into tears. Madame de Polignac lifted him up and started walking towards the house; his short legs began kicking under his petticoats. Madame de Mackau, taking the Dauphin's hand, followed.

The Queen said to Thérèse, Ernestine and Zoë: "Girls, you must rest a while, too. In honor of Saint Teresa's day, there will be no lessons this afternoon. But you must have some quiet time before you play. Thérèse, as a special privilege, you may lie down on my bed in my room. Ernestine and Zoë, you may rest upstairs in your own rooms. Go now, with Madame la Duchesse."

The three little girls followed the others into the main entrance of Trianon. The bare, white walls of the vestibule accentuated the exquisite workmanship of the bronze and blue enamel lantern that hung from the ceiling. They climbed the stairs to the first floor, trailing their hands along the black wrought iron banisters with its curling designs of lyres, caduceus and the gilded monogram "M.A." While the other children went up the stairs to the second floor, Madame Royale went through the antechamber to the dining room, with its carvings of fruits, nuts and trees entwined with mytho-logical animals and cornucopia, then into the billiard room, with its colored panels portraying sylvan and pastoral scenes. It opened into the large salon. Thérèse lingered for a moment to absorb its beauty.

The sea-green panels, on which the white carvings, accented with gold, made a striking contrast with the furniture of red and gold-striped silk. Maman's harpsichord was on one side of the room. On the other was a pianoforte, a harp and a music stand. In the next room, the boudoir, the ceiling became very low, as in a true country house. Roses were carved everywhere, entwined with ribbons, doves, quivers and lyres. The Queen's gilded initials appeared here and there, bordered on each side by two torches, symbolizing the flame of love.

The boudoir led into Maman's bed chamber. Except for the carvings of roses, jasmine and narcissus, it was very simple and plain, with the low ceiling and narrow bed which had muslin hangings embroidered in silk. She loved the bronze clock on the mantel piece, with its Austrian eagles, birds, roses, and shepherds. Thérèse curled up on the bed. A moment later, her Maman came into the room. "I brought you your music box, *ma petite Mousseline la sérieuse.*" She wound it up, placing it on the mantelpiece. The Dresden figurines, a shepherd playing a flute with a dancing shepherdess, went round and round to a delightful tune.

"This will help you to rest." Maman kissed her and went through the bathroom door on the opposite side of the room from where she had entered. Beyond the bathroom was a narrow staircase, leading upstairs. Maman was going to look in on the other children.

Thérèse watched the Dresden dancers. She remembered the New Year's Day when Maman had taken Louis-Joseph and herself to see a marvelous toy display. There were toys from all over Europe: exotic mechanical animals, wax and china dolls, shiny drums, tin soldiers, miniature palaces, and doll houses. The Dauphin's eyes shone. Thérèse gaped, which was very improper, but she could not help it.

"My children, I want you to see these beautiful toys," Maman had said. "You know, Papa and I decided not to give you new toys this year for Epiphany. Instead, the money is being used to buy food and blankets for the needy. It has been a very hard winter, and there are children your own ages who are cold and hungry. It is a noble sacrifice for those little ones and will please the Heart of the Christ Child. But I wanted you to see for yourselves what you were sacrificing, so it will have more merit in God's eyes." Louis-Joseph had looked very solemn and nodded manfully.

Thérèse, swallowing hard, had said, "Yes, Maman. We already have so many nice toys."

Still watching the revolving figurines, she fell asleep. She dreamed that she was at the Opera in Paris. Once, when she was seven, Maman had taken her to the opera. It had been very exciting. She had taken a long afternoon nap, and then, after supper, had ridden in a gilded coach all the way to Paris. She had worn plumes in her hair, like Maman, and a choker of pearls. Maman had never taken her again, however, because the

Parisians had disapproved of a little girl being at the opera. Thérèse did not understand why. Perhaps it was because she had fallen asleep during the second act, and dozed on cushions in the back of the royal box for the rest of the performance.

In her dream, she was once again seated in the royal box, but Maman was not with her. Maman was on the stage. She was singing a beautiful Italian aria. Suddenly, Papa walked on the stage, too. It was so strange, because Papa had never acted in a play; he disliked playacting, unless he was watching Maman perform at Trianon. He was never on the stage at all, but always in the audience. In her dream, people began to laugh at her parents on the stage, then boo and hiss. Her mother kept singing, while her father took her arm and began to guide her off the stage. The angry audience began to throw things at them. Then there was the sound of a bell. . . .

She awoke with a gasp. What a relief that it was all only a dream! The clock on the mantelpiece was chiming a merry little tune. The music box was silent, the dancers, still. Her Maman's singing, however, was real. From the grand salon came the sound of a harpsichord and her mother's lilting soprano, raised in an aria of Sacchini. She slipped off the bed, and went through the boudoir to the salon. Maman was seated at the harpsichord, playing and singing. She had taken off her hat. Poor Maman! thought Thérèse, how gray her reddish-blonde hair had become. At the temples she was almost completely gray! Thérèse was glad to hear her singing. She had hardly touched the harpsichord since Baby Sophie had died.

Maman looked up and saw her. "Mousseline! Come and join us!" Thérèse stepped in, remembering to curtsey to her mother, and the other ladies. Sometimes Maman had to correct her for forgetting to acknowledge people when she entered a room. "Madame la Duchesse has the napkins you are embroidering. You may sit on the footstool near my chair and work."

Thérèse obeyed her mother. The Queen spoke to Madame de Polignac. "Madame la Duchesse, will you play something for us on the pianoforte?"

"With pleasure, Madame." La Belle Gabrielle came forward. "What would Your Majesty have me play?"

"Oh, something cheerful, to go with the day." The Queen took up her own embroidery. She was making new chair covers, pink roses on white silk. "I am so glad it is fine weather for the Kings's hunt. His Majesty has been unable to hunt for more than a fortnight, being so occupied with this tiresome business of the *parlements....*" She trailed off as she noticed Thérèse's questioning gaze. "And other affairs of state. But he shall join us for supper here at Little Trianon."

As Madame de Polignac played a trilling new piece by W. A. Mozart on the pianoforte, Ernestine and Zoë came in from their siesta. They took up their own needlework, and sat on stools near Thérèse without saying a word.

The Queen addressed herself to Madame de Lamballe. "Well, my dear princess, what do you think of this latest work by Monsieur Mozart? I met him in Vienna, you know, when we were both children. He was a genius even then. He came to play for my family. He stumbled and I helped him get up. He asked me to marry him!" She smiled, and for a moment drifted back to a time and a place that were lost to her forever. "It seems he has again surpassed himself."

"Indeed, Madame," replied the princess, in the gentlest tones. "It appears that the Austrians are beginning to triumph over the Italians in music."

"It does not matter to you or to me who triumphs over whom," said the Queen. "For we are both Frenchwomen now. I ceased being Austrian when I crossed the border at Strasbourg seventeen year ago. I have even forgotten how to speak German."

"Truly, Your Majesty?"

"Yes, my dear Lamballe, with the exception of a few words and phrases. It is a strange thing, because I remember my Italian quite well, although I have used it less in conversations than either German or French. I suppose it is because I use Italian so often in my correspondence."

"And in poetry reading, and in singing, Madame," added the princess.

"Oh, yes," the Queen agreed. "And of course, my Italian tutor was the great poet, Padre Mestastio. He made the language so beautiful for me; I loved it so, just as I loved his poetry."

"Please, Madame," the princess asked, "recite for us the lines of Padre Mestastio that His Majesty your father whispered when you were born."

Thérèse glanced up from the design of *fleur-de-lys* she was embroidering on the napkins. She had heard the poem (and the story that went with it)

43

several times before, as they all had, but being associated with her mother's birth, it held a certain magic for her. Madame de Polignac stopped playing to listen.

"Well, you all know," began the Queen, "how my Mama, the Empress, made a wager with my Papa that I would be a girl. Papa wagered that Mama would have a son. When I was born, the Empress said to my father: 'Sire, you have lost your wager.' Papa laughed and whispered these lines in her ear:

Io perdei: l'augusta figlia
A pagar, m'a condemnato;
Ma s'e ver che a voi somiglia
Tutto il mondo guadognato.

"Which means," the Queen interpreted for the benefit of the children: "'I have lost: my august daughter has condemned me to pay; but if she should be like you, then all the world has won.' Papa thought that of all my sisters I most resembled my mother." She smile ironically, concentrating upon on her silk rosebuds.

At that moment, there was a scratching at the door of the salon. The stiff formality of the court was dispensed with at Trianon; Maman wanted everyone to behave in a "natural manner." Nevertheless, it was still a queen's house, and people scratched on doors instead of knocking. A maid opened it, and in walked Madame la Comtesse de Provence, generally known as "Madame." She was the wife of the King's next oldest brother, "Monsieur." Madame was accompanied by the Comtesse d'Artois, wife of the King's youngest brother, and her two sons, the Duc d'Angoulême, age twelve, and the Duc de Berry, age ten. Madame was a devious, eccentric woman with a red nose. She frequently reeked of cognac and Chianti. Always extremely polite, Thérèse somehow sensed she was deeply unhappy and envious of the Queen. She and Monsieur had no children.

The Comtesse d'Artois was Madame's younger sister. She was of small stature, with a long, pointed nose and crossed-eyes. She did not like to bathe. Madame and the Comtesse were the daughters of the King of Piedmont. Thérèse had once overheard her Maman saying to Madame de Polignac that the two Italian sisters, especially Madame, were such avid plotters, ever embroiled in some intrigue. Nevertheless, the three brothers, their wives and children usually supped *en famille* in the evenings at Monsieur and Madame's elegant suite at Versailles. Papa said it saved money for them to sup together rather than at their separate establishments.

Today, her handsome Uncle Artois and her sly, corpulent, Uncle Provence, that is, Monsieur, were hunting with Papa in the forest of Meudon. Her Uncle Provence never rode, but would follow the hunters in a *calèche*. Thérèse asked her mother one day why Monsieur had a stable full of horses but did not ride any of them. Maman told her that he needed the horses for his carriages and that he was not able to ride because there was something wrong with his hips. Thérèse still thought he had far too many horses.

Her cousins, Angoulême and Berry, looked bored at having been brought to play with such little girls and boys. They were at the age when they would have preferred watching military maneuvers or following the hunt. Berry, handsome, quick, and lively like his father, seemed particularly uninterested. Angoulême, thin and hairy, with nothing of the Bourbons about him but his large, aquiline nose, tried heroically to smile at Madame Royale. Thérèse liked both her cousins: Berry, because he was full of fun, and Angoulême, because he was quiet and gentle, and his manner reminded her of her Papa.

"My dear sisters!" said Maman. "My dear nephews! What a pleasure to see you this afternoon of our Thérèse's feast-day. I thought it would be charming to have tea in the Belvédère." She began putting on her hat. "Let us all stroll through the gardens while the preparations are being made. We can watch the children at their play. Monsieur le Dauphin and little Normandie are still asleep, but Madame Mackau is with them, and will bring them over when they awake."

The entire company went through the glass doors onto the terrace and down the steps to the lawn, everyone chattering at once. Madame and the Comtesse d'Artois had brought several ladies-in-waiting and other attendants, so the company now numbered about fifteen. The group divided into twos and threes, ambling by different paths in the general direction of the Belvédère.

"Let us play hide-and-go-seek," suggested Berry to the other children.

"Oh, yes," said Thérèse.

"I will count to fifty, and the rest of you hide," said Angoulême. He leaned up against a tree and began to count in a loud voice. Thérèse dashed off down the path, past the pavilion and the theater, until she became hidden from sight among the trees and shrubbery. There were many places to hide in Maman's gardens. She had only to decide where. The Grotto? No, it was the most obvious place. The Belvédère? No, there would be too many servants, setting up the tea. She ran in the direction of the Temple of Love. It would be a wonderful place! No one would find her there.

She ran towards the canal. The air was crisp and sweet, a blending of the fragrance of chrysanthemums and asters with fallen leaves. Bees were still buzzing on the flowers. Robins and cuckoos sang, as if summer lingered at Trianon, in spite of the autumn colors. The canal was like a mirror, giving a double glory to the golds, yellows, russets, scarlets and emeralds of the beeches, oaks, poplars, yews and cedars. Swans glided across the smooth water. She crossed the little foot bridge that led to the island on which stood the Temple of Love. A cupola upheld by twelve, graceful, Corinthian columns, it had in the center a statue of Cupid carving a bow from the club of Hercules. She hid behind the pedestal of the statue. A moment later, she heard footsteps. She did not dare look. She had nothing to fear, it was only Ernestine, who had followed her.

"May I hide with you, Madame Royale?" she panted.

"Yes, of course, but do hide quickly before he comes!"

Ernestine crouched next to her. She would not be still and kept giggling and peeping around the pedestal.

"Shhh!" said Thérèse. They heard footsteps and shouts. Ernestine peaked out. "Oh, there is Monsieur d'Angoulême chasing Monsieur de Berry!" Another shout was heard. "Oh, no, I think he sees us!"

"Oh, Ernestine, do be quiet and do not move!" whispered Thérèse. But already they heard someone climbing the steps of the Temple of Love, and suddenly, there was Angoulême, grinning at them.

"Ah, ha! I have found you both!" he cried.

"Yes! but you can't catch us!" laughed Thérèse, darting away. She ran in and out of the columns, with her cousin right at her heels. It flitted through her mind that he was letting her get away. Being a big boy, he could catch her if he half tried. He chased Ernestine, too, who screamed and giggled.

Ernestine left the Temple of Love, crossed the bridge, and ran down the path into the glade, in the direction of the rose gardens.

Angoulême hesitated, then took off after her. Thérèse began to follow him, but stopped. She felt an odd tingling up her back, as if someone had called her name. But she had heard nothing.

Then it came again, "Thérèse...Marie-Thérèse!" The words echoed within her. Surely she had not imagined it. She ran around to the other side of the Temple of Love. It was from thence that she felt a pull, sensed a presence. The afternoon sun, beginning to slant, shone into the yellow beech leaves and the red foliage of the Virginia creeper, in a blaze of majesty. It did not seem real. She could only compare it to the stained-glass windows in one of the old churches in Paris. She blinked, because for a second the waving, translucent, prism-like leaves seemed to take the form and figure of the being. She almost thought she saw a face, rippling within the brightness. A joy and peace pierced her to the depths. She felt—no, she more than felt—she knew that God loved her, that He was near her and would always be. A light shone within her; it passed in a flash.

She heard her name called again: "Thérèse! Thérèse! Where are you?" She ran to the other side of the Temple. On the far bank she saw a figure in white. It was a smiling, pretty, young woman, in gauzy white attire such as her Maman wore, with a lace-trimmed cap over her chestnut curls. On her arm she held a basket of silvery sage, lavender, and asters. It was Tante Babette.

"Thérèse!" She called again. "Do come! It is time for tea! Everything is ready at the Belvédère!"

"Oh, Tante Babette, I did not know you had arrived!" She ran across the bridge and towards her aunt.

Chapter Three
The Crimson Rose

"Hear me, ye divine offspring, and bud forth as the rose planted by the brooks of waters." – *Ecclesiasticus 39:17*

Madame Elisabeth of France, late afternoon, October 15, 1787

Madame Elisabeth of France, known familiarly as "Babette," was not beautiful, but attractive. Her mouth was too large, but her smile charming and her cheeks so rosy. Her petite form was at its best in simple costume; the vivacity of her nature was thus accentuated. Her piety was of the kind that captivates others. She sparkled, not with worldly wit, but love of God, a love which had overcome the disappointment for a thwarted vocation to the cloister, ardently seeking fulfillment in service to others. Her smiles hid a thousand struggles with a willful and passionate temperament. Behind her serene countenance there often raged a battle to suppress an unkind retort or a sharp answer, bearing in silence innumerable pinpricks.

On arriving at Trianon, she had greeted her sister-in-law the Queen, whom she found by the smaller lake, saying, "Mesdames Tantes send their regrets. I had word from Bellevue before I departed. Tante Victoire's gout has flared up again, and Tante Adelaïde cannot leave her."

"What a pity," remarked the Queen, not looking remotely sorry. After all, the Mesdames de France, daughters of Louis XV and aunts of Louis XVI, had never really cared for their nephew's wife, Antoinette.

Madame Elisabeth well remembered, even though she had been practically a baby, how obdurately against the "Austrian marriage" her aunts had been. With both parents not long dead, she and her older sister, Madame Clothilde, were often brought to spend afternoons with their four spinster aunts, who liked to embroider vestments while being read to by Mademoiselle Genet (the future Madame Campan). Sometimes, Tante Victoire would play the bagpipes for their enjoyment, or Tante Adelaïde would play the spinet, but usually they sewed and gossiped, while Tante Sophie played solitaire, and Tante Louise read pious books, gazing dreamily out the window.

It was Tante Adelaïde who did most of the talking. She had been quite pretty in her youth, at least according to the huge portrait by Nattier that hung in the palace. She had never married; no prince on the earth was worthy of a daughter of the King of France, from her point of view. Tante Adelaïde had suffered deeply from her country's humiliations at the hands of the English and Austrians during the Seven Years War. To her, the idea of an alliance with their most bitter enemy, the House of Habsburg, was yet another abomination forced upon France by La Pompadour. She spoke vehemently against it, especially after her dear sister-in-law, the Dauphine Marie-Josèphe, who had favored an alliance with her own Saxon relatives, died of a broken heart. From Tante Adelaïde, Princesses Elisabeth and Clothilde derived the impression that Austrians were a haughty and arrogant race who ate too much chocolate and cakes and drank nothing but coffee. They were not sure what to expect of *l'Autrichienne*, which was Tante Adelaïde's only name for Antoinette of Habsburg-Lorraine.

They were surprised when she was not a monster. They were even more surprised when they began to like her, especially since they had been determined to despise her. She laughed rather too much for a Dauphine of France, the girls thought, their own quiet and dignified mother still fresh in their minds. Antoinette loved little children. She asked if Elisabeth and Clothilde could sometimes be brought to her apartments. Clothilde was a staid, obedient and humble child, whereas Elisabeth was proud, headstrong and frequently corrected by their governess, "Mama" Marsan. Clothilde was a bit appalled by her visits to Antoinette's suite. A boxer and two spaniels romped and lolled on the furniture. Children of the servants ran about with sticky fingers and faces. Antoinette liked her servants to bring their children, because being surrounded by their activity reminded her of home. Elisabeth was shocked by the disorderly environment, but completely fascinated.

On that autumn day at Trianon, watching her niece and nephews play hide-and-go-seek, she was transported back to the days when she and Antoinette would enjoy the same game in the Dauphine's rooms at Versailles. They would run from room to room, hiding from each other behind heavy drapes, under beds, behind fire place screens, and in cupboards, shrieking with laughter. Elisabeth was always amazed at how fast Antoinette could run and maneuver her skirts (panniers grew in width every year). She supposed it was partly because Antoinette refused to wear her whale-bone corsets, much to the disgust of the Comtesse de Noailles, whose responsibility it was to turn the harum-scarum Austrian girl into a proper French woman. The fun would usually end when Madame de Noailles walked in the door, her frozen countenance twitching as she tried to conceal her consummate horror at a Dauphine who had spider webs in her hair from crawling under furniture. Antoinette giggled as soon as Madame de Noailles' back was turned, dubbing her "Madame l'Etiquette," since the lady's most frequent words seemed to be: "Your Royal Highness, etiquette prescribes....etc."

In those days, Antoinette was not permitted to ride a horse (their grandfather, the King, considered it too risky for a future Queen), so instead she would canter about the palace grounds on a mule. Once she fell off, but would not allow her ladies to help her up.

"No, no!" she jested. "You must ask Madame l'Etiquette the proper way to get a Dauphine off the ground!" Unfortunately, her Reader and former tutor, Abbé Vermond, who prided himself on being a *philosophe*, ridiculed the court etiquette in front of the impressionable young Dauphine, who had not yet learned that all the minute, meaningless ceremonies protected the prestige of the crown by giving it a glamour, an aura of majesty.

Nevertheless, Antoinette did bring some *joie de vivre* into the bleak lives of Elisabeth and her sister, at a court where the only people who enjoyed themselves were the scandalous Madame du Barry, the favorite of the King, and her clique. Innocent merriment was a new idea for many of the courtiers, who had trouble accepting the fact that a lively, attractive young girl could also be quite wholesome and pure. Indeed, Antoinette was almost prudishly modest, taking her baths in a gown buttoned up to the neck, and making her women hold towels up in front of her as she got out of the tub. She disliked nudes, and would refuse to accept immodest statues or paintings, much to the disdain of the connoisseurs. She said her prayers at a *prie-dieu* every morning, reading a short passage from some spiritual book as her mother the Empress had commanded her, always receiving Holy Communion on feasts of Our Lady, and confessing with regularity. In her own apartments, she delighted in simple attire, to the disapproval of Mesdames Tantes and the Comtesse de Noailles. When returning from a court function, she would joyfully take off her elaborate dresses, exclaiming, "Thank Heaven, I am out of harness!"

She organized her husband's brothers, their Piedmontese wives, who by that time had joined the family, and her young sisters-in-law, Clothilde and Babette, in theatricals in the attic. They had a collapsible stage, that could be easily hidden away in a large cupboard, so most of the court was unaware of the plays. The Comtesse de Provence and the Comtesse d'Artois did not entirely approve, feeling it was beneath the dignity of the princesses of the House of Savoy to perform on stage. They acquiesced; however, their acting was so dreadful, it would have been better if they had been more obdurate. The Dauphin refused to act on stage, which was just as well, because they needed him to be the audience. Elisabeth saw her older brother laugh more than ever before, as he applauded his young wife's talent for drama and comedy. Antoinette made him laugh offstage, too, whenever she scolded him for his unkempt appearance, which he generally had after hunting or working at his forge, or having a wrestling match with his valets.

Madame Elisabeth saw her niece running to her from the Temple of Love. Thérèse's eyes shone; Elisabeth kissed her flushed cheeks, stroking her silky curls. She recalled how Madame Royale had been given the nickname *Mousseline la sérieuse* the day she was born, because even then her expression seemed not quite to approve of Versailles and everything that went on there. "Oh, Tante Babette! I am so glad you are here!"

"Happy feast-day, *ma chère*! I brought some herbs and flowers from my garden to decorate the tea table."

"Oh, thank you, *ma tante*!"

They walked hand-in-hand to the Belvédère. To Madame Elisabeth, coming to Trianon was like entering another world. At Montreuil she had gardens which were quite captivating, but there was something magical about Antoinette's retreat. One always had a sense of expectation, as if there were some hidden enchantment only waiting to be discovered. She experienced a repose in the solitude of its groves and along the winding paths, where one could easily and happily become lost.

They came to the white, octagonal building, with a large window on each of its sides. It overlooked the small lake, and was not far from the grotto. A table with a linen covering was in the center of the one-room, neo-classical structure, the walls of which were decorated with murals of the Four Seasons. In the middle of the table was a silver tea service, with scarlet and white Sèvres porcelain plates, cups and saucers. There were crusty baguettes, gooseberry and apricot jams, fresh fruits, ices, chocolate and cream-filled puff pastries, raspberry tarts, *paté*, sausages, and cheeses. The table was decorated with Elisabeth's lavender, sage, and asters, strewn amongst the dishes. There were large bowls of the Queen's fresh butter, made at the dairy at Trianon, along with pitchers of her cream.

Trianon was a working farm. The purpose of it was to raise revenues to boost the sagging royal pocket-book, as well as to experiment with new agricultural methods and devices. Antoinette raised sheep, goats, Swiss cows, and hens. From her *orangerie*, orange-blossom water was made, with its many medicinal and hygienic uses. In the lakes there were carp and pike. She had an orchard of apricot trees, fields of raspberry and gooseberry bushes, and a strawberry patch. The King had recently built a similar farm at Rambouillet, where there was a dairy, as well as merino sheep, raised for their fine wool. It was all an attempt to be self-sufficient; to give an example to other aristocrats in not relying solely on tax revenues; to lighten the burden of the poor.

Unfortunately, Elisabeth was aware, the Queen was greatly criticized for Trianon, and jealous courtiers called it "Little Vienna." To soothe their feelings, Antoinette had begun opening her gardens to the public every Sunday, so people could see the result of her efforts; that she had been quite industrious for what was good, and not engaged in waste and dissipation. However, people preferred to believe the scandal sheets rather than what they could witness with their own eyes.

The ladies and children sat on benches, chairs and stools, drinking their tea. It was all so very English; the Queen admired English customs. Footmen and maidservants stood along the wall and behind the table, seeing to everyone's needs, and yet the atmosphere was wonderfully informal, compared to Versailles, that is. Elisabeth sat between her sister-in law, the Comtesse d'Artois, and Madame de Lamballe. Elisabeth had befriended the homely, neglected wife of her dashing brother Artois, of whom she was very fond in spite of his fast living. The Comtesse was one of many court ladies who sought Elisabeth at her country house at Montreuil for spiritual consolation and advice. The Queen sat between her two sons, busying herself with tying large napkins around their necks, while making sure they had what they needed to eat. Madame de Polignac sat next to Charles, who was munching a bunch of grapes, occasionally seeing how far one would fly when he threw it. Madame Mackau was beside the Dauphin, holding his tea cup and hers in one hand, with a plate of tarts in her lap. The Queen was speaking to Diane de Polignac, Gabrielle's sister-in-law and lady-in-waiting to the Comtesse d'Artois. Diane was not pretty but known for her intelligence and wit, which attracted all the cleverest *philosophes*, including the famous Dr. Franklin of Philadelphia, to her salon. Diane was always conversant on the latest word from the political arena, as well as on the trends at the opera and the theatre.

"Tell us, Madame, of Monsieur Grétry's latest triumph."

"Well, Your Majesty, it was breathtaking, even though the duet in the first act was practically mutilated by the new soprano they had. I do not know where they found her. The finale was magnificent, all the same."

"Did you see Monsieur Grétry's daughter in the audience? She must be a young lady by now."

"Yes, Your Majesty, I saw her. She was in the front row with Monsieur Bouilly, the librettist, who is her beau."

"Whenever I am at one of Monsieur Grétry's productions, I always blow a kiss to Antoinette," said the Queen. "She is my goddaughter, you know. It has been some time since I last went to the Opera, so I have not seen her."

Madame Elisabeth, aware that her sister-in-law's recent avoidance of the Paris Opera was not only because she disliked being too far from her children in the evenings, but also due to her having been hissed when she last appeared in the royal box. It was a shame, since the Queen attended the Opera not only for her enjoyment but to do her duty as its leading patroness; her presence there meant an increase of the box office revenues.

As the Queen and those near her chatted of the arts, Madame Elisabeth noticed that Princesse de Lamballe looked as if she wanted to speak to her.

"Dear Lamballe," asked Elisabeth, "have you received any news of my sister, the princess of Piedmont?"

"Yes, I have, Madame. Her Royal Highness has been quite busy with her charities, and sends her love. She promises you a letter by your feast-day in November."

"What did Her Highness write in her letter? She always has such admirable thoughts. Is there any sentiment you can share with us?" Madame Elisabeth missed her sister, Clothilde. It has been difficult for her to say farewell to her closest companion from infancy, when the princess married the Prince of Piedmont and went away forever. Clothilde was quite fat, but her pleasant, steady disposition was like an anchor to Elisabeth. After her departure, Elisabeth became more zealous about the life of the spirit, spending hours at various devotions.

"Her letter was interesting," Princesse de Lamballe was saying. "She told me that lately she had fallen to thinking much of Your Highness' grandmother, Queen Marie Lezcinska and how she was consoled in her trials by pondering the vanity of earthly things. A month or so ago, she says, she even dreamed of your grandmother, whom she saw standing beside her bed, weeping. 'Pray, you must pray much, Clothilde,' the old Queen said to her in the dream. Then she was surrounded by the most hideous skulls, all with tears of blood running out of their empty sockets. The image disturbed her very much."

"How odd," said Elisabeth, thoughtfully. "You know, so often I, too, have pictured my Polish grandmother quite clearly in my mind, as if I saw her only yesterday. In the evenings, when I am alone at Montreuil, before returning to Versailles, I can almost sense her presence, and when I close my eyes, I see her before me in those high-necked dark dresses and heavily-veiled black bonnets. I do not remember her wearing anything else. Once or twice, I have said aloud: 'Yes, Grand-mére?' because I feel that she is hovering near, trying to tell me something."

"What of those skulls that your sister saw?" asked the Comtesse d' Artois. "Is that not bizarre?"

"It is," agreed Elisabeth, "but I will never forget how my grandmother loved her *belles mignonnes*, as she called them."

"What are *belles mignonnes*?" asked the Comtesse.

"They were skulls with elaborate, beribboned wigs. How they frightened me so as a little child! I did not want to go near them. But Grand-mére told us they helped her to bear her sorrows and humiliations.

It must be the *belles mignonnes* that Clothilde saw in her dream."

"How could such ugly things help her to bear her sorrows?" asked the Comtesse.

"By reminding her of the shortness of life, I suppose," said Princesse de Lamballe. "When death comes, all earthly pains, as well as joys, will have an end."

"I see," said the Comtesse, swallowing a bite of baguette with gooseberry jam. "Then perhaps I should get my own *belles mignonnes*." Like Queen Marie Lezcinska, the Comtesse d'Artois suffered from an unfaithful husband.

Elisabeth sipped her tea. "At my Tante Louise's monastery, there is a placard over the clock which reads: 'In a little while it will be eternity.' I often ponder how someday I will come before God to be judged. Will I be ready to face Him when the time comes?"

"We must do the best we can," said Princesse Lamballe, "by sharing our earthly goods with those who have nothing, by frequenting the sacraments, and most of all...." She drew out a Sacred Heart badge, attached to her bodice by a ribbon. "We must throw ourselves upon the mercy of the Sacred Heart."

Elizabeth smiled and nodded at her friend, who had endured many miseries in her private life.

"I love my house at Montreuil," said Madame Elisabeth. "It was delightful how the King and Queen presented it to me on my birthday. Her Majesty took me for a carriage ride to Montreuil and stopped in front of the house, saying, 'I wonder who lives here?' She led me up to the front door, and taking a key out of her pocket, unlocked it. I was speechless, and could hardly believe I was being given my own place. The King says I am too young to live alone, and so until my thirtieth birthday I must return to Versailles at nightfall. I am happy at Montreuil; it provides me with solitude. And yet more and more I find that worldly goods bring anxiety and vexation of spirit."

The Queen, meanwhile, had paused in her conversation and was listening to theirs. "How serious you ladies are today!" she exclaimed. "Do take some more tea. How do you find my raspberry tarts?"

"They are quite delicious, sister," Elisabeth gaily replied.

"And the gooseberry jam is wonderful," said the Comtesse d'Artois, wiping her mouth with her linen napkin.

The Queen rose to her feet. "What we need is music and dancing!

Gentlemen!" She called to two of the footmen, who produced a flute and a violin. "Play 'Over the hills and far away,' if you please. Come, Elisabeth, children, we will dance in the English country style for our guests!"

On the lawn before the Belvédère they joined hands, forming a circle, and danced around and around, the Queen and Madame Elisabeth laughing as much as the children. Charles lifted his short chubby legs as high as they could go, to everyone's amusement. As they broke into pairs, Louis-Joseph gently took Zoë's hand, twirling her around, looking very serious. Tall Angoulême matched his steps to Thérèse's as they skipped together. Ernestine, left without a partner, cavorted about alone and unaffected.

"This is what you need, Babette, you somber girl!" laughed the Queen, as she swung passed with Charles in her arms. "I heard you speaking of your grandmother and her *belles mignonnes*—you, who are always the last to leave any ball!"

"And what of you, Madame," retorted Elisabeth, dancing with her nephew Berry, "who used to dance until the sun rose? Now we are fortunate if we can get you to lead a *contredanse* or a *colonne anglaise* during Carnival. Is this the Queen who never once sat down at a masquerade?"

"My bad leg gives me trouble," replied the Queen, breathlessly, as they formed the circle again. "Besides, it is more important for me to be a good hostess at a court ball than to enjoy myself by dancing."

"And here at Trianon you can do both!" said Elisabeth, herself nearly out of breath. She was glad to see her sister-in-law in such a light-hearted mood. Since the diamond necklace scandal, followed by Baby Sophie's death, Antoinette was a quieter version of her former self. Her mother's death six years ago had also altered her. The Queen's grief at that time was extreme; withdrawing into seclusion, she left her rooms only to go to Mass. Elisabeth, only seventeen, had been summoned to console her, and it was then that their friendship solidified.

"How right my husband was," said the Queen, when the dance ended, "to abolish the office of the Lesser Pleasures. We have no need of expensive entertainments! We need only a bit of music, good dance partners, and a little sunshine!"

"What my brother said when he abolished the Lesser Pleasures was so true to the mark: 'My entertainment will be to walk in the park.'"

"Can you not hear him saying it?" said the Queen, taking her sister's arm, as they went to the Belvédère, the children scampering around them. "The King is the soul of frugality. He was and is so determined to cut all extraneous court expenses. He wears the same suits year after year— mostly brown ones—with the Star of the Order of the Holy Spirit as his only adornment or mark of distinction." She lowered her voice. "You know, Babette, as I wrote my Mama, that if I had had to choose for myself among your three brothers, I would have chosen Louis-Auguste, whom God Himself chose for me."

As they were seated again in the Belvédère, the Queen said, "My sister Elisabeth, do tell us of the time the King saved your life."

"We were at a party at the chateau of Meudon," said Elisabeth. "I, who was only three, amused myself by clinging to my oldest brother's coattails, following him from room to room, refusing to let go. The courtiers noticed, and crowded around to see the sight, but pressed in on us so tightly that my safety was threatened. Louis picked me up, hoisting me on his shoulder, saying to the throng: 'Gentlemen, take care you do not crush my little sister, or she will not come to see you again!'"

Elisabeth thought of the man her brother had become. She admired the King's intelligence, courage, and determination to be just, even if it meant offending powerful nobles, which it often did. Elisabeth was aware that her brother was one of the best-educated men at Versailles. An amateur geographer, he loved books of travel, and had personally planned and financed the voyage of Jean-François de la Pérouse to explore the islands of the Pacific, drawing up detailed charts and instructions. He was well-read, and could speak and read Latin as well as he could his native tongue, in addition to Italian, English, and German. The King insisted on reading all letters and dispatches that came in, instead of relying on secretaries. Being overwhelmed with business, he would read his mail at council meetings, while his ministers were presenting their reports. A careful reader, he quite amazingly never missed a word of what his ministers told him, and if later in repeating their reports they left out a single item, he would remind them of it. He made it his business to be thoroughly informed of events, daily reading several newspapers from different parts of Europe. He strove to be a father to his people. To Elisabeth, Louis took the place of the father she had lost, as he assured her he would when their grandfather died, and he became King.

After eating more tarts and pastries, the tea was over. The Queen and her children prepared to take their leave; the others were free to relax in the Belvèdére, or depart if they wished. Antoinette asked Madame de Polignac to take Thérèse and the older children to the *hameau*, her farm on the far side of the gardens. There they could watch the mill, visit the cows, help Valy-Busard the farmer to feed the hens, and play in the Marlborough Tower. The little white tower was named after the song *Malbrouque s'en va-t-en guerre*, which had been the lullaby Madame Poitrine, the Dauphin's nurse, had sung to the long-awaited heir to the throne. So great was the French people's adulation of their new prince, that the lullaby became a popular tune throughout the realm. The Queen built the lakeside tower to commemorate the event; it reminded her of the devotion the ordinary French people had for the Royal Family.

Now, it was too far a walk to the *hameau* for the Dauphin, whose back was beginning to ache. The Queen suggested that Madame Elisabeth and the Princesse de Lamballe accompany her and her sons to the nearby French gardens, where the boys could play quietly or rest.

"It is better for little ones to run and play than to be made to take long walks," she said, as they started across the lawn. The small boys, one still in skirts, the other in a sailor suit, had the blue ribbon of the Holy Spirit draped across their shoulders. They skipped ahead of the three ladies, gathering colored leaves. As the afternoon wore on, the air, becoming damp, had a strong, leafy smell. The sun, slipping lower and lower, sent its rays dancing on the bright foliage. A breeze caused the leaves to swirl into the air and to the ground, as the shadows lengthened. The day was dying, but it was a slow, rapturous dying.

In a low voice, the Queen spoke of her sons. "Louis-Joseph is so obedient and has great self-possession. But Charles is terribly high-strung. He is petrified of dogs; the sight of one makes him hysterical. He has quite a temper and is terribly proud. He hates to say 'Pardon' when corrected. But he is very loving and generous. I believe it is better not to be too harsh with such a child. I try to appear more hurt than angry when I scold him."

"I do agree, Madame," said the Princesse de Lamballe. "Consistency in one's discipline is so important."

"You are so right, Lamballe. I always give my children the reason behind anything I want them to do, so they will not think I am being arbitrary or whimsical."

"As for Monsieur Charles," added the princess, "I am sure as his reason matures he will overcome those little fears."

"Oh, yes, surely he will," agreed Madame Elisabeth.

"I hope he also out grows his impressionability," said the Queen. "He is so quick to believe and repeat anything he hears, building upon it with his imagination, until he himself does not know what is real, and what is mere fancy."

As they strolled past the Queen's theater, Elisabeth imagined she could almost hear the laughter, singing, and recitations from past performances. In her mind's eye she could see her sister-in-law dressed as a servant girl for Sedaine's comedy *La Gageure Imprévue*, or as "Rosine" in Beaumarchais' *Le Barbier de Seville*. The latter was only rehearsed, never performed, due to the outbreak of the diamond necklace scandal, from which the Queen's *joie de vivre* had never recovered.

For the last two years, the little *papier-maché* blue, green and gilt stage had been unused, except for a few children's plays directed by the Queen. Sometimes, young girls from the Maison Saint Cyr, who came to the Queens' household to complete their training, gave performances. Antoinette carefully reviewed the scripts they used to make sure they were appropriate for young ladies.

"I am responsible for the moral integrity as well as the physical well-being of everyone in my care, whether they be aristocratic schoolgirls or servants," she would say. Her theatricals had been organized as a wholesome recreation, not only for herself and her friends, but especially for her husband. He was so busy that it was often easier for him to stroll over to Trianon to see one of his wife's plays than to drive into Paris for a night at the Opera. The problem was that the plays at Trianon had been limited to a few people. Only the King, close family and friends, some foreign guests, and the servants, were allowed to be in the audience when the Queen performed. Many nobles, dismayed by the exclusion, spread rumors that the Queen was having wild parties and lavish, lewd spectacles at Trianon.

They came to the symmetrical gardens, laid out in the days of Louis XV and his favorites. The orderly pattern of lawns, ponds, and flower beds extended between Little Trianon and the charming, white *pavillon français*, which it also encircled. They decided to sit in the pavilion a few minutes so the Dauphin could rest. In the spring, the beds were full of blue hyacinths, the Queen's most cherished flower, as well narcissi, daffodils, and tulips. In October, most of the summer flowers had withered. Only the marigolds, geraniums, asters, and chrysanthemums were holding their own. The beds were bordered by low, manicured hedges and an occasional clipped yew tree.

"Raising children is such a great responsibility," the Queen said, when the Dauphin and his brother were ready to return to their play. "Even when one has the best people to help, being a mother is an all-encompassing business. My worries never cease, yet one joy compensates for a thousand anxieties. I will never know how my Mama managed all sixteen of us, while having to deal with that horrendous man, the King of Prussia, and all the problems of a vast empire."

"God helped the Empress," said Madame Elisabeth. "As He gives His aid to all who sincerely seek His Will."

"Yes, indeed, my sister," replied the Queen. "Nevertheless, I am deeply grateful that the *loi Salique* is maintained in France. Mercifully, only a man can inherit the throne! Women are happier when busy with domestic matters. Leave the politics to the men! It has been such a trial for me, these past few months, to interfere in that unspeakable business with the *parlements*. But since I suggested the appointment of Monseigneur de Brienne, the King thought I should be present at the council from time to time. How happy I was in the old days. Yes, Queens of France are much happier when they do not meddle in politics."

"And women in general, Madame," said Princesse de Lamballe. "Unless duty demands it, as in the case of Your Majesty and your mother the Empress."

"You know I did not interfere in the last war with England," said Antoinette. "But I was very much against it. I could not see the purpose of helping those rebels against their lawful King, especially when they were inspired by the new-fangled philosophies promoted by Dr. Franklin and his masonic cabal. His Majesty said that the American victory was a great help to Roman Catholics in those provinces, who under a Protestant British Parliament did not have the freedom to practice their religion. That is what comes from having a constitutional monarchy; there is little the sovereign can do when Parliament ties his hands. The King of England could not give relief to the Catholic subjects even if he chose to do so."

"Too true, my sister," said Elisabeth. "Aside from the help to religion, we must remember that my brother's victory over the British restored French honor and prestige among the nations. He became the most admired sovereign in Europe!"

"He was greatly admired even before the American victory, sister," said the Queen. "You forget that the war had hardly begun when my brother the Emperor came incognito to Versailles. He wanted to see for himself why my husband was so loved by his people. It was the first time since the days of Charlemagne that an Emperor came to visit the King of France." She paused, choosing her words carefully. "Of course, the Emperor also wanted to visit us as an older brother, to assure us of his love and concern for our well-being." It was a polite way of saying that her brother had come to interfere in her private family matters.

"Madame, let us not forget the visit of the Tsarevitch Paul and the Grand Duchess Maria," reminded the Princesse de Lamballe. "Truly, they came from the ends of the earth to see the glory of Louis XVI and his Queen."

"Oh, I shall never forget!" exclaimed Antoinette. "How well the four of us got on! Grand Duke Paul or the 'Comte du Nord' as he was calling himself, with his odd, flat face, was an eccentric, but very kind man. He respected and admired the King my husband very much. And he took quite a liking to our *Mousseline la sèrieuse*."

"What was it that her Royal Highness said to the Tsarevitch, Madame?" asked Princesse Lamballe.

The Queen laughed, "She climbed on his lap and said, 'I like you. You are a nice man. Someday, I shall come and see you.' Imagine, my little Thérèse going all the way to Russia!"

"Stranger things have happened, Madame," sighed Elisabeth.

"Yes, Babette, but that would be too strange. I did think that the Grand Duchess Maria was a lovely woman. She is quite a horticulturist; she knows everything about plants, and sketches them. She has the most remarkable gardens at Pavlovsk, their country estate, where they live most of the time, to stay away from her mother-in-law. Yes, we had the most interesting talk right here in this pavilion. I can never again hear the name of Empress Catherine without my blood running cold."

"How lovely was the *fête* you gave for them here at Trianon, Madame," said Elisabeth. "The grotto and lake were illumined by torches. The chapel musicians played in the groves. It was heavenly!"

"Just like the *fête* you gave for the King of Sweden, Madame," added Princesse de Lamballe.

The Queen nodded. "Yes, and now he is our closest ally. As for the *fêtes*, they were pleasant. I do have to earn my keep, you know, by entertaining my husband's guests in a suitable fashion, without further depleting the royal coffers." She smiled, her brow touched with concern. "I do everything now to save money. I even have my old shoes resoled. And we have begun to let go of so many of our servants."

"That reminds me, Your Majesty, of the passage I read in my Kempis this morning," said the Princesse de Lamballe. "I have a small edition with me, if you would like to hear it."

"Oh, please do, dear princess," said the Queen. Although Antoinette did not do a great deal of reading herself, she had a retentive memory, and usually remembered well whatever was read to her.

Princesse de Lamballe reached into her petticoat and brought out a small red moroccan volume of *The Imitation of Christ*. Opening to Book I, Chapter 22, she read: "'But take heed to heavenly riches, and thou wilt see that all these temporal ones are nothing; yea, most uncertain and rather a heavy burden, since they are never possessed without solicitude and fear!'"

"How true!" sighed the Queen. "How great are the worries of sovereigns, who have great possessions, compared to those of the simple folk."

"May I share with Your Majesty what I read from Kempis this morning?" asked Elisabeth.

"Please, sister," the Queen nodded. Elisabeth took the book from Princess Lamballe.

"'Son, take it not to heart if some people think ill of thee. . . . '" she began.

The Queen interrupted. "I know the passage! The King has read it to me! Go on!"

Elisabeth continued. "'Let not thy peace depend on the tongues of men: for whether they put a good or bad construction on what thou doest, thou art still what thou art. Where is true peace or true glory? is it not in Me?'" She paused.

The Queen was watching her sons. They were throwing pebbles in one of the circular ponds. "I can never hear those words too often," commented Antoinette. "Especially in these troubled times. Calumny seems to have become an industry by which many in this land earn their daily bread. Please, read to us from the passage about the cross, Babette. It is one of the King's favorites."

Madame Elisabeth found the page easily, it being marked by a ribbon. She read: "'To many this seemeth a hard saying: *Deny thyself, take up thy cross, and follow Jesus.* But it will be much harder to hear the last word: *Depart from Me, ye cursed, into everlasting fire.* For they who now love to hear and follow the word of the cross shall not then fear the sentence of eternal condemnation.'"

The Queen interrupted again. "Charles, come away from that water!" she called to her son. "You might fall in! Go on, Elisabeth, pardon me."

The princess read on: "'The sign of the cross shall be in the heavens when the Lord shall come to judge. Then all the servants of the cross, who in their lifetime have conformed themselves to Him that was crucified, shall come to Christ their Judge with great confidence. Why, then, art thou afraid to take up thy cross, which leadeth to the kingdom?'"

Antoinette's eyes glistened with sadness as she gazed at her sons, one of whom was supposed to inherit the kingdom of France. "My mother always told me that my most important task on this earth was to save my soul. After she died, I began to realize how I was not trying fervently enough."

"It is always the time for beginning," said Elisabeth, gently. "And for trying again."

Antoinette squeezed her sister-in-law's hand. She rose to her feet. "Come, my dear ladies, we must return to the house. There is much to do before supper, and the King may arrive at any time. Come, my children!" She went to fetch the boys.

They started towards the Little Trianon, walking past more clipped hedges. They fell to talking about the Duc d'Orléans, who had recently defied the King.

"I am so glad His Majesty exiled Orléans," said Antoinette. "He pretends to be on the side of the people. Yet when the King tries to relieve the poor of their heavy taxes, and completely abolish the *corvée*, Orléans and his friends, who care about nothing but their own incomes, accuse their sovereign of tyranny. Of course, the Duc will cause just as much trouble at his country estate. What scandal he gives everywhere he goes, especially with that Madame de Genlis! Imagine having such a woman as the governess of one's children!" She shook her head in amazement. "Oh, Lamballe, your poor sister-in-law! What she must suffer in being married to Orléans."

Madame de Lamballe said, "Yes," and lowered her head. It was rumored that the Duc d' Orléans, formerly Duc de Chartres, had made improper advances upon the princess in her youth. After being spurned, he had taken his revenge by corrupting the morals of her husband, the young Prince de Lamballe, causing him to contract a fatal illness. Elisabeth remembered how Antoinette, with great compassion, had befriended Madame de Lamballe and taken her sleigh-riding, in order to help her overcome an almost paralyzing grief.

"I do pray for Orléans," said Elisabeth.

"And so do I," said the Queen.

They were passing the rose garden. Most of the roses were withered or full blown, petals dropping to the ground. The leaves were yellowing.

"I must have these roses cut back soon," said the Queen. "It should have been done a week ago. Perhaps I will have time to speak to the gardener before supper. Or maybe I will just come out early tomorrow and tend to them myself." Antoinette loved working in the garden with her own hands.

"Oh, Maman, look what Charles found!" cried the Dauphin. Little Charles was proudly clutching in his plump hand a rose bud of a majestic crimson hue. He handed it to his mother.

"How lovely, *mon chou d'amour*! How wonderful that they are still producing fresh blooms. Yet I do not remember having roses of this color!" She preferred delicate pinks and whites.

"What an extraordinary shade of red!" exclaimed the Princesse de Lamballe.

"I have never seen anything quite like it!" cried Madame Elisabeth.

"Let me see..." mused Antoinette. "A red rose symbolizes the triumph of love!"

"The triumph of love over hatred, over evil!" sighed Lamballe.

"Here, Babette, do take it." The Queen handed it to her sister-in-law. "It so suits you."

Elisabeth curtseyed, and stuck the rose in her sash, remarking in a thoughtful tone, "A red rose is also the symbol of martyrdom."

"And what is martyrdom," asked Lamballe, "but the triumph of love?"

The three ladies grew quiet. Soon they reached the steps of the terrace.

"Papa! Papa!" Charles exclaimed. Standing against the balustrade, looking down on them, was the King.

Chapter Four
The Son of St. Louis

"For the king hopeth in the Lord: and through the mercy of the Most High he shall not be moved." —Psalm 20:8

King Louis XVI of France, sunset, October 15, 1787

The King of France stood on the porch of Little Trianon. The sun was partially hidden by the trees on the western horizon, and there was a fading splendor upon the French gardens where his family was walking. He leaned with his large hands and massive arms upon the balustrade, realizing for the tenth time that day that he needed to lose weight. His was the sort of build that required plenty of strenuous exercise. When he did not get it, his muscle quickly turned to fat, as his neck and waist bore witness. But the events of the past year had often kept him from the saddle. With his aquiline, Bourbon nose, his was a strong yet gentle countenance, weathered from exposure to the elements; tanned, except for his high, slanting forehead, which the brim of his hat protected from the sun. Deep lines had begun to form around his large, full mouth and under his deep-set, heavy-lidded eyes, which, nevertheless, continued to have an expression of kindness, almost of sweetness. His powdered hair was his own, and was tied at the nape of his neck with a broad ribbon. His blue serge jacket with crimson cuffs was the official uniform for the King's Hunt. His big jack boots were splashed with mud from wading on his horse through streams after the stag. He was a reckless rider, and his gentlemen always found it difficult to keep up with him.

He saw his wife before she saw him. Although he was nearsighted,

65

he knew which of the blurry white forms was hers, even before she came into focus. Squinting his eyes, as he did when aiming at his quarry, her image took on greater clarity. In her white muslin dress, the sheer fichu draped carelessly yet artfully around her neck and shoulders, veil fluttering off the side of her wide hat, she was a vision of beauty that always, when he had not seen her for a few hours, left him breathless.

"Papa! Papa!" His sons had seen him, and ran towards him. Antoinette looked up, smiling in her sweet, childlike way that had never changed. She curtsied, as did his sister, Elisabeth, and Princesse de Lamballe. They had come far from the moment of their first meeting, he thought, as he went down the steps to his wife.

*****

Into his mind flashed a distant scene of May in the forest of Compiègne, where the newly unfurled leaves were luminous and fresh. The birds were trilling and chirping as if it was the first spring day they had ever known. The bird song was drowned in the din of the oboes and drums of the chapel musicians, who played a triumphant march. Musketeers in grey and black stood at attention. Cordons of the Royal Bodyguards lined the road for a quarter of a mile in their blue, white and red uniforms. He was a slender, gawky youth of fifteen, whom many had expected would die as a child, standing near the gilded, royal coach at his grandfather's side, the entire court assembled around them in glittering array. It had entered into his mind that they were not far from the spot where Jeanne la Pucelle had been captured by the Burgundians. (He knew such an obscure fact because he knew everything about the forest of Compiègne and its environs; it was one of his favorite haunts and he had composed, charted, and printed a little guide book about it.) They were waiting for the arrival of the Austrian girl to whom he had been married by proxy for almost a month, but whom he had never seen.

"Be careful, Berry," Tante Adelaïde, his godmother, had warned him back at the palace. She persisted in calling him "Berry," even though he had been Dauphin of France for nearly five years, ever since his father's death. "*L'Autrichienne* will try to dominate you, and through her Choiseul will rule France. And remember, that confiding in her will be like confiding in the Austrian ambassador, Comte Mercy-Argenteau. She will tell everything to him, and he to the Empress. Austria will then have control of French policy. You must exercise the greatest prudence and caution."

His aunt's words were not news to Louis. The Duc de Choiseul, as a prime minister whom the late Marquise de Pompadour had put in power, had carefully and stealthily maneuvered freethinking *philosophes* and atheists into both government and Church positions, in order to systematically de-Christianize France. It had come to pass that many bishops and priests no longer made any mention of Christ in their sermons, and neglected to wear clerical garb. Choiseul himself would hypocritically attend Mass, the covers of his missal hiding a racy novel, or the works of Voltaire. Choiseul's worst enemy had been Louis' father, Louis the Dauphin who, in defiance of the mockery of Choiseul and his friends, erected an altar to the Sacred Heart in the chapel of Versailles. Choiseul did his best to alienate King Louis XV from his pious son, humiliating the Dauphin in his father's presence, and belittling him in his eyes. The minister despised the Dauphin's children (Louis and his brothers and sisters), referring to them disparagingly as the "Dresden knickknacks." All of this had occured because Louis' grandfather had been ruled by a woman.

Louis was determined it would not happen to him. Tante Adelaïde, his own godmother, had drummed into him that it must not. He could never allow any woman, no matter how beautiful, to ensnare him. Now that his father was dead, all of Choiseul's malice was focused on Louis. The Austrian marriage was the triumph of his wily career, his *magnum opus*, because through the lovely Austrian girl he planned to manipulate the young heir to the throne, whom he took pleasure in describing as "dull," "barbaric," "uncouth," and even "imbecilic." The devout and upright young man enraged him. Tante Adelaide's words were the truth, and they echoed in Louis' mind as he stood beside his grandfather Louis XV, amid the springtime glory of Compiègne, waiting for the princess who was to be his life's companion.

Louis was devoted to his Papa-King, and his grandfather practically adored him, although each strove to conceal his affection for the other. For Louis XV and his grandson, family relationships were usually seared with pain, so they feigned an attitude of indifference towards those whom they loved best. The boy's greatest happiness in life was hunting with his Papa-King. Then they were only an old man and his grandson, rather that the King and the Dauphin, as they chased through the forests after a stag or a boar. They spoke to each other more while hunting than they did at the palace. Louis was never good at the mincing small talk at which courtiers must excel. He liked down-to-earth conversation, just as he liked down-to-earth things and people. In the woods, Louis felt he could make his grandfather proud of him, since on horseback he never experienced the awkwardness that overwhelmed him elsewhere. In the evenings after hunting, they would go to hunt suppers together, where they would talk about nothing but the chase, about their guns, hounds, and horses, about how many stags or birds they had caught. Louis immensely enjoyed himself at the hunt suppers, even though Madame du Barry usually presided. Madame du Barry was Madame Pompadour's replacement, but she was not nearly as intelligent as La Pompadour had been, and therefore not as dangerous.

For most of his life, Louis had been regarded as too sickly to ever inherit the throne. Therefore, most of the courtiers ignored him, preferring to fawn on his younger brothers. Louis had had an older brother, the Duc de Bourgogne, a brilliant, handsome boy, generally regarded as the pride of the House of Bourbon and the Hope of France. He was precocious, independent, strong-willed, and assertive; a Louis XIV born again. Bourgogne, however, had become ill with consumption. Berry, as Louis had been called, was only five and still dressed in skirts in the nursery with his governess, Madame de Marsan.

In order to console and cheer his dying brother, he was taken from his beloved Mama Marsan, given a thorough medical examination by several physicians, dressed in "men's" clothes, and handed over to the grave, pompous, royal tutor, the Duc de Vauguyon. He had cried three days for his Mama Marsan. He eventually became resigned, and sat pale and quiet at the bedside of his pain-racked brother, who coughed up blood. Soon little Berry began to vomit blood, too, but so great was Burgogne's importance to the realm, it was thought better to risk sacrificing the less promising child.

Burgogne died, anyway, on Easter Sunday 1761, and Berry's constitution had never really recovered. His poor eyesight, frail health, and natural reserve inclined most of the court to consider him a political nonentity, and they did not scruple to exclude or humiliate him.

His Tante Adelaïde worried that he was so quiet, yet she sensed there was a hidden anger rising within him. She told him to come to her apartments, and there she bade him to run and shout, break china or anything he wanted. Louis refused. He wanted to master his anger, not give vent to it, and as he grew older he sought to master his other passions, rather than give them free rein, as was the general custom at Versailles. He turned to God, and to his forge in the attic, where he could hammer out his frustration and annoyances, gain control of them and of himself. And always, he turned to religion. The hypocrisy of so many of the courtiers, including his tutor, Monsieur de Vauguyon, sickened Berry. To him, Christ was a Person, his Friend. The sacraments and rituals of the Church were not mere forms to be observed through tedious custom, but living links to his God, sources of strength and peace.

On December 24, 1766, Louis made his first Holy Communion; what a sublime day for him to receive the first tender embrace of the Christ Child. Two days later, on December 26, Feast of St. Stephen the first martyr, he was confirmed, receiving the special sacramental grace to be a soldier of Christ, to die, if necessary, for his faith. He had been baptized at birth, but was not christened until he was about age six. Because his birthday occurred right before the Feast of St. Louis (August 25), he was given the name of "Louis-Auguste," which was exactly the baptismal name of the holy crusader-king himself. On the day of the christening, their father had taken Berry and Provence (his younger brother, who had also been christened) to see their names in the parish register of Versailles.

Their father pointed out to them the name of the child of a poor artisan, saying, "You see, *mes chers*, when it comes to religion, all distinctions vanish. The only true superiority is that conferred by virtue. In the eyes of men, you will be greater than this humble child, but if he has better morals than either of you, then he will be greater in the eyes of God." It was a lesson Berry never forgot. His father also took them on visits to the cottages of the poor. He saw the straw beds, the hard bread, the smoky hovels. He resolved that someday he must do everything he could to help his people.

Louis' father saw to his thorough religious and secular education. From Fathers Soldini and Berthier he not only received instruction in sacred scripture, but imbibed a profound devotion to the Sacred Heart. He was taught dancing, fencing, mathematics, physics, writing, geography, history and carpentry. His true love was geography, especially map making, because in the study of those disciplines he was able to mentally travel to all of the distant, fascinating lands that he would never see. He was enchanted by metal work. His health improved with physical exercise, not only at his forge, but especially on horseback.

While Louis never fit in with the empty-headed courtiers, he felt very much at home with the ordinary French people. He would stop and converse with peasants in their huts and fields, occasionally taking a turn at the plow. He would speak to workmen at Versailles, asking them about their building projects, and often removing his jacket, rolling up his shirt sleeves, to give them a hand. The elegant *philosophes* were full of talk about the people and the plight of the common man, but most would have preferred death to actually rubbing shoulders with grimy, sweaty laborers, never dreaming of trying to speak to them about their hopes, fears, and concerns, as did the young prince.

He saw it all as preparation for his future vocation as King. He composed for himself a political catechism covering the duties of a sovereign, including piety towards God, benevolence towards men, strict justice towards all, to avoid war if at all possible, devotion to the happiness of the people, winning their affection through kindness. He had written an earlier work as a present for his grandfather. It was entitled *Maximes morales et politiques tirées de Telemaque*. On his little press he printed and bound twenty-five beautiful volumes, which he was very pleased to present to Papa-King. Louis XV, however, found it a reproach to read in his grandson's book about the high standard of morality which a King should uphold. He ordered the type broken up, so it could never be printed again. It crushed the young prince, but he quietly continued to prepare himself for his future role. Meanwhile, his parents died, and his Polish grandmother, too. He had to tread water in an ocean of grief.

Before he knew it, the time had come to prepare for his marriage. He resolved not to give in to whatever he might feel towards his bride. Initially, he must appear bland and impassive, so as not to convey the impression of vulnerability. The welfare of the kingdom depended upon it.

Soon it was May 14, 1770, the fateful day of their meeting, and there he was in the forest of Compiègne. He was aware of a blurred feminine form running towards them. As she came into focus, he realized that it must be his bride. He was surprised she would run, instead of walking in a slow, stately manner as the occasion demanded. She dropped into a deep curtsey at his Papa-King's feet. His grandfather raised her up, kissing her cheeks. He, Louis, held his head high, trying to look detached and aloof, but when his turn came to embrace her, in a sweeping glance he absorbed as much of an impression as he could.

He was shocked. From everything Tante Adelaïde had said, he had half-expected a bold, flaunting woman like Madame du Barry. But his wife did not appear to be more than twelve years old! He had been told she was fifteen; he soon discovered that she was only fourteen. Heavy powdering covered her hair, reported to be of a reddish color, as his brothers had liked to tease him. With a high forehead, a thin, aquiline nose, the full Hapsburg lower lip, hers was a comely and bewitching visage. Her large sapphire eyes looked into his own, with unabashed curiosity. His feeling of consternation combined with a strong urge of protectiveness towards this foreign child. Somehow, he must shield her from the intrigues of the court. He himself was not quite sixteen; he did not know how he would protect her, just as he did not know how he could be expected to be a husband to such a little girl. In an instant, he realized he would have to wait to love her, wait for her to grow up, giving himself time to win her affection and respect. And there, leering at her side, was the Duc de Choiseul, looking like an overdressed ape. Louis had much with which to contend.

Seventeen years later, in the glow of an October sunset, he raised his wife from her curtsey, kissing her hand. On her other hand gleamed a gold band. On May 16, 1770, with what trembling he had given it to her, placing it first on her thumb, saying, *"In nomine Patris,"* then on the second finger with *"et Filii,"* then on the third with *"et Spiritui Sancti"* and then on the fourth saying "Amen." He had not seen her for more than a total of six hours, but he promised to be faithful to her until death, and she promised the same to him. They knelt side by side before the high altar in the Royal Chapel, he in his blue and gold robes of the Order of the Holy Spirit; she in an elaborate silver dress that was too bulky for her slender frame. The Archbishop of Rheims joined their hands; binding them with a stole, he pronounced the nuptial blessing. Louis also wore a ring on his left hand. Inside, it bore the inscription "M.A.A.A." for "Marie-Antoinette, Archduchess of Austria." The new Dauphine made a blot on the register when signing her name. They were both terribly nervous, but it was only the beginning of an exhausting day.

*****

He swung his little sons into the air. "Oh, Papa, oh, my Papa!" exclaimed Charles, stroking his father's face. "We played outside almost all afternoon, Papa," said Louis-Joseph. The king was seized with concern

71

about his oldest son, whose cheeks were pale even after hours of fresh air.

He greeted his sister, and Madame de Lamballe, then turned to his wife. "I trust you have had a pleasant day, Madame?"

"Yes, Sire," replied the Queen, playfully straightening his cravat. "Forgive us for not being in the house at your arrival. We lingered too long in the gardens. How was Your Majesty's hunt?"

"We killed two stags," he replied shortly. "And how were our children, Madame?"

"Oh, we had a lovely afternoon. Our Mousseline played hide-and-go-seek with Ernestine, Zoë and her cousins."

"Did you milk the cows? Did you churn any butter?"

"No, Sire, not today. But we had some of my butter at the tea. If I may be so bold, I think it is perhaps the most excellent butter in your realm."

She slipped her arm through his, and they began to walk along the porch, the children and ladies behind them, as the sky turned to orange, purple, and gold. He remembered how they had first begun to walk arm and arm, in the gardens of Versailles, so many years ago, when they had first begun to love each other. It had started a trend, since husbands and wives customarily hardly even spoke to each other in public and never displayed signs of affection.

"Sire, have you given an audience to Monseigneur de Brienne today?" asked the Queen.

"Yes, Madame, I saw the . . . the Archbishop this morning." He acknowledged Lomenie de Brienne's ecclesiastical rank with reluctance. The prelate had lived such a debauched life that he had a loathsome skin disease. The King refused to touch any papers he had handled.

"Oh, Sire, I know that Monseigneur's private life has sadly not been above reproach. However, Abbé Vermond praised him so highly as a shrewd and careful administrator. His charity to the poor in his diocese of Toulouse is quite admirable."

"Madame," said the King, a hint of impatience in his voice. "You must realize that there is a profound difference between Christian charity and what the *philosophes* describe as programs of 'civic welfare' and 'social justice.' The Archbishop de Brienne is an agnostic. That means he is not sure whether or not he believes in God. He does not provide for the poor because the love of God inflames his heart. He does it only for political ends! And there are some who would have had such a man made

Archbishop of Paris! Mercifully, the see of Paris is under Monsiegneur Juigné, a believing Roman Catholic, although he does not quite take the place of our late beloved Cardinal de Beaumont, God rest his soul."

"But, Sire," said the Queen. "Monseigneur de Brienne has saved your treasury a great deal of expense. Look at all the posts he has abolished, all the pensions he has cancelled."

"I sometimes wonder if creating more unemployment is the answer," said the King. "I think Monsieur de Calonne had wiser ideas. He was a financial wizard if there ever was one, much better than Monsieur Necker that everyone raves about. His borrowing has only increased our national debt."

"Sire, you yourself said that Monsieur de Calonne's bullying way of dealing with the Assembly of Notables and the *parlements* only alienated them all, and was a greater hindrance to your proposed tax reforms." The Queen carefully weighed her words. "Which was why Your Majesty had to ask him to resign."

The King was silent. He remembered the heated argument he and his wife had had over Calonne last winter. For the first time in their marriage, he had raised his voice to her. It would be so much better for her if she were excluded from politics, as she had been earlier in his reign. But now that he was surrounded by so many enemies, by so much deception, he had begun to confide in her more and more. Unfortunately, there were those, such as his cousin Orléans, who loved to portray the King as a weak man, subjugated by a scheming Austrian woman. The country's financial troubles were blamed solely on her and she was labeled "Madame Deficit." Occasionally, when exhausted from a long day of hard work and hunting, Louis was seen to stagger with weariness. This gave rise to the rumors that the King was befuddled with drink; indeed, that *l'Autrichienne* was getting him drunk, in order to make him sign anything she wanted.

"Well, Madame," said the King, changing the subject. "I must return to the palace to wash and change for supper. I will return in about an hour and a half."

"Supper will be ready when you return, Sire." Antoinette gave a little curtsey.

"Will you play with us before your supper, Papa?" asked Louis-Joseph.

"No, dear," said the Queen. "Papa is very busy, and you and your

73

brother must go to bed early tonight. You have had a long day."

"I will come to see you before you go to bed, my sons," Louis promised. "And we will have a story."

The King kissed his sons, and nodded to the ladies. He walked to the courtyard, where he mounted his horse for the five minute ride to the palace. Now that his afternoon of hunting was over, a thousand worries began to crowd into his mind. In spite of his labors and sacrifices there was widespread discontent in the land. He thought of all the humanitarian legislation he had effected for his people, such as the reform of prisons, of hospitals, and of the wine trade. He had partially abolished the *corvée*, a practice by which the peasants had to leave their fields at a certain time every year to repair the roads. He was trying to have it abolished in the entire country, but the nobles resisted, knowing they would have to supply tax money to pay soldiers to do what peasants had done for free. He had reformed the army, bringing an end to forced recruitment and abolishing the death penalty for deserters. He established military academies for the training of officers. He built a navy which had defeated England, the mistress of the seas. He had opened the Louvre to the public, so everyone could enjoy the art treasures that formed the royal collection. His striving to give state positions according to personal merit and ability had slighted many nobles, who believed custom and privilege naturally accorded them offices in the government and at court.

He rode into the vast courtyard of Versailles and dismounted, handing the reins to a groom.

"I will ride again at seven o'clock," he said, going up to his apartments.

He could not help thinking of how much Antoinette had offended people during her first years in France. She had particularly outraged Madame du Barry by refusing to speak to her. His grandfather's favorite had retaliated by allowing a bucket of slops to be thrown out of a window onto Antoinette, as the latter walked in the gardens with one of her sisters-in-law.

Antoinette had marched right upstairs to King Louis XV's rooms, saying, "Oh, Papa, just look at my dress! You really must keep your household in better order!"

The old King apologized but did nothing, and soon it was being whispered that Madame du Barry was scheming to have Louis and

Antoinette's marriage annulled, so that the Austrian girl would be sent home to Vienna. The Duc de Choiseul was no longer in power, but he had been replaced by Madame du Barry's friend, the Duc d'Aiguillon, who was an enemy of Antoinette and the Austrian alliance. It truly appeared as if heaven and earth were conspiring to keep them apart.

During the summer which followed their marriage, Louis was sick and feverish for weeks. He had been exhausted and overwrought by the festivities; by the coarse jests and speculations about his conjugal relations with the girl whose affection he had resolved to win before living in intimacy with her. His Tante Adelaïde had been right. His wife confided in her mother's ambassador, Comte Mercy-Argenteau, as the Empress had commanded her. Mercy had Abbé Vermond, Antoinette's Reader, as a spy, and both men twisted every account of Louis' behavior to make him appear like a weak numbskull, ruled by his child-bride. The servants, too, were in Mercy's pay. Even the Duc de Vauguyon, Louis' tutor, listened behind keyholes, as Louis and Antoinette once discovered when a valet had suddenly opened the door of the room where they were talking. At least they were afforded with a moment of merriment to see the pompous, rotund old Duc bending his ear to a keyhole that disappeared!

Louis could not woo or win his wife when he had no privacy. His own awkwardness was also a liability. The only girls he had ever been around were his little sisters. Besides, he had never met anyone like Antoinette. For one thing, he never knew what she was going to say or do next, and her outbursts of either enthusiasm or distaste for a person or a thing she liked or disliked always embarrassed him. He was not accustomed to people who expressed their feelings, especially with such frankness. His kindness to her had to be mingled with aloofness and restraint, so as to rid her of any notions of controlling him. He could not open his heart to her, for fear it would be reported to Mercy, and thus his ardent and affectionate nature remained hidden.

He did not have the faintest idea of how to be romantic and tried to recite passages from his favorite playwrights for her enjoyment. He recited to her one day a scene from Racine's *Andromaque* which was particularly moving to him. He repeated the tragic words of Hector's widow, Andromache:

> *J'ai vu mon père mort, et nos murs embrasés;*
> *J'ai vu tranchu les jour de ma famille entière,*

Et mon époux sanglant trainé sur la poussière
Son fils, seul avec moi, reservé pour les fers.
Mais que ne peut un fils? Je respire, je sers . . .
Qu' heureux dans son malheur, le fils de tant de rois. . . .

"How unspeakably sad!" Antoinette interrupted him. "Oh, please do not recite anymore! It is inconceivable, a poor princess whose husband was killed, and then to have her little son taken away! Oh, I cannot bear to hear another word!"

He discovered that she preferred comedy, and he found himself laughing at her plays in the attic. She also loved to dance. Louis arranged supper parties to be held for her every Monday night in her apartments, asking his brother Artois to dance with her, since he himself had two left feet.

Eventually, he began to feel less awkward around his wife, especially when he discovered her compassionate heart. During the public fireworks display that celebrated their marriage, a stampede occurred, killing hundreds of people and injuring thousands of others. Antoinette was inconsolable when she heard of the disaster, weeping for days. Louis was shaken, and both of them gave all of their private spending money for a year to relieve the victims and their families. They would have given even more if they could. He was touched to find how Antoinette cared for an old peasant, injured during a hunt, staunching his wound with her handkerchief. He was pleased to see that her character did have a serious side—she said her prayers, she read history books, she loved children and the outdoors, as well as riding and hunting. Those were things they had in common.

*****

In his private bathroom, the King had two tubs—one for soaking and one for rinsing. His valet, Cléry, helped him to put on his olive green velvet jacket with white breeches, and to carefully comb and powder his hair. He knew how important it was to Antoinette that he be clean and neat. Their first argument had come about because of his unkempt appearance.

*****

It was a hot July day, more than a year after they were married. There was a spring in his step as he went to her apartment, after an afternoon of hawking with his grandfather. He was in high spirits, and

76

eager to see his pretty little wife.

"Oh, Monseigneur!" she exclaimed as he entered. "You should see yourself."

He looked in one of her mirrors. His hair was dishevelled from being in the wind; his clothes soiled, not only from hawking, but also from stopping to help some workmen mix their mortar.

"Forgive me, Madame," he said with a bow. "I was hunting with the King."

"Oh, hunting, always hunting!" she scolded him.

He had heard that women could be this way.

"And your nails! Oh, Louis-Auguste, you must learn to keep them clean!"

He realized his nails were blackened from working at his forge.

"Are you a prince, or are you a Vulcan?" she asked, her voice becoming shrill.

He was stunned, and could not respond. Then he, too, became annoyed. This must be her way of trying to dominate him. He pulled himself up to his full height (he was now almost six feet).

"Madame, I shall return when you are disposed to receive me in a cordial manner." He turned his back on her and left, feeling pleased and surprised that it was so easy to put her in her place. He started walking through the maze of rooms to his own apartments. Then he heard the clicking of feminine heels and the swishing of petticoats coming from behind. He did not look back, but he realized to his horror that she was following him. He did not know what to do except keep walking.

"I have more to say to you," she said in an intense whisper, as she caught up with him.

He arrived at his rooms, wishing he could lock the doors against her, but he could not. After all, she was his wife. He hoped none of his gentlemen-in-waiting or *valets de chambre* were around.

"You were hunting yesterday," she burst out, as soon as the door closed behind her. "And hunting again today! And last night you were at another hunt supper with that...that creature!" She was referring to Madame du Barry.

"My grandfather the King required my presence at all of the—the events you just mentioned, Madame." He spoke in the firmest tone he could manage. Antoinette's cheeks were scarlet beneath the round patches of rouge prescribed by etiquette; her eyes glistened.

"But that creature...she is an insult to every decent woman in the palace! She has many times gone out of her way to humiliate me!"

"She insults you, Madame, because you have refused to utter a kind word to her. Everyone has advised you to speak to her—my grandfather the King, Her Majesty your mother . . ." His voice remained steady. "And myself. A word or two will not compromise your morals, but will show respect to the King our grandfather, whose...whose . . . friend she is."

"Friend, indeed! It is not right that she should reside at Versailles, and have so much authority over everyone. One of my ladies has been exiled from court because of her!"

"Antoinette," he said. He had hardly ever called her by name. "To criticize me is one thing, but I cannot permit you to criticize the King. It is his will that she live here, and how she conducts herself is his business. And furthermore—there is much that you know nothing about." His grandfather had once hinted to him that he planned on secretly marrying Madame du Barry someday, but that was practically a state secret, and it would never do to tell his angry little wife.

"Oh, Louis-Auguste!" She stamped her foot. "There is much you know nothing about. For one thing, you do not know how to have fun. None of your family does! My Mama said so, and that is why the King seeks his recreation with creatures like La Barry!"

He knew she was right. His reserve was broken. It seemed to Louis that suddenly his lonely boyhood, combined with his humiliating marriage, were closing in on him. It was as if the people he cared for the most always brought him the greatest pain. He stared at her, unable to say another word. He felt tears uncontrollably well into his eyes. His hands trembled, as he covered his face, and even with the greatest effort he could not suppress a choking sob.

"Please...go..." he said to her convulsively, sinking into a chair, his tousled head in his hands.

She stood motionless, then she, too, began to weep. "Oh, forgive me, forgive me!" She sank onto the floor beside his chair. They cried together for a long while.

*****

The King went to say goodnight to his sons. His wife was generally with them at that time, except for the occasional evenings she supped at Trianon. He told them about Charlemagne and his paladins, then said

78

prayers with them, making the sign of the cross on their foreheads. As he rode back to Trianon, he breathed in the damp crispness of the autumn night. A lone nightingale was singing. He could not help thinking of summer; of a particular summer, the summer of 1773. Then, he had begun to know happiness.

*****

It all started on June 8, 1773, when he went with Antoinette to make her official entry into Paris. He and his brothers had taken her to the masked opera ball in Paris during the previous Carnival, but they had all gone incognito. Now, the citizens of Paris were to formally meet their future King and Queen. Louis and his wife were cheered all the way into town. Their reputation for virtuous living had preceded them. The people had heard of Antoinette's beauty and generosity. Louis' plain, blunt manner appealed to one and all. Stories of his magnanimity were repeated everywhere. He was surprised to discover that in the eyes of the nation he had become the Hope of France. He was determined to do whatever he could for his people, make whatever sacrifices were necessary for their happiness.

They drove through the streets of Paris to the welcoming blare of trumpets and thunder of cannon. After Mass at Notre Dame, they went to the church of Saint Geneviève, where they prayed at the tomb of the shepherdess who protected the city. They dined at the Tuileries palace. On the balcony of the palace, they showed themselves ten times to a mixture of silent awe and ovations of delight. Afterwards, they walked arm-in-arm in the open gardens, the crowds thronging around them, but Louis ordered the guards not to push the people back. The Dauphin answered all of the speeches in a calm, polite and gracious manner, which touched many hearts. Antoinette was so moved by the acclaim that tears rolled down her cheeks.

The Governor of Paris said to her: "Madame la Dauphine, two hundred thousand people have fallen in love with you."

The Dauphin looked at his wife. She was seventeen. Her wonderful hair was piled into a high coiffure, with long reddish-blonde ringlets hanging half way down her back. Her blue eyes were dark with emotion. She had finally begun to wear her corsets, which set off her figure to perfection. She was no longer a little girl, but an enchanting woman. He, too, had fallen in love with her.

79

That summer the court moved to the château of Compiègne. Louis and Antoinette were able to go riding and hawking in the forest and lush countryside. He was a magnificent rider, completely fearless in the saddle. At eighteen, he had become the tallest, brawniest man of the court. None of his gentlemen could keep pace with him as he cantered through the forest, jumping over fences and splashing through streams and rivers. He was surprised when Antoinette was willing to take the same risks he did in order to ride at his side. She rode side saddle in a dark blue English riding habit, with a beplumed shovel hat; her hair in a loose chignon, on a grey horse caparisoned in azure and silver. Once or twice, he caught her gazing at him amid the relatives and retainers who usually surrounded them. Their eyes would meet, and for an instant the others disappeared.

In a smaller palace, with fewer people around, and a simpler routine, they seemed to have more time alone together. They spent long evenings in her apartments, while she tried to improve his dancing, and he helped her memorize the lines for her newest play. He was happy watching her at whatever she was doing, whether it was chattering or embroidering, deciding on fabric for a new dress, playing the harp, rustling around her rooms and romping with her dogs. On clear nights they would slip out to the gardens. To Antoinette, moonlight walks were one of the joys of existence.

"Oh, see how the moonbeams sparkle on the fountains—like living diamonds!" she exclaimed one evening.

With her arm through his, he experienced an almost sublime exaltation. He could hardly respond to her bubbling comments, except to say, "Did you know that the light of the moon is only the reflected light of the sun?"

"Oh, is it?" she replied. "I do think someone told me that once! Then it is like gold changed . . . into silver! What enchantment!"

It was a June night, warm with the scent of jasmine. Somewhere, a nightingale was singing, and a robin. There was much in his heart that he longed to express to her, but he could not find the words. He wanted to tell her that she was the loveliest, most beguiling girl he had ever seen; that he wished he could lay all of France at her feet; that he did not know why he, of all princes, had been given such an exquisite bride. All he could say was: "I think of you...all the time."

"And I think very often of you," she softly replied.

He stopped abruptly. Putting his hands on her shoulders, he turned her towards him. "Do you love me?" he asked in a husky voice.

She looked straight into his eyes. "Yes, I do," she said, firmly. "And what is more, I respect you."

It was the answer he had been longing to hear. "Oh, truly?" he asked, kissing her hands.

"Yes," she said, a slight tremor in her voice. "Truly."

He folded her into his arms, lost in the happiness of their first real embrace.

The months that followed found them always together. The Dauphin was so enthralled with his wife, he kissed her even in public, and other married couples, including his own brothers and their wives, began to imitate them by going about together in such an affectionate manner. When he was not with Antoinette, Louis made ready to shoulder the duties of King that someday would descend upon him. He subscribed to the Dutch *Gazette de Leyden* and to the London *Morning Chronicle* so as to become thoroughly informed of the political climate abroad. He found a wise man to secretly tutor and advise him in matters of state—the Marquis de Pezay, who because he did not have a position at court was free from all petty intrigue, and had more objective opinions. He put his regiment through maneuvers to keep himself and his soldiers in practice. All honest men admired his serious and noble bearing, while the *philosophes* and free thinkers feared him, in spite of their derisive and nasty comments. Hope gleamed on the horizon for France. Then, in the spring of 1774, his grandfather died.

Louis would never forget the Holy Thursday preceding his Papa-King's death. For once, they had a fervent priest to preach in the Royal Chapel. At the beginning of the sermon, he stared right at Louis XV and said, "Forty more days, and Nineveh shall be destroyed." Afterwards, the old King came down with small pox. By May 7, 1774, it was clear he was not going to survive. Louis and Antoinette knelt outside the King's room while the dying man made his confession to the half-blind and saintly Abbé Maudoux. Madame du Barry had already been sent away.

The once handsome face of Louis XV was black, swollen and pocked, as he pressed to his lips a crucifix sent to him by his Carmelite daughter, Madame Louise. He sent Cardinal de Beaumont, Archbishop of Paris, to the large antechamber where the court was assembled, to beg pardon in his name for the scandal he had given. On May 10, shortly past three o'clock in the afternoon, the candle in the window of the King's room was extinguished. It was the fortieth day. The reign of Louis XVI had begun.

The nineteen year old King knew that the cross that had been given him would be a heavy one. The needs of the nation must now come before all personal joys. He was immediately overwhelmed with so much business that he hardly had time for Antoinette. He chose as his chief minister and advisor the elderly and experienced Monsieur de Maurepas, whose respect for tradition was shared by the young king. His other ministers he chose according to their ability and the recommendation of those whose opinion he valued; with their guidance he set about attempting to reform the economy. Louis had inherited a deficit from his predecessors. He refused to raise taxes to correct it, but wished instead to design a plan in which the tax burden would shift more onto the shoulders of the wealthy. He knew little of financial matters. He had to learn about them, and the business of governing as he went along, spending hours examining documents and having lengthy discussions with his advisors.

Meanwhile, Antoinette had been getting into trouble. While receiving the homage of the greatest ladies of the realm, one *dame d'honneur* sat on the floor behind the wide dresses of the Queen and her attendants, making funny remarks and playing tricks. Antoinette hid her face behind her fan in order to repress a smile. The noblewomen noticed it, and were insulted that the Queen had "laughed" at them.

Then she began making the etiquette of the court less strict. With her family in Vienna, there had been great dignity combined with a free and easy atmosphere. It was not so at Versailles. The Queen could not ask for a glass of water without setting in motion an elaborate ritual of precedence and etiquette. She had five hundred people to wait on her, all of whom were excessively jealous of their privileges, yet somehow the mantelpiece in her bedroom never got dusted. She was required to dress in front of several ladies, with the garments handed down a long line from princess to princess, while she shivered from cold and embarrassment. She tried to reorganize her household in a more practical manner, but in doing so affronted many aristocratic families, who thought she was trying to impose Austrian customs on them. They began to sing songs and ballads against her.

Louis often had to say to his wife: "Madame, I have business to attend to." She did not realize what a sacrifice it was for him not to watch her rehearse for a play, or go for a walk in the garden, but now his people came first, and he was so anxious to be a good King. Antoinette retaliated by bombarding him across the table with pellets of bread at dinner, which was usually eaten in public. There was no end to her teasing and tricks. Once, while he was giving audiences, a Grey Nun, with lowered countenance and humble, shuffling gait, was ushered into his study. She knelt before him, and in a strange muffled voice began to present a petition. He noticed the nun was shaking convulsively and he wondered if she were ill.

"Good sister," he began, rising from his chair. Suddenly, the nun threw back her head and to his surprise it was his wife, laughing so hard she was crying.

"Antoinette!" he exclaimed.

She smiled up at him. "Oh, Sire, it is the only way I am able to see you! You are always surrounded by your ministers, and by mountains of books and papers!"

They laughed together, but Louis realized that since he himself did not have time to be with his wife, he must make other arrangements. There were numerous persons at Versailles who would be willing to amuse an eighteen year old Queen, to her own destruction. He asked his brothers and their wives to take her into Paris, since she so loved the opera, but the drawback was that he was usually already asleep when she came home, so they saw even less of each other.

Then he decided to give her Little Trianon. She had hinted that she liked it, and the gardens proved to be a wholesome diversion for her. Furthermore, being there would remove her from the intrigue of the court at large; she would be safe, almost sheltered, as in a secret garden. She would also be kept out of politics, which she did not understand, and when she did, it was from an Austrian point of view. He had only to make certain she chose the right friends.

*****

Upon arriving at Trianon, Louis found the entire company in the billiard room. The gentlemen were gathered around the billiard table. His daughter, who had been watching her cousins play backgammon, came running to him.

"Happy feast day, Mousseline," he said, kissing her cheeks.

"Thank you, my Papa," she replied.

His wife, leaving the game of lotto she was playing with Madame de Polignac, came to him with her usual manner of playful deference. For supper she had changed into a red velvet, sable-trimmed gown, which suited her magnificently. He was aware that people blamed Antoinette's dress expenditure for ruining the economy, but he happened to know that she spent less on clothes than did his old Tante Adelaide. The economy had been in a shambles long before Antoinette had even come to the throne, and as Queen it was demanded that she dress like one.

The King and Queen led the guests into supper, just like any bourgeois couple at their country home. In the dining room there was a bust of himself on the grayish-black carved marble mantelpiece, between two ebony and gold vases, supporting candelabras with bunches of golden lilies in various stages of bloom. Louis sat at one end of the table, the Queen at the other, their guests between them. They only had a few people with them that evening. In addition to his daughter, his brothers and their wives, his nephews, his sister Madame Elisabeth, they had the Princess de Lamballe, the Duc and Duchesse de Polignac, and the Baron de Besenval, a white-haired Swiss soldier and one of the Queen's oldest friends. When everyone was at table, Louis asked the blessing, and the soup was brought in.

In the candlelight he watched his wife across the table. Her once luxuriant hair had become thin after the strange fevers she experienced in the mid-seventies and then the miscarriages she had in the early eighties. Monsieur Léonard was always able to dress it so that it looked elegant and presentable. She tried to keep the conversation light and diverting.

"My dear Lamballe," she asked, "have you heard from our dear Lady Spencer?"

"Yes Madame, she plans to come to Paris again in the spring."

"I hope Duchess Georgiana comes with her," said the Queen.

"It will be a marvel if she does, my sister," said Artois. "How you shocked her poor old mother with that naughty word."

"I was just having Lady Spencer help me with my English lessons," said the Queen. "I did not realize that 'breeches' was not an acceptable word to her Ladyship."

"I will never forget how she ran from the palace," laughed the Duchesse de Polignac, "waving everyone out of the way with her cane!"

"Honestly, I did not mean to upset her so," said the Queen

At the King's left hand sat Madame de Polignac, in a plain but shimmering gown of azure crêpe. The Duchesse always dressed simply and never wore diamonds. She had become one of the most hated women in France because of her closeness with the Queen. Louis remembered how he had encouraged Antoinette's friendship with her. She was from an old Gascon family and her husband was from an equally old Auvergnat family. Whatever their private peccadilloes were, they did not flaunt them, and stood unflinchingly behind the principles of a traditional monarchy.

In La Belle Gabrielle's company, his impressionable wife would not pick up the liberal political opinions with which many noble ladies were obsessed. The Polignac family had been impoverished, so Louis had more than willingly provided them with positions and income so that they could afford to live at court. As much as he was fond of Princesse de Lamballe, and respected her sincere piety, she had many English friends, and was related by marriage to the Orleanist clan, who were themselves Anglophiles, promoters of English fashions, customs, and politics. What the Duc d'Orléans wanted more than anything else was to make France into a constitutional monarchy like England. Louis did not believe his country was ready, if it ever would be, for such a form of government. There was not as large of a strong, educated middle-class in France as there was in England. In France, the peasants would only be manipulated by the liberal forces, to the destruction of religion and virtue. In such a situation the decline of morals would infiltrate every class of society, where now it was mostly the nobility who were infected with vice. La Belle Gabrielle, a protegée of Louis' faithful minister Maurepas, had steered Antoinette away from the Orleanist circles.

The Polignacs also kept Antoinette away from the Guémenés. The Princesse de Guémenée was lovely and charming and had been Madame Elisabeth's governess. Antoinette, naively fond of her, as she was of witty, high-spirited people, kept her on as the governess of their children. However, Madame de Guémenée was addicted to horseracing, and her salon was a gambling hell. For Louis, the last straw was when she fell under the spell of Mesmer, the quack of quacks, and began to imagine that spirits were communicating to her through her dogs. He was relieved when the Guémenés went bankrupt, and had to leave the court. Madame de Polignac was not only governess of the children, but like an older sister to Antoinette, keeping her out of harm's way.

The *paté* was served. Louis enjoyed it as he sipped a crisp red bordeaux. The Queen addressed herself to Madame la Comtesse de Provence. "Do tell us, sister, how is the work on your new music salon coming along?"

"Very well, Madame," said the Comtesse, unctuous as ever. "I hope soon Your Majesty will grace it with your presence."

"I would be delighted," said Antoinette. "What charming musical evenings we will have there!"

*****

In the early years of his reign, his little wife had continued to get into scrapes. For one thing, Madame de Guémenée had passed on to her a fondness for horse-racing. Louis thought it was highly inappropriate for the Queen to appear at such events, especially when she cheered and clapped, which was just not done. He told her she could go on occasion to the Bois de Boulogne for the races, but she must *not* cheer so loud. By age twenty she had become enthralled with Paris, especially the Opera balls. One evening, her coach broke down, and she had to ride in a hired carriage.

"I came in a *fiacre*," she laughed to everyone at the ball, "is it not droll?" But people were scandalized.

On another occasion, she went sleigh-riding through the streets of Paris without an escort. Louis' aunts had been horrified. Their Polish mother, Queen Marie Lezcinska, would have died a thousand deaths before committing such an indiscretion. He was aware that in Vienna it was thought charming for a monarch to behave like a private citizen, but in Paris, it lowered the prestige of the monarchy. He was happier when she became more and more involved with her gardening projects at Trianon.

How distressed he had been when he discovered his beloved wife took such great pleasure in gambling. At Versailles, card-playing was dictated by etiquette and a certain amount of gambling was normal; even his devout Polish grandmother had occasionally lost money to her daughter Madame Adelaïde. It was a revelation to Louis that at the Court of Vienna it was customary to play for very high stakes, and that Antoinette, as an adolescent, had been taught by her parents, the Emperor Francis Stephen and the Empress Maria Theresa, to preside over such games. For Antoinette, the higher the stakes, the more exciting the game. Louis detested gambling; it took him years to break her of it, and then he finally had to forbid her completely. She obeyed, but her last game was a thirty-six hour marathon that began on the Vigil of All Saints Day and ended on All Souls' Day (her birthday), to the great disedification of the faithful (even though she had left the card table to go to Mass). Afterwards, he gave her a sound scolding, saying that she and her friends were a "worthless lot."

*****

The main course was served. Louis, who liked plain, simple food, was glad to see the cutlets, vegetables and fried potatoes. He had encouraged the cultivation of potatoes as a staple crop for his people, since they were nourishing and filling.

"Sire, remember on the Feast of Saint Louis two years ago, when you were first presented with the potato plants?" the Queen asked.

"I stuck the potato blossoms into my button-hole, and you, Madame, used them to adorn your dress," said the King.

"Thus potatoes became the rage in Paris," commented Provence, dryly.

"Our little Mousseline loves fried potatoes," said the Queen.

Madame Royale was sitting at the King's right. She was studiously eating her potatoes. How ecstatic were he and Antoinette when they discovered, after eight years of marriage, that she was going to have a child. Her brother the Emperor Joseph had visited them. Outspoken in the most embarrassing way, he had told Antoinette that she must not go so often to Paris in the evenings. December 19, 1778 was one of the happiest days either of them had ever known. But it was the last time that he ever permitted one of his children to be born in public. His wife had fainted because of the crowd in her room, and would have died if he, Louis, had not happened to possess the strength needed to wrench open the sealed windows, letting in a gust of wintry air.

When their little Dauphin was born, the spectators were kept in the antechambers and on the staircase. People were angry that another old custom was being flung by the wayside, but Louis thought it was one custom which certainly needed to die.

The birth of his son and heir nearly coincided with his victory over the British at Yorktown. With the American War he had hoped to dampen public enthusiasm for everything British. Sympathy for the American patriots had shown his people the flaws in the English parliamentary system. France had been restored to her position as first nation in Europe. How he had been cheered when he went to inspect his navy at Cherbourg! "Long live the King!" everyone shouted and he responded with: "Long live my people!" It seemed that all his labors, his self-denial, were reaping the fruits of prosperity. The harvests were good, inflation was dropping, new houses were being built in Paris, tourists were coming from all over the world to see the churches, museums and palaces of the capital, spending generous amounts of money on French furniture, soaps, perfumes, silks and other items. He and his wife had three children with another on the way. Antoinette was settling down, showing herself to be a devoted mother. And then—the diamond necklace scandal befell them.

Diamond bracelets sparkled on the Queen's wrists as she ate and talked. How strangely it all began! The court jeweler Boehmer had approached Louis with a fabulous diamond necklace. For years, Boehmer had been gathering the finest diamonds in the world to create the necklace to end all necklaces, the dream of every jeweler.

"Your Majesty, this is the masterpiece of my career," said the elated craftsman, who originally created the necklace with Madame du Barry in mind, but since she was no longer in power, he hoped to sell it to the Queen of France.

"Oh, sire, we need ships, not diamonds," Antoinette replied in the merchant's presence, and privately she told her husband: "It is the most vulgar necklace I ever saw, so heavy, so gaudy." She preferred aerial, subtle creations. Anyway, she possessed enough jewelry, preferring to have old pieces reset rather than buy new ones. She did not need or want a breastplate of five hundred and forty diamonds.

Months passed after the interview with Boehmer. Suddenly, the Queen began to receive strange notes from the jeweler, thanking her for her "purchase," and hinting that her first "payment" was due.

"The poor man must have become deranged," she sighed, discarding the notes without another thought. Then he began to pester Madame Campan, the Queens' maid, while the latter was on holiday in the country. Madame Campan persuaded her mistress to receive him.

On August 12, 1785, he came to Versailles in a state which bordered on hysteria. He claimed that the Queen had secretly bought the diamond necklace from him, using Cardinal de Rohan, the Grand Almoner of France, as an intermediary. The necklace was delivered to the Cardinal in February, but he, Boehmer, had not yet been paid the first installment, due August 1. As he saw the Queen's blank expression, and realized she knew nothing of any such transaction, he fell to his knees, sobbing, "I am a ruined man!"

On August 15, 1785, the Feast of the Assumption of Our Lady, the patronal feast-day of the kingdom, the King summoned the Cardinal to his cabinet, interrogating him in the presence of the queen and two of his ministers. Antoinette had never spoken to Cardinal de Rohan, ever since he had insinuated his way into the post of Grand Almoner eight years before. He was a worldly prelate who, as former French ambassador to Vienna, had behaved so disgracefully that the Empress Maria Theresa had longed to expel him from the town. He ridiculed the Empress in a letter, which had found its way into the hands of Madame du Barry, who read it aloud at a supper for the enjoyment of her lackeys and sycophants. It was an insult Antoinette never forgot; the Cardinal was the last man she would have asked to help her in any such matter.

The Cardinal was infatuated with the Queen, and tried in a thousand ways to win her attention, even by coming uninvited to one of her *fêtes* at Trianon, which only infuriated her the more. On that August day, Louis was distressed at the sight of his wife's tears, as the Cardinal admitted to buying diamonds from Boehmer for the Queen. He showed the King a contract, ostensibly from Her Majesty, signed "Marie-Antoinette de France."

"This is neither the Queen's writing nor her signature!" cried Louis, feeling more and more that he would like to throttle the handsome Cardinal, in spite of his red pontifical robes. "How could a Prince of the House of Rohan and a Grand Almoner of France think that the Queen would sign 'Marie-Antoinette de France'? Everyone knows that Queens sign only their Christian names."

The Cardinal paled as if he was about to faint. The King, in an effort to calm him, told him to sit down in the royal study and write out his story on paper. It appeared that a woman calling herself the "Comtesse de la Motte-Valois" had pretended to be an intimate friend of the Queen's, and had tricked the Cardinal into acquiring the necklace through forged letters. The Queen had never heard of any such Comtesse, but whoever she was, the necklace was in her hands. The Cardinal begged not to be arrested.

"I must do my duty as a king and a husband," said Louis. He did not like the way the Cardinal looked at his wife.

In the months that followed, the sordid affair was brought to public trial. The Queen desired everything to be as open as possible, but the Parisian lawyers were delighted that the case proved to doubly besmirch the Church and the Crown. As the story unraveled, it came to light that the Cardinal had often consulted an alchemist, who styled himself the "Comte de Cagliostro," a dabbler in the occult. Cagliostro claimed not only to be two thousand years old, but to possess prescience of future events. He had even conjured up a vision of the Queen in a carafe for the benefit of the Cardinal. The motto of Cagliostro was *Lilia pedibus destrue*, "Tread underfoot the Lilies."

The implications of Cagliostro's involvement horrified the King and Queen, as much as did the Cardinal's story about a nocturnal rendezvous with the Queen in the palace gardens. Most people believed the tale about his encounter with a lady in white, who handed him a rose, since it was common knowledge that Her Majesty loved to take walks in the moonlight. However, the Cardinal had been duped again. The LaMotte woman had paid a streetwalker to impersonate the Queen, attired in a white dress and veiled hat.

In the end, the Cardinal was acquitted of all guilt, and was allowed to go free. When Louis refused to have the man back at Versailles, he was accused of tyranny. Meanwhile, Antoinette's name had been dragged through the mud. Many thought the Cardinal was her lover, that she had used him to get the necklace for her, afterwards abandoning him to his fate. The LaMotte woman, who made a fortune by having the necklace broken up and the diamonds sold separately, escaped from jail to England, where she wrote and published obscene books about the Queen's "private life." Antoinette's reputation was in shreds. She was hissed at the Opera, and compared to every wicked and wanton queen who had ever lived, including Jezebel and Messalina.

*****

The fresh fruit and cheese were served. "I wonder how Monsieur Necker is occupying himself these days?" asked Monsieur. The King raised an eyebrow. Leave it to his brother Provence to bring up politics at a family supper, and such a controversial subject, too. Louis did not reply.

The Queen eased over the awkwardness. "Dear Mademoiselle Necker, that is, I should say, Madame de Staël! Remember how her train fell off when she was being presented to us?" The King nodded.

"I felt so embarrassed for her," Antoinette continued, "and I

90

brought her to my rooms to have her dress mended. She still felt so shy that the King said to her: 'If you cannot be at ease with us, then you cannot be at ease with anyone.' Afterwards, she relaxed a bit. Do you remember, Sire?"

"Yes, my dear," he replied. A glass of Madeira was poured for him, which he always drank at the end of a meal. Coffee and cognac were served to everyone else. As usual, his wife drank only water; she never imbibed anything else, except for coffee or chocolate first thing in the morning. Again, he eyed his brother Provence, sitting at the Queen's right, placidly sipping some cognac. The King was stout, but Provence could be described as corpulent. What a sly fellow he was! Always the cleverest of their family, people had thought Louis-Stanislaus would make a better king than Louis-Auguste, even when the brothers were children.

What a blow the birth of the Dauphin Louis-Joseph had been for Provence! He had been first in line for the throne; now after little Charles' birth, he was only third. Louis never knew what his brother would be plotting next. They could be having a friendly family supper, laughing and talking, while Provence, smiling pleasantly, kept the wheels of his mind turning incessantly, weaving ambitious and devious designs. Last week, in the Oeuil-de-Boeuf, one of the antechambers of the King's apartments, a bundle of pamphlets was found, containing vicious cartoons of the Queen that were surely from the depths of hell itself. One of Louis' valets had intimated to him that there were underground presses in the palace that were printing some of the same filth. One of his gentlemen-in-waiting had hinted that the Comte de Provence owned such a press and was behind some of the calumnious obscenities.

The preceding evening, the King received a very disturbing letter from his secret advisor, Marquis de Pezay, who as an outsider, sometimes had the clearest picture. His letter said:

Sire,
Information has come to me by one of my most trusted contacts that Versailles has become the newest site of the séances that have spread throughout the land. To be more precise, Monsieur de Modéne, gentleman-in-waiting to His Royal Highness Monsieur le Comte de Provence, has become quite practiced in the black arts and in occult incantations. It is said he has called up the Devil for the purposes of His Royal Highness, for reasons that can be known

to Monsieur alone.

Your humble servant,

Pezay.

Louis wished he could have the entire palace exorcized. That such things would happen under the very roofs where his wife and children slept made him ill. He had heard that his cousin, the Duc d'Orléans, frequently consulted with the Evil One through the spells of the diabolists Chavigny and Beauregard, but to hear that his own brother had sunk to such depths!

As for Artois, even though he was completely given over to women and luxury, he occasionally displayed a sense of traditional morals and politics, and might turn out alright in the end.

Sometimes, in his dreams, Louis saw the ships he had sent to explore the Pacific under the guidance of La Pérouse. The urge to sail away with his family, away from the plots of hell, often came over him like waves crashing on the shore. But his heart told him that he was already on his ship; France was his ship, and he was the captain. As long as he lived, he could not abandon the storm-tossed vessel.

He rose, taking the Queen's arm, and together they went into the Grand Salon. After thirty minutes or so of listening to music, he begged leave to retire. It was ten o'clock. His little Thérése was already slumbering on the sofa; her cousins were stifling yawns. He had much work to do before bed. Bowing to the company and embracing his wife, he left Little Trianon. He must rise at six if he wanted some time to read and work at his forge before his lever at eight thirty, when he would officially rise from bed in the presence of the great nobles. It was a never-ending nuisance for him to leave what he was doing, return to his bedroom and throw on his nightshirt again, but the lever was an institution; one of the smaller sacrifices a monarch was required to make.

He mounted his horse in the courtyard, recalling the spring day, shortly after his accession to the throne, that he and Antoinette had ambled over to Trianon, with an assortment of little children trailing behind.

"Since Trianon has always belonged to the mistresses of the King, it is only right that I should give it to you," he had said to her.

She had thrown her arms around his neck in gratitude and joy. She never ceased to be enraptured with her garden retreat. He felt she so belonged to its beauty and simplicity. As he slowly rode away, her voice came to him, singing an aria from Gluck's *Iphigenia*, her fingers lightly plucking and dancing across the harp strings. It was a cross for him to leave her company, but to wear the crown was to live alone. At his coronation, he was given the grace to bear the loneliness of heart that was the lot of every monarch, of every serious, business-like monarch, at any rate. For Louis, to be with Antoinette as much as he would like would mean neglecting his duties, as his grandfather had done with women.

Again, he made an interior surrender of his will to God, the same assent he had made when prostrate at the foot of the altar at Rheims before his anointing and crowning. He summoned to his mind the image of the Sacred Host on the Corpus Christi following his coronation, when he had walked in procession behind the monstrance, his eyes on his God, rapt in ecstasy.

"Sweet Jesus," he whispered. As he trotted away, Antoinette's voice faded into the darkness.

Chapter Five
The Grotto

"Fear and trembling are come upon me . . . And I said: Who will give me wings like a dove, and I will fly and be at rest?" —Psalm 54: 6, 7

Marie-Antoinette, Queen of France, afternoon, October 5, 1789

A woman in a white cotton dress, a ruffled scarf of diaphanous muslin crossed over her bodice, with a wide-brimmed straw hat, swept down the steps from the porch to the lower terrace on the south-west, French garden side of Little Trianon. She glided across the terrace where, as a young Queen, she had danced in the light of *flambeaux* at many a mid-summer *fête*. There was a deliberateness to her stride; she had much to do that afternoon. First of all, some of her plants needed watering, even though it did look like it might rain. She planned to inspect her dairy and, if she could find her gardener, give him instructions for the winter preparations. The blue sky was becoming overcast. The beauty and serenity of the gardens, of the lawns and dales, of the trees whose leaves were deepening into gold, made a striking contrast with the leaden clouds and thunderheads that were creeping up from the western horizon. Her heart was heavy, as she avoided the French gardens. They reminded her too much of a little boy who would never play there again.

Passing her theater, she recalled with a glimmer of bitter humor how the deputies of the Third Estate first came to Trianon last spring, searching high and low for a pillared room studded with diamonds, sapphires and rubies. They were disturbed when they could not find it at Trianon, and went away convinced that she, the "Austrian Woman," was concealing it from them.

One evening in her apartments, she discussed the incident with her husband the King. "But where, Sire, would they get the notion of such a room? There is no gem-studded chamber in all of Versailles, much less at my Little Trianon. Do they not know that I long for, and delight in, simplicity rather than ostentation?"

Her husband was silent. "I believe I know where the idea came from," he said, thoughtfully. "I remember, years ago, perhaps even in Madame du Barry's time, that there was a theater prop at the Versailles opera with colored glass that sparkled, and from a distance it resembled jewels."

"Oh, I do remember," she said. "But how could they connect it with Trianon?"

He looked at her, his sad, sweet eyes full of a tenderness that was reserved for her alone. "I do not know, my dear. All I can say is that the pamphleteers have been busy."

She buried her face in his shoulder; she felt the strange trembling coming on, from which she had suffered as a child, but lately began to experience more frequently. Only in her husband's arms could she regain her self-control. "But what have I done to them that they should hate me so?"

"Jealousy, envy, calumny," he murmured. "And I suppose it is true enough to say, that in the days of my predecessors, the calamities and misfortunes of the land were blamed on the mistresses of the king, on a Pompadour or a Du Barry. The Queen was never held responsible when things went wrong." He chuckled to himself. "I, on the other hand, have as my mistress none other than a beautiful actress with red hair named Antoinette, whom I refuse to give up."

"My hair is not red anymore; it is gray," she said, her voice muffled by his silk waistcoat. Then she looked up at him. "And because you are a virtuous man, they blame everything upon your wife, who becomes the scapegoat for the ills of the nation. Oh, sire, if I knew that my death would save your kingdom, how willingly I would offer it as a sacrifice."

"Nonsense," he brusquely replied. "Nonsense. If I ever thought you or the children were in serious danger, I would send you out of the country."

She pulled away from him, putting her hands upon her waist. "Louis-Auguste, please understand one thing. I will never agree to leaving

95

you. If I die, it will be at your feet, with the children in my arms. My place is at your side; to escape without you would be cowardice, and only playing into the hands of our enemies. Whatever storms assail us, we will face them together."

"We shall see," he replied, gravely.

"And furthermore, Sire," she said in a teasing tone. "I do have a rival for your affections."

"Oh, do you?" he asked, kissing her hand. "And who is the lady? I seem to be unaware of her."

"The lady," she replied, "is France. The kingdom of France became my rival the day you ascended the throne. I lost you to a jealous mistress, one more conniving and desirous of power than ever La Pompadour dreamed of being."

He shook his head. "There are others desirous of power, Madame. The people themselves are innocent of connivance. It is the lawyers and politicians who manipulate and incite the poor and uneducated, most of whom are still loyal, in spite of the crop failures last year, and the difficult winter."

"We have done the best we could to relieve their misery, have we not?" demanded the Queen. "We sold our table silver to buy bread for the citizens of Paris, and have ourselves taken to eating the coarsest, cheapest, barley bread there is. I do not complain; I would willingly do more. Yet Orléans spreads his slanders that we are doing nothing, and he is believed!"

"Unfortunately, Orléans is not alone in his black work," said the King. "There are others."

She knew he was referring to his brother Provence, but it pained him to say so. She was also aware that the famine was worsened by profiteers who bought up the crops in prosperous regions of the country. She wondered if they, too, were not under the direction of Orléans and his friends. The Palais Royal was the hideout of every brand of criminal conspirator, but the police were not allowed to enter Orléans' domain, he being a Prince of the Blood. Pamphlets were printed there, and the dregs of society were organized and sent out to instigate riots. Perhaps, Provence, too, was behind some of the propaganda. But there was no way of telling.

She sighed, "How happy we were in the days of your grandfather Louis XV. We had no care but to love each other."

It was last April when Antoinette and her husband had spoken thus, right before the convocation of the Estates General. The calling of the Three Estates was the last recourse open to the King in his effort to correct the situation of unequal taxation in France. If his reforms could become law, it would reverse many of the country's economic problems. The *parlements* had resisted registering his edicts. By summoning the Third Estate, which was comprised of the elected representatives of the common people, he hoped to appeal directly to those citizens whom his programs would most benefit. By doing so, he was taking a tremendous risk, because many of the people's elected representatives were disciples of Voltaire and Rousseau. Not only that, but the powerful nobles and clergymen, who would lose money from Louis' tax reforms, sought to agitate the bourgeois representatives against their King.

Meanwhile, Louis had decided that the Third Estate should have as many deputies as the clergy (First Estate) and the nobility (Second Estate) combined, extending the franchise to all male tax payers over twenty-five. He was giving concessions that no king had ever granted before, hoping to win the commoners to his side. He was determined to make the Estates-General a success, and had devoted all the last year to preparing for it. If successful, it would mean a new era of prosperity and civil peace for France. In accordance with the character of his reign, he planned to protect religion and the good old traditions, while pruning away what was cumbersome and obsolete. But he needed to have the nation behind him.

*****

Antoinette walked the wooded path towards the big lake and the *hameau*. The rustling of the trees eased her mind, as if they were whispering secrets to her. It felt wonderful to be alone, entirely alone. On one hand, she savored parties and gaiety, but she also craved solitude the way others crave food. She had desperately needed to leave the tensions at the palace, and lose herself for awhile in the glades of Trianon.

She came to the lake. On the far side was her rustic Norman cottage; it was reflected in the smooth surface of the water. A willow tree mournfully brushed the lake, on which floated clusters of water lilies. The banks were spiked with bulrushes and reeds. A swan glided near her, ignoring the fish that would occasionally splash up after a dragonfly. She realized that it was nothing but a dream of enchantment that she had made tangible. She was much censured for her dream. It was considered extravagant, but all she had sought to do was create a garden enclosed, where she and her family and friends could come and be safe, happy, and free—free from gossip and scandal, from malice and plotting. But, as she had learned, there was no escaping the wickedness of the world, at least not permanently. Only in Heaven was there true peace and freedom.

Her eyes fell upon the white Marlborough Tower and quickly the image blurred. She had also discovered there was no escaping pain, the pain of memory, the sword-like piercing of her heart whenever she saw or thought of anything that brought to mind a small boy in a velvet sailor suit, with whom she had once walked along those banks. The little tower had celebrated his birth. She realized that it, too, was only another illusion. Happiness cannot be built on illusions. The illusion and the dream now gave her only pain.

*****

Last spring, while her husband was feverishly preparing for the Estates-General, he had taken every available opportunity to dash over to the chateau of Meudon where their eldest son had been sent for his health, the air being purer and fresher there. She spent every free moment at her little son's side. Louis-Joseph was stretched out upon a billiard table, which mitigated somewhat the torment caused by his displaced and projecting vertebrae. By the end of April, 1789, their Dauphin was in the final stages of consumption of the bones. His patience was remarkable for a child; he read books far advanced for his age.

With his hyacinth-blue eyes shining in spite of his pain, he would tell her about his reading. "Maman, I am reading of the reign of King Charles VII. The times were exceedingly dangerous! France was almost lost to the English, and the good Duc d'Orléans was imprisoned by King Henry V. Then God sent Saint Michael to Jeanne la Pucelle. With Dunois' help, she saved the kingdom. She led the Dauphin to Rheims where he was anointed and crowned. Then the Burgundians captured her at Compiègne, and the English burned her at the stake."

Antoinette fought back tears as he spoke of Rheims, where he would never go for his coronation. To watch one's child die was an unendurable torture. As the deputies of the Estates were convening at Versailles, he entered into his agony, and his agony was her own.

On May 4, 1789, she put Louis-Joseph and his sister with Madame de Polignac on a balcony above the stables so they could watch the magnificent Eucharistic procession which marked the opening of the Estates-General. The procession wound from the Royal Chapel, across the vast courtyard of the palace, through the streets of the town of Versailles, to the Church of Saint Louis. The monstrance, in the hands of a bishop, was under a rich canopy carried by Provence, Artois, Berry, and Angoulême. Everyone held a candle, except for the standard bearers, with the fluttering silken banners, and the royal falconers, with falcons on their wrists, looking both noble and fierce. The King, with a lighted taper, walked directly behind the monstrance. He wore a cloth of gold mantle and a plumed hat with the famous Regent diamond. He was wildly applauded by the crowds that lined the route. But when Antoinette, who with her ladies followed the King's household, passed by in her gown of gold and silver tissue, every tongue fell silent. She could almost taste the hatred. It frightened her.

When passing beneath the balcony where her sick boy was lying, she glanced up to blow him a kiss. The cry "Long live Orléans!" resounded in her ears. The extent of the malice overwhelmed her. That someone could hate her so much that they would use her child's suffering as an opportunity to humiliate her; that they would praise her known enemy at a moment when as a mother she was most vulnerable, within the hearing of her pain-wracked Dauphin, stunned her as much as if she had been whipped or burnt. She halted, dizzily, then turned to see who had insulted her. In doing so, she staggered, but before she lost her balance, Princesse de Lamballe took her arm and steadied her.

During Benediction at the Church of Saint Louis, the bishop preached against the luxury of the court which, he said, was causing the martyrdom of the French people. Antoinette felt everyone's eyes turn towards her. At the end of the sermon, there was an outburst of clapping. It jolted her more than anything else that had happened that day—people applauding in the presence of the Blessed Sacrament. Surely, such an outrage had never been done before.

After the services, her ladies somehow got her back to her rooms, where she collapsed in a fit of convulsions. She trembled so violently, her pearl necklace and diamond bracelets broke. Madame de Lamballe and Madame Elisabeth tried to calm her, but they had to cut off her dress in order to get her to bed.

She recovered enough the next day to be at the King's side in the Hall of Lesser Pleasures at Versailles, where he gave his welcoming address to the deputies. Her husband, in his golden robes, was heartily applauded, while she, in her lavender-blue silk dress covered with silver spangles, received a few weak cheers.

The King's speech was magnificent. "Gentlemen," he began, his voice echoing with all the ardor and majesty of the Bourbons. "The day I have been awaiting with eagerness has arrived at last. I see myself surrounded by the representatives of the Nation it is my glory to command."

His Keeper of the Seals, Monsieur de Miromesnil, then presented the King's program of reform to the deputies: he wanted the clergy and nobility to share in the burden of taxation. The day appeared to be a success, in spite of a long, sonorous speech by the finance minister, Monsieur Necker. But in the following weeks, the King's worst fears were realized.

The deputies demanded more than the King thought it was possible to give. The Third Estate wanted to abolish all class distinctions and privileges of rank. They were not really interested in economic reform, but demanded the restructuring of society, the only society France had ever known, and they wanted it to happen immediately. They did not want a fatherly king who would grant them concessions from above, rather, like rebellious adolescents, they wanted to wrest power and authority for themselves. On June 17, without the King's permission, they created what they called the National Assembly—the basis of what they hoped would become a constitutional monarchy. And there were some who wanted no monarchy at all.

*****

Antoinette came to her dairy. Turning up her skirts, she pinned them in the back so that her blue and white striped petticoat was exposed. She put on an apron that hung near the porcelain crockery and bowls. She walked around the stalls and the rooms for making butter and cream. Everything was clean and in order. She loved to come there in the evenings to help with the milking. There was something about manual labor that relieved an anguished soul. Madame Valy-Busard, the farmer's wife, and the dairy maids, were busily churning butter, pouring the finished product into crocks, kept cool by the springs under the dairy. Antoinette drank some of the fresh milk. She had found in the past that it calmed her frayed nerves.

*****

Throughout the month of May, while her husband was having it out with the deputies and Monsieur Necker, Louis-Joseph's body became increasingly twisted and tortured. His mind became tormented, too, and he believed Madame de Polignac was trying to poison him with her perfume. Antoinette wondered if Monsieur d'Harcourt, the Dauphin's governor, was engaged in some power struggle with the Duchesse de Polignac, and was trying to influence the child against her by putting ideas into his mind.

"Maman," Louis-Joseph moaned to her one day, "why do you love Charles more than you love me?" From a dying seven year old, the question cut her to the heart. "Oh, my darling," she replied, "I love you and your brother equally." Any doubt of her devotion to him was like a wound.

As he became more confused, he would not allow her to feed him, but accepted only what his doctors gave him, as if he suspected his own mother of wanting to poison him, too. On June 2, Forty Hours devotion began, and the bell of Notre Dame tolled, summoning the people to pray for the dying heir of the Bourbons. In all the churches of Paris, the Blessed Sacrament was exposed. On June 4, the curtain of the *Théatre Français* was lowered after the first act, and the death of the Dauphin was announced. At one o'clock that morning, his agony came to an end, but Antoinette's was only beginning. According to etiquette, she could not weep beside her son's body, but had to tear herself away from where he lay, already surrounded by twelve candles and by monks chanting the Office of the Dead. He was dressed in a golden crown and spurs, laid in a white coffin, and carried in procession to the Cathedral of Saint Denis, where he was buried in the royal crypt with his ancestors. Custom did not permit the bereaved parents to follow their son to his tomb. Instead, they went alone to the chateau of Marly, to mourn together for a week, until duty recalled them to Versailles. The King, incessantly badgered by deputies, was overcome by his son's death, and cried out to them: "Are there no fathers among you?" He and Antoinette arranged for a thousand Masses to be said for the soul of Louis-Joseph, paying for the stipends with what was left of their silver plate.

*****

On the trail back from the dairy, Antoinette encountered the gardener, pushing a wheelbarrow. They walked along, discussing the various plants, and what would be best for each one.

"The clematis needs to be well-mulched, don't you think, my friend?" she asked.

"Yes, Madame. And I will cut back the roses tomorrow."

"Good, very good. And would you please divide the hyacinth bulbs in the French gardens?"

"Yes, Madame."

"Last year was such a hard winter that the sage and rosemary plants almost did not survive. In fact, we did lose a few. Perhaps tomorrow you had better bring them in."

"That I will do, Madame."

*****

While the King and Queen mourned a dead child, their enemies were busy. Orléans devoted himself to stirring up the people. By the end of June, there was rioting in the streets of Paris. The King saw to the replenishment of the grain supply, but the citizens were not appeased. To protect Paris and Versailles, and restore law and order, Louis summoned six regiments from the eastern frontier. He was accused of tyranny, and on July 14 an enraged mob stormed the Bastille. Monsieur de Launay, the Governor of the Bastille, who treated with great benevolence the seven criminals who were housed therein, was tricked by the leaders of the mob, including the dreadful Marquis de Sade, and brutally murdered. Louis, on hearing of the infamy, was stunned.

"My heart is rent asunder," he said. "It is inconceivable that the orders I gave to my troops are the cause of this." Three days after the carnage, the King went to Paris, alone and without an escort, to attempt to come to an understanding with the National Assembly.

Antoinette begged him not to go. "It is futile, Sire. They want a reconciliation only on their terms. If they do not get it, I fear they will turn on you as they did on the Governor of the Bastille, and it shall be your head they carry through the streets on a pike!"

He calmly put on his hat. "Then it is a good thing I confessed and received Holy Communion this morning. In the event I do not return, I have told my brother Provence that he is in charge."

"Provence!"

"Yes, my dear. Letting him feel important for a few hours will keep him out of trouble while I am gone. But I will return before supper, I assure you."

He embraced her, and went out the door, without the least sign of agitation in his slow, swaying walk. As soon as he left, Antoinette was seized with one of her trembling fits. Once again, Princesse de Lamballe, Madame Elisabeth, and her ladies were not able to calm her. All she could say was: "He will never return! Oh God, spare my husband!"

She sent for Count Axel von Fersen. Count Fersen was attached to the Swedish embassy, and as a close friend of their ally, the King of Sweden, he had many times proved himself to be of indispensable value on diplomatic missions, not only to Sweden, but to other countries, too. They had known him for many years; the King had given him a commission in the American War, where he had showed himself a loyal and able soldier. He was also a dedicated monarchist, and as quite the cosmopolitan man-about-town, he had thousands of contacts all over Paris. A seasoned diplomat, he always managed to have a firsthand knowledge of events.

The Count was one of the men the scandal sheets named as being Antoinette's lover—any handsome man with whom she was friendly was immediately assumed to be having an illicit relationship with her. She was fond of the Count—he was one of the few people to whom, like Gabrielle de Polignac, she could frankly and openly express her thoughts without being misunderstood or misinterpreted. The King also liked Count Fersen, and refused to send him from the court, because to do so, he said, would be like giving credence to the ugly rumors.

"Oh, Count Fersen!" cried Antoinette, as she lay on the sofa in her *méridienne*, with Madame Elisabeth sitting at her side. "I implore you, if the King is taken prisoner by the National Assembly, to please go to all the embassies in Paris, and beg them to put pressure on the National Assembly to release him."

The gallant Swede knelt and kissed her hand. "I will do whatever I can, Your Majesty."

"And if they will not release him, then please enjoin the Assembly to allow me to share my husband's imprisonment."

She asked to be left alone for awhile. Lying in the cool, white and gold octagonal chamber, with its sky-blue upholstered furniture, she could see herself reflected in one of the mirrors—all of her, except for her head. She composed and memorized a short speech she would say to the National Assembly, if they decided to deprive the King of his liberty. She pulled on a long cord, and Madame Campan, her maid, entered.

"Madame, let me recite for you my speech. If the King is

imprisoned, I will go with my children to the National Assembly, and say: 'Gentlemen, I come to put in your hands the wife and family of your sovereign. Do not suffer those who have been united by Heaven to be put asunder on earth.' How does that sound?"

"They could not help but be moved, Your Majesty."

"Oh, but I fear he will never return!" She began trembling again. "Please, Madame Campan, send word to the stables for them to ready my horse, so I may go to him when he needs me." Unable to eat or rest, she sent for her children, and the sight of them calmed her.

"Maman," asked Charles, who was now Dauphin of France, "where is Madame la Duchesse de Polignac? I cannot find her anywhere."

Tears came to Antoinette's eyes, as she hugged her four year old son. "*Mon chou d'amour*, do you not understand, that Madame la Duchesse and her family have had to leave us?"

"Oh, but why, Maman?" he asked.

"Because there are people who are very angry at her, and they might try to . . . to hurt Madame la Duchesse." She could not bear to tell him that his former governess was hated only because she was the Queen's friend. Louis had ordered the Polignacs to leave the country for their own safety, as well as the Comte d'Artois and his family. In the last few weeks, dandified Artois had surprisingly shown a great deal of backbone for the cause of the traditional monarchy, making himself quite hated and feared by the Assembly.

"Why did our cousins go away, too, Maman?" asked Thérèse. "Berry and Angoulême, what could they have done to make people angry?"

"Well, of course they must go with their Maman and Papa," answered the Queen.

"Versailles seems empty today, Maman, with Papa gone, and so many friends."

"Yes, Mousseline," agreed Antoinette. Indeed, the palace was like a tomb. Scores of courtiers had left Versailles the day before, now that the Revolution had begun in earnest.

The agonizing afternoon wore on. At last, the King's coach could be seen coming through the palace gates. In a few minutes, he was up the stairs, and at the door of her apartments, with Count Fersen and other friends behind him. Antoinette flew into his arms, her face transfigured with joy. She choked with happy tears, feeling like one who had died but come to life again.

"We might be able to ride out the storm," he said to her when they were alone. He had been well-received by the National Assembly even though they had made him walk through a Masonic arch of swords. "We must try to stay in the eye of the hurricane. To flee Versailles, to leave the hub of events, would be to play into the hand of Orléans. He would love for me to be out of the way so he can be the king if a constitutional monarchy is declared. We must hold on as long as we can, without giving in to panic."

"Yes, Sire," she agreed, resolving to make an effort to be cheerful and courageous. For the rest of the summer, tensions seemed to subside. Some people even said the Revolution was over. Antoinette found a new governess for her children, Madame de Tourzel, and devoted herself to the upbringing of the son and daughter who were left to her. Then on October 1, the Royal Bodyguards at Versailles gave a banquet at the palace Opera for the Flanders regiment, who had recently arrived as reinforcements to protect the Royal Family.

"I have never heard of people dining in a theater, Maman," said the Dauphin Charles.

"No, my dear child, it is generally not done. But the Bodyguards are giving a dinner for the good Flanders regiment, and the Flanders soldiers are so brave that the guards chose the finest place they could think of to entertain them, which is why they chose dining in the gay, painted theater."

"Oh, Maman! Oh, Papa!" exclaimed the little boy. "How I should like to see them!"

"Let us go," said the King, "to satisfy the child."

They walked over to the opera with both of their children, and the troops welcomed them with thunderous cheers and acclamations. "Long live the King! Long live the Queen! Long live the Dauphin!"

Then the soldiers began to sing a song from Grétry's opera *Richard Coeur de Lion*:

> *O, Richard, O mon Roi*
> *L' univers t'abandonne.*
> *Sur la terre il n'est donc que moi*
> *Qui m'intéresse à ta personne.*

The little Dauphin went with one of the soldiers, and proudly walked the length of the large horseshoe table without upsetting a single glass. Antoinette had not wanted to appear at the banquet, and although she was heartened by the loyal cheers and singing, she feared the incident would somehow be distorted by the gazettes.

She was right. Unfortunately, within a couple of days, the banquet was turned into a story of a wild orgy in which she, the evil Austrian woman, trampled on the red, white and blue revolutionary cockade, inciting the soldiers to cry: "Down with the Assembly!" She dreaded what the outcome of it all would be, but perhaps it would come to nothing, and everything would be alright. Perhaps they would be able to ride out the storm.

*****

Her walk led her to the grotto. Crossing the narrow foot bridge over the ravine, she sat on the dry, mossy couch in the rocky, sheltered alcove, where the spray of the little waterfalls rose around her. The gentle roar of the water helped to soothe the confused thoughts, which darted in and out of her mind like gnats. So many loved ones gone! Dear Gabrielle, with her easy charm and lisping, Occitan accent, who always found the right words to console her, with whom Antoinette could be herself. It so distressed her to be separated from the friend who took the place of the older sisters she had left in Vienna; she could not even say her name.

She also missed her son, Louis-Joseph. In her antechamber hung the portrait by Madame Vigée-Lebrun of herself in a red velvet dress, with Mousseline at her side, Charles on her lap, and Louis-Joseph standing by Baby Sophie's empty cradle. She could no longer endure the sight of it.

The death of a child was a never-ending pain; even if it dulled, the sense of loss never went away, like an amputated limb that ached on rainy days when it was no longer there. Her eldest son, her Louis- Joseph, gentle and bright, for whose birth she had implored Heaven, was no more.

*****

The day Louis-Joseph was born, her husband came to her bedside, his face studiedly sober. She did not yet know whether the baby was a boy or a girl.

"I have been a good patient. Can you not tell me?" she asked.

"Madame," he said, his eyes shining with an almost ethereal joy, "Monsieur le Dauphin begs leave to enter." He embraced her; their tears

106

mingled. "You have fulfilled my dearest hopes and those of France. Madame, you are the mother of a Dauphin!"

What a happy day! What rejoicing! Paris was illuminated and peopledanced in the streets. Craftsmen and merchants came to the palace, bringing gifts for the new prince. Her husband walked among them, examining their varied and curious products, as they all strained their arms to touch their King, who was the father of a son and heir. The continuation of the dynasty was assured. With what acclamations did she go to her churching at Notre Dame, as the choir chanted in Latin Psalm 23:

> *Who shall ascend into the mountain of the Lord: or who shall stand in his holy place?*

She processed down the nave surrounded by her ladies, whose jewels glittered in the colored light of the windows.

> *The innocent of hands, and clean of heart, who hath not taken his soul in vain, nor sworn deceitfully to his neighbor. He shall receive a blessing from the Lord, and mercy from God his Savior.*

Alas, for the fickleness of human hearts! In seven years, everything had changed. The life of Louis-Joseph had come and gone as if he had never been, forgotten by everyone except his mother.

"He is in Heaven," she murmured to herself. "He is better off. " With what was coming upon them, the dead were truly more blessed than the living.

*****

Her mind was tired and at that moment, she felt overwhelmed by life. She did not know if she could bear any more sadness.

"I must endure whatever God wills for me," she whispered aloud. Her hand touched the bodice of her dress, where next to her skin was a lock of her mother's hair.

"Oh, my mother, pray for me," she said. She became conscious of the scapular, which she also wore beneath her shift. It had been sent to Antoinette two years ago by Tante Louise, Mother Thérèse of Saint Augustine, only three months before her death. Tante Louise had died on December 23 after receiving an anonymous package labelled: "Relics of the Eternal Father."

"What nonsense can this be?" the old nun said, opening the package to find it contained nothing but feathers, and an odd, white powder. Antoinette was convinced the powder had been poison, because the next day Tante Louise was vomiting and ill. Her last words were: "Full gallop, into Heaven!"

"A Bourbon to the end," sighed Antoinette. Louis was devastated to lose one whose wisdom he relied upon in such crucial times.

Another crushing disappointment for the King was the news that the expedition to the Pacific under La Pérouse, that he had so painstakingly outfitted, had met with disaster. The explorers had encountered some hostile natives who were fierce cannibals, so most of the crews of the two frigates perished miserably. Mercifully, one man had been sent across Asia to Europe with charts and records that pinpointed the exact location of hitherto unknown Pacific islands; the quest had not been entirely in vain. The tragedy destroyed the theory of the *philosophes* that man in his primitive state is peaceful and benign.

And now the ship of state was foundering! There were so many breathlessly waiting for the King to abandon the ship, so they could step in behind the rudder. In the minds of many, the King was no longer the representative of God, but the Nation had become a god, and Antoinette knew that a false god was a demon. Orléans seemed to be the foremost high priest of the worship of the Nation, of the new "Temple of Man," where the only doctrines were the "rights" of the citizens. If Orléans did not succeed in stepping in, then Provence would. He would be delighted to become a regent if anything happened to the King.

*****

Her mind traveled back to an autumn day at the *château* of Fontainebleau when they were very young, before her husband became king, and she and Louis were walking together to the stables to see a new horse. They came upon Provence slapping about a young groom for not currying his horse properly. Her husband, only about eighteen at the time, went pale. He could not bear the sight of cruelty or injustice. He grabbed his brother Provence by the collar and yanked him away from the groom, who scampered off.

"Do not let me catch you striking the little lad again," said Louis-Auguste. "As if it matters so much what your horse looks like!" After all, Provence did not even ride. Louis turned and began walking away, but

Provence jumped on him from behind, saying,

"You great ox!" Antoinette, in the doorway of the stable, let out a little scream. She had seen her husband tussle with Provence before, but this time the younger brother seemed particularly livid. He began pummeling Louis with his fists. He might as well have been striking iron, because Louis was practically unaffected, and flung him off, then knocked him into a mound of dirty straw.

"You __ __." Provence let fly a torrent of ugly words that Antoinette had never heard before, at least not when she was studying French in Vienna. Louis said nothing, but took her arm and they left the stables.

How rough her husband and his brothers could be! Really, they were more like their Saxon and Polish forebears than their French ones. At least she was married to the strongest brother—stronger morally and spiritually as well as physically. Provence had always seemed compelled to compete with Louis, to prove he was superior, even if he was not the eldest. The old rivalry had only taken on a subtler, more insidious form.

While Provence was plotting, Louis studied the Scottish historian David Hume's account of the tragedy of England's King Charles I, who was tried and beheaded by his own parliament. He was determined not to make the same mistakes as his ancestor the king—he would not raise his sword against his people, which in the case of Charles brought about the horror and widespread destruction of civil war. He read aloud to her the parts about Queen Henrietta Maria, Charles' wife, which Antoinette remembered from reading the book as a young girl.

"You need not fear," she said to Louis. "I am not Henrietta of France. Not even to save my life will I ever willingly be separated from my husband, my son, or my adopted country. My life or my death must be encircled in your arms and in the arms of my family. With you, and with you only, will I live or die!"

It was only a repetition of the argument they had had several times during those months of crisis.

"Madame," replied her husband, "by imitating the brave Queen Henrietta you would be showing prudence and wisdom, not cowardice, in fleeing the country. After all, does not the Gospel say: 'If they persecute you in one town, flee to another?' "

"Matters have not yet come to such a turn for the worst," said the Queen, resolutely. "Hopefully, they never will. If you flee, I will, too. But I shall never go anywhere without you." They both knew it was not the last time the topic would be discussed.

*****

Lightly, she brushed her hand against the scapular, recalling Our Lady's promise of final perseverance to those who wear it worthily. She had learned from her mother not to fear death, as long as one's soul was at peace with God. She was not afraid of anything that could happen to her personally, but as a wife and mother she was tormented by anxiety about what lay in store for her kind and gentle husband and her innocent children. She only hoped they would not be compelled to suffer for her sins. Her sins were not what the gazettes made them to be; rather, pride was her besetting sin. Pride had kept her from speaking to Madame du Barry for so long. How difficult it had been for her to finally throw a random phrase at the woman! She had long forgiven the misguided creature, as she hoped to be forgiven by God for her many imprudences and follies. Since she had ardently begun to follow the way of devotion, she tried by prayer and charity to the poor to atone for the faults and negligences of her youth. She and her husband had attempted to make virtue a reality at Versailles; marital fidelity and charitable works had even become fashionable in some circles. But to certain people, clean living was a reproach, to be either scoffed at, or denied, or twisted into something decayed and unnatural.

She began to pray. All she could do was commend her family to God's mercy. "Oh, Lord, not my will, but Thine be done. Most Sacred Heart of Jesus, I place all my trust in Thee." As she prayed, the rush of water drowned out all other thoughts. She did not even notice that the sky had become dark, and rain drops were beginning to fall.

Antoinette glanced up. There was someone at the entrance of the grotto. It was a young page. He was gasping for breath.

"Oh, Madame," he panted. "I come from the Comte de Saint-Priest. He begs Your Majesty to return at once to the palace! Paris is marching on Versailles!"

"What?!" She stood up.

"A mob, a huge mob, Madame, with long knives, clubs and pitchforks, is coming this way!"

"*Sacré bleu!*" she cried. "The King is hunting at Meudon! Has anyone sent for him?"

"Yes, Your Majesty, they are trying to find him now. But, please,

110

come, do come, Madame!"

She left the grotto, plunging into the rain, behind the running page. The hour of trial had come at last. Her fears vanished like the rising mist from the falls. She was calm, and fortitude filled her heart, readying her to face the storm. She ran through the wet gardens, the hem of her white dress becoming green with grass stains. At length, she reached the house, and was soon at the gates. She did not look back at Trianon, as it receded from view, veiled behind a curtain of rain.

Part II
THE CROSS

Chapter Six
The Priest

"I will take the chalice of salvation and I will call upon the Name of the Lord." —
Psalm 115:13

Abbé Edgeworth de Firmont, late afternoon, January 20, 1793

On a narrow street in a dingy Paris slum, a coach halted in front of a row house. A tall, slender man in his forties, wearing a dark hat and overcoat, left the house and climbed into the coach. He had chiseled features, high cheekbones, a Roman nose, and a solemn expression. He was no stranger to sacrifice; his life from childhood had been a series of renunciations for the sake of Christ, but he was at that moment embarking on a mission which would be the crown of his priestly career. He was being called to risk his life for a soul at the hour of its supreme trial. The coach was taking him to minister to a condemned prisoner, and by answering that prisoner's request for a priest, he was exposing himself to death, because the condemned man was none other than His Most Christian Majesty Louis XVI, by the grace of God, King of France and Navarre.

Without a thought to his own safety, the priest went to succor his sovereign. He went with the same adherence to God's will with which he accepted the Catholic faith as a child, along with his father, a former Anglican minister, and the rest of his family. Their conversion meant that under the anti-Catholic penal laws they no longer had a right to the vast Edgeworth holdings in Ireland, but had to leave relatives and homeland for France where they would have the freedom to practice their faith.

Although he had grown up in the Irish colony at Toulouse, young Henry Essex Edgeworth de Firmont thought of himself as a loyal subject of King Louis; French became more familiar to him than his native tongue. Educated at the Jesuit College in Toulouse, he was ordained a secular priest, and went to work with the poorest of the poor in a run-down neighborhood on the left bank of Paris.

With him in the coach was an official of the revolutionary government. Closing the coach window, he exclaimed, "Great God, what a dreadful commission this is!" His name was Garat, and he had the dubious title of Minister of Justice. He spoke of the King. "What a man! What courage! No, human nature alone could not give such fortitude. He possesses something beyond it."

Abbé Edgeworth was amazed to hear an avowed republican refer to the royal prisoner in such a manner. By all accounts, the King's quiet dignity and unfailing graciousness had touched the hearts of his enemies. The Abbé did not reply. The slightest slip of the tongue on his part could be used as an excuse for keeping him from his royal master, who longed for the ministrations of a priest faithful to the Holy See.

"Louis XVI has been 'set for the fall and for the rising of many in Israel,'" he thought, "and if my life could save him, I would gladly offer it."

How France had changed in the last four years! Now there was always a scarcity of bread, unemployment was rampant, the beggars had multiplied; the increase of crime had brought France to the brink of anarchy. The revolutionaries spoke of liberty, equality, and fraternity, but there was no liberty for those who did not conform their minds to the government policies. Freedom of conscience had disappeared. Priests were hunted men if they refused to take the oath to the Civil Constitution of the Clergy, which acknowledged the French government as head of the Church in France, severing the ties with Rome, plunging the nation into schism. Clerical dress and all external religious symbols were outlawed as well. Already, thousands of priests and laity had been killed for refusing to break with the Pope. Last September, there had been a five-day blood bath in which fourteen hundred prisoners were slaughtered by a crazed mob. The victims included many priests, religious, and devout lay people such as the Queen's friend, the Princesse de Lamballe, and little girls as young as ten.

During the drive to the Temple prison, Abbé Edgeworth turned over in his mind the web of events that had brought him to this moment. Through the bond of faith, his life had become inextricably woven with that of the King. In 1789, he had been living on the Rue de Bac at the Seminary of the Foreign Missions (the slums of Paris being considered mission territory), on the other side of the river from the Tuileries.

On October 6, 1789, the King, Queen and their children were taken prisoner at Versailles by the mob, most of whom were the most depraved elements of the city, stirred up by Orléanist propaganda. It was comprised of many men dressed up like women, and they proclaimed their desire to make a cockade of the Queen's intestines. The Queen was almost killed in her bed, escaping down a secret passage to the King's room, moments before a band of rabid fishwives slashed her sheets and mattress to shreds, leaving a trail of murdered Swiss guards in their wake. With heads of the guards carried on pikes ahead of their coach, the Royal Family was brought through the rain and mud to Paris, amid the rabble hurling filthy epithets at them. Abbé Edgeworth and every decent citizen were filled with horror at the tale. Once the King's person was threatened, then no one was safe.

The unfolding of events revealed that the attack on the royal sovereignty coincided with an attack on Church authority. In November of 1789 all Church property was confiscated by the government. The legislation was backed by anti-clerical propaganda, including plays which either ridiculed the Church, or portrayed priests and nuns as being wicked and licentious. In July of 1790 the National Assembly voted to nationalize the Catholic Church in France under the Civil Constitution of the Clergy. Henceforth, bishops and priests would be elected by the State, and no longer invested by the Pope.

On November 27 of the same year, the Assembly passed a decree mandating every priest and bishop to swear an oath to the Civil Constitution of the Clergy, and the King was pressured to sign the decree. The King appealed to the Pope for advice, and the Holy Father appointed two archbishops to guide him. When his two advisors urged him to sign the decree, the King did so out of obedience to the representatives of the Vicar of Christ, but against his conscience, as everyone knew. While the worldly clergy freely took the oath, the more fervent, learned priests and bishops refused; they began to be hunted and turned out of their parishes. The King's aunts, Mesdames Adelaïde and Victoire, would have nothing to do with the new national church, and escaped to Rome, in spite of public indignation. The King became gravely ill. Abbé Edgeworth refused to take the oath, and hid with his mother and sister in a private home where he could still minister to his flock.

On March 10, 1791, the bull *Charitas* of Pope Pius VI condemned the Civil Constitution of the Clergy as being schismatic. The Holy Father declared all bishops elected by the State to be invalid and their consecrations a sacrilege. He suspended every priest and bishop who had taken the oath. When the bull was made public, the persecution began in earnest, with the burning of the Pope in effigy in Paris. Grey Nuns were beaten in the streets by fierce *poissardes*. In so many ways, however, Abbé Edgeworth reflected, *Charitas* came as a relief. Now all faithful Catholics knew exactly where they stood, including the King, who would not now receive Holy Communion from a juring priest. Underground Masses became the norm.

On March 17,1791, a week after the papal bull was published, the Abbé Edgeworth made his first visit to the Tuileries Palace as the new confessor and spiritual director to the King's sister, Madame Elisabeth of France. Her former confessor had taken the oath. The Abbé went as unobtrusively as possible to the Tuileries, where he entered by a side entrance as he had been bidden to do. He was conducted to the apartments of the twenty-six year old princess, who received him with gratitude. She wore a simple, modest dress with a kerchief around her neck, her hair bound in a turban-like scarf. She immediately fell on her knees and begged for his blessing.

"Oh, Monsieur l'Abbé!" she exclaimed. "You know not what consolation to this penitent is the presence of a priest loyal to the Holy Apostolic See."

The Abbé found the princess to have an insight into the life of prayer that many seasoned religious lacked. Like the Queen, who could be seen about Paris visiting hospitals, orphanages, factories, and mental asylums, Madame Elisabeth occupied herself in charitable works. Even outside of the confessional, she shared with him personal questions that troubled her.

"My father," she once said, "I have no doubt that the Revolution is evil. I believe that as Roman Catholics, and descendants of King St. Louis, we should have no part in it. Yet my brother the king and my sister-in-law the Queen think differently. There is no end to our arguments on how to deal with these troubled times. My good brother is clearly aware of the wickedness of the new order, but he tries to conciliate with the moderate forces of the Revolution, who still desire an anemic form of monarchy. He says that as King he must continue to intervene in public affairs as much as possible — that to withdraw from the Revolution will be to become a political nonentity. 'Then everything will be lost,' he says, 'but as long as we are on amicable terms with the Assembly, we can win many of the moderates over to our side.' The Queen handles the King's correspondence with the moderates and she also has maintained a correspondence with the foreign powers, her own relatives included, whom she hopes will at least promise to make a stand in our defense if the situation becomes desperate. I, Monsieiur l'Abbé, believe we should boldly appeal to all the leaders of Christendom, begging them to help us crush the Revolution with fire and sword, and restore my brother the King to his rightful, God-given authority. My brother Artois at Coblenz is in full agreement with me. But the King refuses. 'I will never raise the sword against my own people, and will not be the cause of a civil war. We must continue to pursue what other courses of action are open to us.'"

By Passiontide of 1791 it became clear to the King that his only recourse was to escape from Paris. He was no longer a free man, as he discovered on Monday of Holy Week when, with his family, he tried to leave for their country estate at St. Cloud, where he planned on privately receiving his Easter communion from a non-juring priest.

A mob surrounded the coach and would not let it leave the courtyard. They had to give up going anywhere that day, and returned to the palace. Plans for an escape were made. A few days after Trinity Sunday, the Royal Family slipped out of the Tuileries in the middle of the night, and fled to the countryside, with the help of faithful Count Axel von Fersen. When the Royal Family's absence was discovered, the Parisians went wild, tearing the *fleur-de-lys* off of all public buildings. The King, however, had no intention of leaving France; believing the citizens of the provinces to be faithful, he planned to go to Metz, where he meant to rally all loyal troops and subjects in order to hold the revolutionary government at bay.

The unfortunate family were betrayed and captured at Varennes on June 25, 1791, and were brought back on the Vigil of Corpus Christi surrounded by a bloodthirsty throng. The people viciously murdered an old nobleman, who had had the courage to salute his King. The berlin slowly creaked passed altars set up on the roadside, adorned with flowers, ready to receive the Saving Victim in the monstrances, borne in the Corpus Christi processions. Meanwhile, the men along the road kept their hats on, and soldiers reversed their arms, pointing the barrels of the muskets to the ground, as signs of disdain for the King and Queen. Abbé Edgeworth thought it was a miracle they had not all been dragged from their coach and killed.

After returning to the Tuileries, the Royal Family were under a closer guard, with two gendarmes sleeping in the antechamber of the Queen's bedroom. One needed a special pass in order to enter the royal apartments. It was with great difficulty that Abbé Edgeworth occasionally managed to see Madame Elisabeth in order to hear her confession. He found it easier to enter in the mornings, when many tradesmen were going in and out of the palace.

Often, he noticed lingering at the gates of the palace a drummer boy with a very dirty face, speaking in a lively but rather common accent with the guards, who laughed at the lad's repartee. He was surprised that once on the old back staircase that he used, he heard the identical voice but this time, speaking in very cultured tones. He looked at the speaker, and saw it was a young milliner's girl with a large hat box in her arms, conversing on the staircase with a veiled lady, in French spiced with Italian and English phrases. He was mystified, especially when the two ladies fell silent as they saw him.

"It is Monsieur l'Abbé," said the veiled lady, nodding to him, but quickly retreating. The young girl smiled and curtseyed, then tripped lightly down the staircase, as if off on some Sunday jaunt. He told Madame Elisabeth about it.

"Oh, do not be perplexed, Monsieur l'Abbé." Her eyes sparkled. "That was only our little Mademoiselle Hyde. She is an English orphan whom the Princesse de Lamballe found in an Irish convent in the city. She is not only musically gifted, but a mistress of language and accents, and has become indispensable to the Princess, not only as a secretary, but as a source of information. She knows Paris well, and goes all over the city in various disguises; as a drummer boy, a milliners' girl, a seller of ribbons or snuff, sitting in on the sessions of the National Assembly-one of our main ways of knowing what is said there. She has recently been confirmed in our holy faith, and has proved herself to be trustworthy and devout."

"And what of the veiled lady, Madame?" asked the Abbé.

"That was Her Highness the Princesse de Lamballe. She has been a most faithful friend to my sister the Queen. Although she was safely away in England, the princess returned to Paris to share the Queen's troubles and will not be parted from us."

The Abbé admired such courage. Many stouter hearts had fled from their sovereigns without a tinge of remorse, but that the Princess, who was known to be delicate and extremely sensitive, should choose to remain with the Royal Family as their situation became more dangerous, filled him with admiration. Meanwhile, the Pope had written to the King and Queen, imploring them to take refuge in his dominions. But they were now too closely watched to be able to escape together. They begged Madame Elisabeth to go, but she refused to leave them, not even with her brother Provence and his wife, who managed to get away. The King tried to get the Queen to leave, but she would not go without him. The moderate revolutionary Mirabeau and loyal Count Fersen then implored the King to flee with the Dauphin, but he did not want to leave the rest of his family alone at the hands of the mob. And so the summer of 1791 slipped away.

In August, the King of Prussia and the Emperor of Austria declared that they were ready to help the King if his life was threatened, much to Madame Elisabeth's joy, although they made it clear they were not eager to invest too many of their resources in restoring France to her former prestigious position. Then, on September 14, 1791, the Feast of Exaltation of the Holy Cross, the King was forced to sign the new constitution, in which he had very few powers, except that of the veto. He unflinchingly used the veto on November 29, 1791, when the Assembly decreed that priests who had refused to take the oath were to be punished.

The Jacobins, the radical party of the Revolution, so named because they congregated at the Dominican monastery of St. Jacques, were livid. They began a horrible campaign of calumny and slander against the King and Queen, calling them Monsieur and Madame Veto, and worse. Abbé Edgeworth could no go out into the street without being subjected to pamphlets with caricatures of the Queen in obscene poses. Especially vicious was the procurator Hébèrt's gazette *Père Duchesne*, which urged the people to crime and violence.

On April 20, 1792, the violent feelings were somewhat pacified when the Assembly voted to have the King declare war on Austria. It showed, at least, that he was not in league with his wife's relatives. France was in no condition to fight, but the Assembly was eager to spread the principles of the Revolution to other lands. Madame Elisabeth hoped that now the Austrians and the French *émigrés* would come to rescue them. She confided to the Abbé that the King feared that with war, all was lost for them, because if anything went wrong for the French, the Queen would be accused of sending military secrets to her nephew the Emperor. The past spring, they had lost their staunchest supporter, King Gustavus III of Sweden, stabbed to death at a masked ball.

On Good Friday, 1792, the Assembly passed a decree forbidding priests to wear clerical dress, and prohibiting Christian emblems. The worldly, juring clergy had long abandoned priestly garb; those like Abbé Edgeworth had already gone underground. On June 19, 1792, the King vetoed the Assembly's decision to deport twenty thousand priests to the jungles of Guiana for slave labor because they had refused to deny the papal supremacy. The next day, Paris marched on the Tuileries, chanting, "Down with the veto! Down with the priests!" The Royal Family was again in danger.

Madame Elisabeth later described the horror to Abbé Edgeworth: "I clung to my brother's coat, refusing to leave him, and together we went to the first floor to meet the mob. Both men and women were armed with everything from axes and pikes to sticks and paring knives. Many of the intruders were already rampaging through the palace, looking for the Queen. They were determined this time to kill her, but she was hiding in a secret passage with the children. She had to leave her hiding place when the mob began hacking at the doors and walls with axes, so a nobleman dragged her into the Council Room, where she and the children were barricaded behind a table. She begged her ladies and the guards to let her go to the King. 'It is only with me the people are angry. I am going to offer them their victim. Let me go the King, my duty calls me there!' Of course, the guards prevented her from going. Meanwhile, the rabble thought I was the Queen, as I hoped they would; I did not fear to die so the others would be spared. Yet my brother's gaze seemed to calm their murderous rage. He held the bulk of them at bay for almost two hours, in spite of their insults. They were amazed that he did not appear to be afraid, or even the least bit shaken. 'Put your hand on my heart, and see if it beats any faster, ' he said to them. Eventually they stopped shouting, 'Down with the veto!' and several unspeakable descriptions of the Queen.

They handed the King a bottle of wine and a red cap, which he put on, drinking to the health of the nation.

"At last, that rascal of a mayor, Pétion, arrived and told the people it was time to leave. My brother calmly asked if they would like to see the State apartments, and so in a procession that could almost be called orderly, they traipsed through the Palace, filled with awe. Eventually, they came upon my poor sister and her children, but did no harm except for one fierce old fishwife, who screeched, 'You vile woman!' at the Queen. My sister calmly replied, 'What harm have I ever done to you?' Soon, the people filed out of the palace, and we all nearly fainted into my brother's arms. Since then he has been quietly strengthening the defense of the Tuileries, in case such an outrage occurs again."

"I know," said Abbé Edgeworth, "and so do the Jacobins. They are doing all they can to turn the city against the King. Under Danton, they plan on seizing the government and declaring a republic. They are using the Brunswick Manifesto as propaganda." The Duke of Brunswick had recently declared that if any harm came to the Royal Family he would use military force on Paris.

"Yes," replied the Princess. "And the King is horrified by it. He disavowed the manifesto before the Assembly. It was a miracle he was not torn to pieces last July 14 on the Champs de Mars. The Queen and I were frantic as we watched him taking the oath to the constitution, surrounded by another violent, cursing horde of people. Yet they ended by shouting, 'Long live the King!' His courage seems to affect them that way.

"We have tried to convince the Queen to flee to Vienna. At one point she agreed to go with Princesse de Lamballe. She secretly confessed and received Holy Communion, and packed, but at the last minute changed her mind. She cannot bring herself to leave the King or her children. Meanwhile, we are insulted even while at Mass or at Vespers, with the chapel musicians playing that hideous song *Ça ira* when the King and Queen enter. People congregate outside the Queen's windows with lewd drawings and placards, sometimes even exposing themselves in indecent ways. It cannot go on like this much longer. The King and Queen have been advised to wear special iron vests under their clothes to protect them from assassination attempts, but both have refused. 'Whoever assassinates me will be releasing me from a truly wretched existence,' said my sister. And so, father, this is the extremity to which we have come."

It was August 9, 1792 that they spoke thus. It was to be their final meeting. Madame Elisabeth gave the Abbé her last will and testament, and letters for her brothers abroad, to be delivered to them if she should be killed. The city was brewing and bubbling, like a pot about to boil over. The princess confessed before the Abbé said Mass.

"I will receive as if it is my last Communion, my viaticum," she whispered. He knew the Queen, too, attended secret Masses with an anonymous confessor. Before departing, the Abbé gave her a final blessing, and then said, "Remember, my princess, what I have always told you. Keep always in your mind three things: your last end, the Blood of the Cross, and the Face of your Judge. Would that we could be worthy to shed our blood for Christ! Adhere to the remembrance that 'the sufferings of this time are not worthy to be compared with the glory to come, that shall be revealed in us.'"

"Yes, my father. I entrust Your Reverence to the mercy and protection of the Sacred Heart. If we do not meet again on this earth, may it please our Redeemer that we will meet in the garden of Paradise." He took his leave, his soul feeling like it had been pierced.

That night the air was stifling and breezeless. All of Paris was drenched in perspiration. Then the tocsins began to ring from the districts of Saint-Antoine and Saint-Marcel, the most fearsome, revolutionary quarters in the city. Abbé Edgeworth could not sleep—the very heat and darkness seemed to ferment with rage. When dawn came, it was flaming red. There could be heard the tramp of feet, along with the *Marseillaise* and *Ça ira*, peppered with howls and an occasional scream. A mob was again marching on the Tuileries. It was August 10, the Feast of Saint Laurence, who had been roasted on the gridiron.

The Abbé spent the exhausting days that followed comforting his frightened family, friends and parishioners, while gleaning all the information he could about the fate of the Royal Family. He learned that the revolutionary authorities advised the King, for the sake of his wife and children, to leave the palace, the champions of liberty being either unwilling or unable to control the people.

Accompanied by their most faithful attendants, the Royal Family escaped through the palace gardens, where very strangely the premature shedding of leaves had already made deep piles on the ground, to the National Assembly, where they took refuge in the stenographer's box, called the Logographe. The servants and Swiss guards who remained in the palace were butchered and mutilated by the indignant citizens. Even children threw heads in the air and caught them on sticks. The enraged populace poured into the National Assembly, and screamed at the beleaguered family, who had little to eat except what the English ambassador's wife sent over. They spent three days in the cramped box behind the President's chair, and three nights in a deserted convent, where they were always within earshot of the screeches of: "No more kings!" or "Down with the Fat Pig!", and especially things like "Death to the Austrian harlot!" The crowd had plundered the palace, and mocked the Queen with her possessions they had rifled, including some jewels. Most horrible of all, they had stolen a golden ciborium full of consecrated hosts from the palace chapel.

After long debates, it was finally decided by the Assembly to imprison the family in the medieval fortress known as the Temple. The Temple was the former headquarters of the Knights Templar, who had been disbanded by the Church in the 1300's because of accusations of occult practices. It was not clear to Abbé Edgeworth whether or not the Knights Templar had been guilty; he had the impression that many of them had been mixed-up in the occult. At any rate, it never failed to shock him whenever he read of the knights' torture and death at the hands of the French King Philip the Fair, who was himself rebellious towards the Pope. And now Philip's dethroned descendant was to be humbled on the very site of the former infamy. Abbé Edgeworth received furtive messages from Madame Elisabeth, wrapped in balls of silk. He learned that Princesse de Lamballe had been separated from the other prisoners, and was being held in the dreaded prison of La Force.

"The fortitude displayed by my brother and sister amid this death and chaos is truly admirable," she wrote. She went on to describe the conditions at the Temple, where they were constantly derided by the guards. The King and Queen responded to the mockeries with either silence or courtesy, forbidding their children to complain, and insisting that they be polite to their captors, who reacted by writing graffiti on the wall which read "Strangle the cubs."

On September 2, 1792 there began five days of carnage unlike anything Paris had experienced since the days of the barbarian invasions. The streets ran with blood, as the prisons were emptied, and the hapless inmates thrown to the sea of knives and hatred. Fourteen hundred people were slaughtered, and the murderers were seen to dip their baguettes into the blood of the victims. After refusing to renounce her allegiance to the King and Queen, the Princesse de Lamballe was handed over to two lines of criminals with sharp instruments. The first man to strike was a former protegé of the princess, whose baptism and religious instruction she had provided, but whom she had been forced to send from her service when he took to immoral ways. The blow killed her; her corpse was mutilated and defiled. The princess' head was borne to a hairdresser who, under duress, arranged and powdered the luxuriant, blood-splattered tresses. The head was then carried in triumph to the Temple, where the maniacs vowed to make the Queen kiss the cold face of her friend. Among the garments that had been stripped from the dead princess' body were found a red moroccan volume of *The Imitation of Christ* and a Sacred Heart badge.

In late November, Abbé Edgeworth received a message from Madame Elisabeth written in a shaking hand. The King had been separated from his family.

"There is no need for it," protested the princess. "They want only to break his spirit before bringing him to trial."

The King was brought before the Commune of the new republic on December 26, 1792. The charges leveled against him were quite flimsy; the trial was a mockery. He was accused of distributing money to the poor for the purposes of "enslaving the nation."

"I always took pleasure in relieving the needy," he candidly answered, "but I never had any treacherous motives." When accused of shedding the blood of his own people, his composure, it was reported, clouded with pain and disbelief, since he had avoided violence at great cost to himself and his family. The dignified resignation of his manner, the straightforward honesty of his replies, the serenity in his eyes, brought even his most virulent enemies to a confused and admiring silence, so that even a cry of "Long live the King!" would not have seemed out of place. With the help of his lawyers, Messieurs de Séze and de Malesherbes, he insisted that he had always upheld the Constitution, he had not broken any of the new laws, and could not be held responsible for his political actions before his acceptance of the Constitution.

When the Commune voted for his death, the deciding vote was cast by the King's own cousin, the Duc d'Orléans, now known as *Philippe Egalité*, a fervent revolutionary. To everyone's disgust, he voted when he could have legally abstained. On January 18, 1793, the King was sentenced. Abbé Edgeworth was sent for, the King having heard of him through the recommendation of Madame Elisabeth. His own confessor, a Eudist priest, had been killed during the September massacres.

As Abbé Edgeworth approached the Temple on that murky January afternoon, he saw young boys hawking copies of *The Trial of Charles I* in the chilly avenues and alleys of the city. When they arrived at their destination, the first gate was readily opened to them, and they climbed out of the coach. After a fifteen minute wait in the darkening courtyard, two commissaries conducted them into the enclosed garden, which they crossed to reach the tower. In the tower was a low, narrow door. Iron bolts and bars were drawn back, and the door groaned open.

As he bent to enter, the Abbé was overwhelmed by a sense of the presence of evil. It wafted over him like a cold wind, as if the demons of the past lingered there, gloating and malicious. The walls dripped with venom. He was led through a hall filled with slovenly guards, into a larger hall which looked as if it had once been a chapel. There were twelve commissaries with long unkempt hair and hats that looked as if they had been put on backwards, typical of Jacobin array. Abbé Edgeworth interiorly recoiled before their icy glares, their deliberately coarse manners and speech. They were the sort of men who reverenced nothing. Into his mind intruded the thought: "There is no crime to which these men would not sink." In a low voice, the minister Garat read to them from some papers he had with him, then motioned to the Abbé to follow him. The commissaries stopped the priest, and after whispering together for awhile, some of the group went upstairs with Garat.

The others undertook to meticulously search the priest, one of them apologizing for the indignity. How relieved the Abbé was that he did not have on his person a pyx with the Blessed Sacrament! They opened even his snuff box, examined the snuff and carefully inspected a steel pencil case to see if it concealed a dagger. Then he was escorted up the stairs.

The priest climbed the narrow, winding staircase, wide enough only to mount in single file. Barriers were placed at various intervals along the stair, and at every barrier stood a guard. The guards were the roughest, crudest *sans culottes* the Abbé thought he had ever encountered—he, who had lived for twenty years in Paris slums. The men reeked with wine and liquor and shouted vile remarks back and forth to each other, their harsh voices resounding on the stones of the fortress. He could not imagine his gentle princess, Madame Elisabeth, held in the same place with such lewd fellows, nor the good King and his beautiful Queen. Especially he could not imagine tender young children, the Dauphin and his sister, kept month after month in that tower of dread.

Finally, the priest reached the apartment of his King. Immediately, he was struck by the calm and tranquil stance of his sovereign, who had just been read his death sentence by Garat. The commissaries squirmed and flinched in Louis XVI's presence, as if they, not he, were the ones condemned to die the next morning. Abbé Edgeworth would never forget the sweetness and benignity of the King's gaze. He knew at once that he had found a brother and a friend. As soon as the King saw the priest, he dismissed the others with a wave of his hand. To the Abbé's surprise, they quietly trooped out of the room as if it were the Oeuil-de-Boeuf at Versailles, instead of the dreary Temple prison. The two men were alone.

Abbé Edgeworth had never seen his King at such a close range. The face of Louis XVI was worn, almost haggard, from sorrow. He was plainly but neatly dressed, hair powdered and tied behind his neck. The drab, stark surroundings, his simple attire, only heightened the majesty of the fallen King who, like a lion in captivity, did not cease to emanate dignity and strength. The sight of the foremost monarch in Europe brought to such a nadir of circumstances caused the priest to fall to his knees, speechless and weeping.

The King appeared to be more moved by the tears of the man who had come to console him than by the death sentence he had heard only minutes before. With his big, sturdy hands he raised the Abbé from the ground, saying, "Forgive me, forgive me, Monsieur l'Abbé, a moment of weakness, if such it can be called." The Abbé felt the King's tears on his own hands. "For a long time I have lived among my enemies, and habit has accustomed me to them. But when I behold a faithful subject, it is to me a new sight! A different language speaks to my heart, and in spite of my utmost efforts, I am melted."

Drying his eyes, the King led him into a small alcove built into one of the turrets of the tower. It contained a broken-down stove, a table, and three chairs. They sat down. "Now, Monsieur," said the King, "the great business of my salvation is the only one which ought to occupy my thoughts. It is the only business of real importance! What are all other subjects compared to this? This must, however, be delayed for a few moments, because my family are coming to take leave of me. In the meantime, here is a paper that I wish you to read."

It was the King's will, written on Christmas Day, less than a month before. Abbé Edgeworth listened, as the King read it aloud. At the beginning, his voice was quite strong and firm, as he forgave his enemies, and implored the forgiveness of any he had offended. But as he came to the mention of his family, his voice broke, and he continued with trembling.

> I commend my children to my wife. I have never doubted her maternal tenderness for them. I charge her particularly to make of them good Christians and honest men, to make them look on the grandeurs of this world (if they should be fated to experience them) as dangerous and transitory, and to fix their eyes on the sole and lasting glory of eternity. I beg my sister to continue in her tenderness for my children, and to be a mother to them, should they have the misfortune to lose their own.

He paused a moment, to regain his composure.

> I beg my wife to forgive me all the evil she is suffering for my sake, and the grief I may have caused her during the course of our marriage, as she may be sure that I hold nothing against her, if she should think she had anything with which to reproach herself.

At the end of the document, the King made his profession of Faith. "I firmly believe and confess all that is contained in the Symbol and commandments of God and of the Church, the sacraments and mysteries, such as the Catholic Church teaches them and has always taught them." He surrendered himself to the judgment of the Church, and renounced any former actions of his that were not in accord with her decisions. "I finish by declaring before God, and ready to appear before Him, that I do not reproach myself with any of the crimes which are advanced against me. In two copies. December 25, 1792. Louis."

Night had fallen. How dark was the Temple on a winter's eve, with the flickering tapers only heightening the menacing shadows! When his family did not arrive, the King questioned Abbé Edgeworth on the state of the Church in France, and the condition of the faithful clergy, many of whom he heard had fled to England.

The King eagerly inquired after the Archbishop of Paris, who was in hiding. "Tell him that I die in his communion, and that I have never acknowledged any pastor but him. I have never answered his last letter because of being so closely watched by my enemies. He has so much goodness of heart, that I am sure he will pardon me." The mention of forgiveness brought to the King's mind his cousin, the Duc d'Orléans, who had voted for his death. "I did not know that there could be such men," the King said in wonderment. "What have I done to my cousin that he should persecute me?" He sighed. "I feel terribly sorry for him, and would never change places with him. His lot is much unhappier than mine." There was no bitterness in his voice, only pity for his misguided relative.

One of the commissaries burst in. "The family of Louis Capet is here to see him!" he barked. The King leaped to his feet, and hurried out of the little alcove, closing the door behind him. Abbé Edgeworth could hear footsteps, and several voices, the King's included, raised in sobs and wails. He listened to the violent weeping of a woman mingling with a child's cry, which pierced the walls of the fortress, echoing in its outer courts. The priest was numb with agony, as he listened to the King's last meeting with the family he had not seen in two months, from whom he was about to be severed by death. The crying gradually softened into conversation, as the King spoke in calm, reassuring tones to his family.

After an hour or so, the melancholy reunion ended, and the King returned to the Abbé, with a pale and tearstained face, a tremor in his voice. He collapsed into a chair. "Oh, Monsieur, what an interview I have gone through." He buried his face for a moment in his hands. "Why should I love so tenderly?" he murmured. "And why should I be so tenderly beloved?" He sat up, wiping his face with his handkerchief. "But it is past. Let us forget everything else for that alone which is now of importance— to that which I should now direct all my emotions. I have much in my heart I wish to confide, Monsieur l'Abbé, before I mount the scaffold on the morrow."

Again, they were interrupted. This time it was Cléry, the King's valet, announcing that supper was ready. The King hesitated a moment, then rose to partake of the pan-fried chicken wings, vegetables, sponge cake and wine that comprised his last meal. He ate with a spoon, all sharp instruments having been taken from him.

"They think me so wicked that I would try to take my own life," he commented to the Abbé.

Abbé Edgeworth was determined to say Mass for the King, so that the condemned man could receive Holy Viaticum. "Please, Sire," he said, "grant me permission to try to acquire what I need to celebrate Mass in your chamber."

"Oh, Monsieur," said the King, "there is nothing that would console my heart more. But you are already risking so much by your presence here. I fear to compromise your safety."

"Please, Your Majesty, I beg you to allow me to try! I promise to conduct myself with prudence and discretion."

The King nodded. "Go, then, Monsieur, but I fear very much that you will not succeed, for I know the kind of men with whom you have to deal. They will grant nothing which they can refuse."

The Abbé knew what he meant. Persons who usurped authority which was not rightfully theirs usually abused it, thinking that the capricious, arbitrary wielding of power displayed their strength, when it really only betrayed their weakness. He hurried down to the main hall. The commissaries were disconcerted by his request, and made several lame excuses, but he persisted. "My demand is just. To refuse me would be against your own principles." After all, the Constitution guaranteed freedom of religion. He was led into a great deal of rigmarole, as they hinted that he might try to poison the King with the Host, but they began to weaken. They finally insisted that he put the request in writing. All true revolutionaries have a love of legalism to rival the Pharisees of old. He noticed that the officials spoke of "Louis Capet" like another dull statistic, another name on a long list of criminals with whom the weary wheels of bureaucracy had to deal.

"How frigid are these new republican ways!" thought the Abbé. "How cold is this liberty!"

He wondrously received permission to say Mass first thing in the morning, with one of the officials bringing what was needed from a neighboring church. The King, who had been waiting with great trepidation, was relieved. The two men retired to the alcove again.

"Monsieur l'Abbé," said the King, "darkness has descended upon my poor family. As for myself, the night is almost spent. I stand on the edge of eternity. Before the sun has again reached its summit, a new morning will have broken upon me. For me, the blackest of nights was two years ago, during Lent. I had recently signed, much against my conscience, but in obedience to the Holy Father's representatives, that reprehensible edict, the Civil Constitution of the Clergy. The revulsion of my soul plunged me into the most severe mental agony."

"Is that when you became so ill, Sire?"

"Yes, Monsieur. I took to my bed for a month, coughing and spitting blood. In my physical weakness and spiritual distress, I could do nothing else but invoke the mercy of the Sacred Heart. I plunged my anguished soul into that wounded Heart, ever compassionate to the repentant. I came upon a prayer card of the Sacred Heart illustrated by my aunt, sent to me by the Carmelites after her death. I fell to pondering the meaning and mystery of the devotion, given to my predecessor by a French Visitandine nun. I sent for some books from the palace library, and began in my sickroom to study the history of the revelations at Paray-le-Monial. My confessor at the time was a holy, Eudist priest Fr. Hébert, who is now in Heaven; he guided me. I resolved, in spite of my illness, to consecrate France to the Sacred Heart. The full, solemn consecration, requiring liturgical ceremonies, would be reserved for later."

The King closed his tired eyes a few moments. "The prayer I wrote to my Redeemer is graven on my soul: 'Oh God, you see all the wounds that tear my heart, and the depth of the abyss into which I have fallen.'" The fire in the pathetic little stove seemed momentarily to burn warmer and brighter. The King paused, then continued. "I vowed to revoke all the laws that were contrary to the faith, as soon as the Vicar of Christ made his pronouncements concerning them. I placed myself and my realm under the protection of the Sacred Heart, promising to build a Church, and institute a solemn feast in His honor as soon as I would be in a position to do so. I promised to go to Notre Dame in Paris within three months of my liberation and there, after the offertory at Mass, publicly pronounce an act of dedication to the Sacred Heart of Jesus. I sealed the document containing my consecration within the walls of my apartments at the Tuileries, with other private papers, where the spies of the Revolution could not find it." He fell again into a profound silence. Time stood still, lost in the wavering shadows on the walls and ceilings of the turret alcove. Abbé Edgeworth was no longer conscious of the darkness of the January night. Then the King spoke.

"Monsieur, my consecration of France to the Sacred Heart has come too late to save the kingdom. For my tardiness and that of my fathers in fulfilling the will of Heaven I repent, my heart and soul torn with compunction. Many innocent people will suffer because of my negligence. The Church is rent asunder, and wolves have entered the sheepfold. Much that is good and beautiful will be swept away forever. With the last beat of my heart I will renew my consecration to the Heart of my Savior, imploring Him to accept my life, united with His Sacred Passion, as an atonement for the sins of my ancestors, and those of the entire nation. May He have mercy on my soul."

Abbé Edgeworth prayed long before he responded to his sovereign. At last, he said, "Oh, my King, love is the central mystery of the devotion to the Divine Heart. Love, indeed, is the wound in the Sacred Heart, because love can never be separated from sacrifice. In the days of the Old Testament, victims had to be consumed by fire before they could rise to Heaven as an odor of sweetness. Truly, love is a flame which requires a holocaust. Blessed is he who has been found worthy to be such a whole burnt offering, to die for Christ, one's soul sundered and rent by love. Sire, Heaven has accepted your consecration. France, after centuries of self-indulgence, is being renewed. The worldly and evil-living clergy have left the Church; the good are being purified. And Sire, France is being crowned with martyrdom. So many have given their lives for the Faith, and many more will do so, before this abominable Revolution runs its course. France has been given a glory that not even Charlemagne or the Sun-King gave it. The Church will rise from the ashes of the Revolution, with a fresh purity and brightness, in bridal array. God will raise up great saints in France, martyrs, confessors, and virgins, who will in fervor and deeds match and even surpass the early centuries of faith. And the Mother of God herself will bless your consecration. She has not abandoned the kingdom which is dedicated to her holy Assumption. She will bless the land that is newly seeded with the blood of many martyrs, with your own blood, Sire, and will manifest her graces in unprecedented ways."

The King's eyes were moist. "I hope that your words will come true, Monsieur. I believe that they will. But at the present, the darkness is impenetrable."

"Remember, Sire, the words of Our Lord to Sr. Marguerite- Marie concerning those devoted to His Sacred Heart: 'I will console them in all their troubles. They shall find in My Heart an assured refuge during life and especially at the hour of death.' And remember the words of the

Apocalypse: 'Fear none of those things which thou shalt suffer. Behold, the devil will cast some of you into prison that you may be tried: and you shall have tribulation ten days. Be thou faithful until death: and I will give thee the crown of life.'"

"It troubles me, my father," said the King, "that I was not able to perform the solemn, liturgical consecration to the Sacred Heart, and build a Church in His honor."

"Leave it for your heirs, Your Majesty. It will be accomplished in God's own time."

"Oh, father," the King burst out. "For myself, I am willing and happy to die. It is with greatest anguish, however, that I leave my family without protection. The anxiety for their safety is so consuming, I fear it will cause me to falter on the steps of the scaffold."

"Sire, you must commend them to God's mercy. Place the Queen under the mantle of Our Lady of Dolors, and Madame Elisabeth and Madame Royale under the protection of the holy virgin Saint Génevière, patroness of Paris."

"And my little son?"

The Abbé hesitated because at that moment, an icy knife of fear passed through his being. "Commend him to the patronage of the Infant Christ."

The tower bells of the churches of Paris began to strike the midnight hour. It was January 21, the feast of Saint Agnes, whose name means "the lamb."

"I will be with you every step of the way, my King," said the Abbé. "If they allow me, I will accompany you to the feet of the guillotine."

"Good Father," replied the King. "How your presence would console me! Yet I fear the mob would turn on you. My death will only cause your own."

"It would be an honor for me to die at your side, Sire."

"To die at the side of 'Louis Capet'?" asked the King with the flicker of a smile.

"No, Sire. Not 'Louis Capet', but Louis the Martyr."

It was time to retire. The Abbé slept in a small chamber next to the King's, usually occupied by Cléry. He could hear the King giving a few directions to his valet. He fell asleep.

The next thing he knew, Cléry could be heard awakening his master. It was five o'clock in the morning.

"I slept well," he heard the King say. "I needed it. Yesterday was exhausting. Where is Monsieur de Firmont?"

"He is in bed," replied Cléry.

"And you, Cléry, where did you spend the night?"

"On this chair."

"I am sorry for it," said the King. As soon as the King was dressed, he sent for Abbé Edgeworth. They went into the alcove for almost an hour, at which time the King made his confession. When they returned to the King's chamber, Cléry had prepared everything for Mass, with a chest of drawers as a makeshift altar. The Abbé vested for Mass in Cléry's room. He had asked only for the essentials necessary for the saying of Mass, but the commissary had brought much more—candles, altar linens, full vestments, even incense. "I will give to priests the power of touching the most hardened hearts," Our Lord had said to Sr. Marguerite-Marie.

The Abbé said the Mass of the virgin-martyr Saint Agnes. The King knelt throughout the liturgy on a flat cushion that he habitually used at his prayers. He received Holy Communion with the greatest devotion. The Abbé left him in silent prayer as the mass ended, and he went to remove his vestments. Then he sat once more with the King by the miserable stove, and together they recited the Divine Office. The King used not only the breviary of the archdiocese of Paris, but was accustomed to praying the Office of the Order of the Holy Spirit on a daily basis.

"My God," said the King," how blessed I am in the possession of my religious beliefs!" He seemed refreshed by prayer and the Eucharist. "Without my faith, what would I now be? But with it, how sweet death appears to me. Yes, there dwells on high an incorruptible Judge, from Whom I shall receive the justice refused to me on earth." He closed his breviary. "Last night, I promised the Queen I would see her today for a final farewell."

The Abbé recalled the weeping of the previous evening. It would be too much for the condemned husband and father to go to the guillotine with such sounds in his ears. "Sire," said the priest, firmly, "do not put the Queen to a trial that would be more than her strength could bear."

"You are right," said the King. "It would kill her."

The King left the cabinet, and Abbé Edgeworth heard him speaking to Cléry. "You will give this seal to my son, and this ring to the Queen." The Abbé saw the King slowly remove a gold band. He assumed it was the King's wedding ring. "Tell her I am leaving her with the greatest pain. This little packet contains locks of the hair of my family; you will give her that also. Tell the Queen, my dear sister, and my children that, although I promised to see them again this morning, I have resolved to spare them the ordeal of so cruel a separation. Tell them how much it costs me to go away without receiving their last embraces once more." His hand brushed his eyes. "I bid you to give them my last farewell."

He returned to the priest. Together they prayed the rosary, then the litany and prayers for the dying. The bells tolled eight o'clock. A loud knock came on the door. It was the commissary who had escorted the Abbé up to the King's room the night before. His name, the Abbé discovered, was Santerre, and he was head of the National Guard.

"Monsieur, it is time to go," he announced.

"I am busy," said the King, firmly and abruptly. "Wait for me. In a few minutes I shall be with you." Louis XVI closed the door on Santerre. At that moment, his calm seemed to vanish. He threw himself at the Abbé's feet.

"It is . . . finished," he gasped. "Monsieur, please give me your final benediction and pray God that He will sustain me until the end."

The Abbé made the sign of the cross over the prostrate King. He got to his feet, composed and collected, and opened the door. Several guards and commissaries were standing there; none of them removed their hats. The King, who wore a white jacket and grey breeches, refused the offer of an overcoat, but put on his three-cornered hat with its red, white, and blue cockade. He said good-bye to Cléry who, bathed in tears, unabashedly asked for the King's blessing.

"Messieurs," said the King, "I wish that Cléry might stay with my son, who is used to his care." The only response was a stony silence. He handed his last will and testament to an official who seemed quite impressed with his own dignity; the official refused to take it.

"I am charged only with conducting you to the scaffold," the man pompously proclaimed. Another official quietly took the document.

"I hope Cléry may be allowed to enter into the Queen's . . . into my wife's service," the King said. Again, the only response was a sort of nervous twitching and fidgeting.

"Let us proceed," said the King. It was as if they could not take him to his death until he gave his consent. They left the tower. It was a cold, drizzly morning. Paris was grey and silent, except for the steady beat of drums. As they crossed the courtyard, the King twice looked back at the prison where his family were confined. The Abbé could see that it took every ounce of his strength to walk away from them.

They climbed into a coach. Two gendarmes insisted on riding with them, so they could have no private conversation. The King sank into a profound silence, until the Abbé offered him his breviary. Together they recited the seven penitential psalms.

"*Domine, ne in furore tuo arguas me, neque in ira tua corripias me.*" The Abbé began Psalm Six. (O Lord, rebuke me not in Thine indignation, nor chastise me in Thy wrath.)

"*Miserere mei, Domine, quoniam infirmus sum: sana me, Domine, quoniam conturbata sunt ossa mea,*" the King responded. (Have mercy upon me, O Lord, for I am weak: heal me, O Lord, for my bones are troubled.)

The streets of Paris were ominously quiet, except for the monotonous sound of the drums, as the coach rolled along. All windows were shuttered and doors closed along the route of the King's via dolorosa. Cordons of soldiers, standing four deep, lined the streets. The Abbé expected to hear taunts and insults, but none came. Instead, to his astonishment he heard a lone voice, man or woman, he could not tell, call to the coach: "Sire, your blessing! Give me your blessing!" But the King was deep into Psalm Thirty-one.

"*Quoniam die ac nocte gravata est super me manus tua, conversus sum in aerumna mea, dum configitur spina.*" (For day and night Thy hand was heavy upon me: I turned in my anguish while the thorn was fastened in me.) It was an interminable drive. The Abbé could not help noticing the expressions of the gendarmes, whose eyes were as wide as children's, as they stared at the King they had been taught to hate. They had never been so close to him, and were seeing him now not as a bloody tyrant, but as a stout, pious man, such as could be found praying in any parish church in France.

"*Quoniam ego in flagella paratus sum, et dolor meus in conspectu meo semper,*" read the King. (For I am ready for the scourges, and my sorrow is continually before me.) Near the Saint Martin's gate a young woman cried out, a wordless, agonizing cry. The Abbé knew there was a plot afoot to rescue the King, even at the foot of the scaffold, but he saw from the heavily guarded streets that any such attempt would come to nothing.

"*Domine exaudi oratione meam, et clamor meus ad te veniat,*" prayed the King. (O Lord, hear my prayer, and let my cry come unto Thee.)

"*Non avertus faciem tuam a me; in quacumque die tribulor inclina ad me durem tuam,*" the Abbé responded. (Turn not away Thy face from me: in the day when I am in trouble, incline Thine ear unto me.)

They came to the Place de la Révolution, formerly called Place de Louis XV, after the King's grandfather. A statue of the old King had once stood there. The Royal Family had been forced to watch the dismemberment of the statue, before being imprisoned in the Temple. They were reaching the end of the penitential psalms.

"*Auditem fac mihi mane misericordiam tuam, quia in te speravi,*" read the King. (Make me to hear Thy mercy in the morning: for in Thee have I hoped.)

"*Notam fac mihim viam in qua ambulem, quia ad te levavi animam meam,*" the Abbé answered. (Make me to know the way I should walk: for to Thee have I lifted up my soul.)

"*Eripe me de inimicis meis, Domine, ad te confugi,*" the King sighed. (Deliver me from my enemies, O Lord: unto Thee have I fled.) Thousands of people had come to see the execution of the King. A large space had been left around the scaffold, the crowd spilling out from it as far as the eye could see. The coach stopped.

The King spoke to the two gendarmes before they jumped from it. "Gentlemen, I recommend to you this good man." He was referring to Abbé Edgeworth. "Take care that no one insults him after my death. I charge you to prevent it." He spoke in majestic tones.

"Yes, yes, we will take care of him," one said, menacingly.

"Leave him to us!" mocked the other, but the Abbé was too concerned about the King to feel threatened or afraid.

As Louis XVI climbed out, the crowd began to buzz, "There he is! There he is!" At the foot of the scaffold steps, three guards came towards the King, trying to remove his jacket. He shook them off, and himself removed his hat, his jacket and neckcloth, unbuttoning his shirt and arranging it so his neck was exposed. The guards then made as if to seize his hands.

"What are you attempting?" cried the King, pulling away from them.

"To bind you," they answered.

"To bind me!" exclaimed the King. "No, I shall never consent to that! Do what you have been ordered, but you shall never bind me!" A knight must never be bound like a criminal, as if he might try to run in terror from the face of death. The guards called on others to help them. The Abbé feared they might strike the king, which for him would be worse than dying. The King looked steadily at the priest, mutely begging for a word of advice.

"Sire," said the priest, "in this new insult, I see only another trait of resemblance between Your Majesty and the Savior Who is about to be your reward."

The King raised his eyes to Heaven, and his expression shone with a soft radiance, as if his gaze had pierced the clouds and glimpsed the Kingdom which awaited him.

"You are right," he said. "Nothing less than His example should make me submit to such a degradation." He turned to the guards. "Do what you will. I must drink the chalice to the dregs."

They bound him, and the executioner Sanson cut his hair. With the Abbé holding his arm, he mounted the scaffold. At the top of the stairs, he suddenly left the Abbé, and strode with a firm step to the edge of the platform. With a nod, he silenced the drummers.

He began to speak, his words ringing throughout the square. "I die innocent of all the crimes of which I am accused. I pardon those who have occasioned my death, and I pray to God that the blood you are going to shed will never fall upon France . . . ." The drums began again. The executioners grabbed the King, dragged him over to the guillotine, and threw him roughly upon the plank. The blade fell.

Abbé Edgeworth heard a strange, disembodied squeal, rather like a pig's. He discovered later it was a couple of guards with an inflated pig's bladder underneath the scaffold, trying to bring ridicule upon the King at the moment of his death. Then came the sound of a loud, almost unearthly voice, which rose into the air, and could be heard even over the drums.

"Ascend to Heaven, Son of St. Louis!" He was afterwards told the voice was his own, but he could hardly believe it, being at the moment practically unable to breathe or move, except to fall to his knees as the King's head was lifted out of the basket. Suddenly, many things began to happen at once. The crowd was silent as the King's head was held high for them to see. While the executioner walked around the scaffold with the head raised aloft, he made obscene gestures.

Then cries of "Long live the Republic!" were heard. People rushed forward, dipping handkerchiefs into the blood of Louis XVI. The Abbé, dazed, did not know how he climbed off the scaffold. He could only notice that some of the blood from the severed head had splashed upon his clothes. Meanwhile, Sanson was selling locks of the King's hair, pieces of his jacket, his buttons, his hat. Someone began to play the *Marseillaise*, and people joined hands, dancing and cavorting around the guillotine, "like the prophets of Baal," thought the Abbé. A cold mist had descended upon Paris at the moment of the King's death, but above, and beyond it, was the sun.

As he edged away from the scaffold, Abbé Edgeworth was aware of thousands of eyes on him, and expected at any moment to be seized by violent hands. But no one touched him. In a few minutes, he was hidden among the crowd and veiled by the mist. It was almost noon. He found his way on foot through the streets of Paris to the house of the King's lawyer and faithful friend, Malesherbes.

The priest gave him an account of the King's death, and the old man wept. "You must leave Paris," Monsieur de Malesherbes urged him. "It would be even better if you left France."

Upon returning to the street, he was amazed to see how calm the city was. It was like an ordinary Parisian day, with people gossiping in the cafés, shopping, and going to the theatres. The tall Irishman hailed a cab, and went to a friend's house outside the city. As he left Paris, his thoughts fled to the Temple, where a disconsolate widow was mourning the best of husbands, who had also been the best of kings.

Chapter Seven
The Sacrifice

"Here is the patience and faith of the saints."—Apocalypse 13:10

Marie-Antoinette, Queen of France, morning, October 14, 1793

The Grande Chambre of the Palais de Justice, renamed the "Hall of Liberty," was overflowing with people. In the name of liberty, the famous Crucifixion scene by Dürer had been replaced by a large reproduction of the Declaration of the Rights of Man and Citizen, the rights of man having supplanted the duties toward God. In the galleries were the *tricoteuses*, the rugged women of Paris, who hovered about like birds of prey at every revolutionary event, bringing their knitting with them. The trial of the Austrian she-wolf was not to be missed.

At eight o'clock in the morning, the door opened, and a woman entered, unshackled but surrounded by *gendarmes*. A ripple of consternation passed over the spectators as she moved through the hall. They had been waiting since dawn to see the beautiful, wicked Antoinette, the bogey-woman of France, who was personally responsible for all the miseries of the Nation. But here she was . . . an old woman! She was emaciated, and the blackness of her widow's weeds and *crêpe* mourning veil heightened the pallor of her skin. Her hair, the little of it that showed, was as gray as a woman of sixty.

However, they had no doubt she was truly the Queen. No other would hold herself so straight, and walk with such dignity, in spite of the slight tremor in her step. Indeed, it seemed that her legs could hardly support her! She was led to a raised platform, where she could be heard and seen by all, in front of a long table, at which sat young Nicolas Hermann, the President of the Revolutionary Tribunal, and five other judges. Hermann was a great friend of Robespierre, whose Committee of Public Safety now ruled France with an audacity that the Sun-King never dared or dreamed of. As it was commonly known, once Robespierre decided someone needed to be gotten out of the way of progress and liberalism, the person was usually abandoned to Mother Guillotine, bribes and pleas having no effect on the heartless "incorruptible." Robespierre and his friends thought France was overpopulated anyway, and needed to be thoroughly purged, of peasants as well as aristocrats, the peasants being the ones who clung so adamantly to superstitions like Roman Catholicism. Therefore, not much trouble was taken to see if those accused were truly guilty or not.

Little effort had been exerted to gather solid testimony against the former queen. After all, the whole world knew she was guilty of every imaginable crime! Standing in the shadows was the public prosecutor, Fouquier-Tinville, a pale man with thick black eye-brows. Both he and Hermann wore medals on which were inscribed the name of their new god *La Loi*, for whose sake they were prepared to break all the old laws of decency and morality. The men were clothed in the deepest black; even their round hats, turned up in front, had black ostrich plumes. The wretched woman was made to stand while forty-one witnesses took their oaths. Then Hermann said: "The accused may be seated!"

Antoinette slowly sat in the chair that had been provided for her. She could not see very well, being half-blind in one eye, but at least it was daylight. The first time she was brought to the Grande Chambre for the preliminary hearings, it had been the middle of the night, with only two candles on the table to give light to the vast hall. How startled she had been when she heard the movements of invisible spectators in the gallery.

"What is your name, surname, age, position, place of birth and residence?" asked Hermann, as if he did not know.

She replied clearly and steadily. The *tricoteuses* leaned forward, straining to hear the Queen's soft tones. "My name is Marie-Antoinette of Lorraine-Austria, aged about thirty-eight, widow of the King of France, born in Vienna. At the time of my arrest I was in the session hall of the National Assembly." A clerk then began to read the eight page indictment.

She appeared not to listen, her fingers running over the arms of her chair as if over a clavichord, as he mumbled off the accusation of orgies and elaborate feasts, of extravagances, of engineering a famine, of printing pamphlets slandering herself so as to gain sympathy, of dominating her husband, of being a counterrevolutionary, of dissipation and waste of the money earned by the sweat of the people. Behind her chair stood her lawyers, two very brave young men. They had only been given one day to prepare their case, and would pay with their lives for undertaking her defense. She did not think it was worth the risk of anyone's life, since the Revolution was determined on her death; she herself had little desire to live.

She had resolved to fight, however, hoping against hope that if she won, she might somehow be reunited with her children; she might somehow be able to save her little son from his tormentors, and heal his wounded mind with her tears and kisses. Her neck never stopped aching from the vise-like grip with which his short arms had locked around her, refusing to let go, as the commissaries began to drag him from her arms. His cries of "Maman! Maman!" echoed within her still. Nothing they could do now could hurt her. Her heart was not broken, it was gone.

The clerk finished reading the accusation. Hermann spoke. "This is what you are accused of. You will now hear the testimony against you. First witness to the stand!" The first witness was a deputy of the convention, formerly second in command of the National Guard at Versailles. She vaguely remembered him. He began to drone on and on about orgies he had witnessed at the palace. His testimony would have been merely ridiculous if it had not been so disgusting. He went on for two hours. Eventually, her anguished mind became unable to follow him, and she slipped into her own thoughts. She would never understand the audacity that enabled an individual to lie so shamefacedly, in such elaborate detail and at such great lengths about events that existed only in his mind, or in another's equally depraved. Had her poor husband gone through this, she wondered? Surely, he had; now it was behind him, and he was in Heaven.

The thought of her husband steadied her nervous fingers, yet roused painful remembrances. The evening before his death, at their last farewell, her daughter fainted as Louis left the room. Antoinette passed a sleepless night, in one of her trembling fits, unable to comprehend the horror of it all. The next morning, she, Elisabeth, Thérèse, and Charles were up at dawn waiting for the King to come once more, but by ten o'clock, the beating of drums and distant cheers told them they had waited in vain. As they recovered from their storm of weeping, she took her daughter's hand, and together they knelt before Charles.

"The King is dead," uttered Antoinette. "Long live the King!"

"Long live King Louis XVII!" echoed Elisabeth, kneeling behind her. He did not have much of a court, this child-king of seven; he was imprisoned and in danger. Yet his was the crown of St. Louis; his was the mantle of Charlemagne. Upon his thin shoulders fell the burdens of the whole nation. And he was the son of a martyr.

No one would ever fully comprehend what her husband had suffered. It was only in the aftermath of his execution that she herself clearly saw the pattern of sacrifice which so characterized his life. Few had appreciated his goodness. Even the *emigrés*, aristocrats who had fled abroad, had snickered at Louis, calling him "King Log." They did not think he was dealing energetically enough with the Revolution, but from a place of safety it was easy for them to criticize the King, who was left with only a handful of loyal supporters, and was for all practical purposes a prisoner in his own palace.

She could never forget the fateful September 14, 1791, when after he was compelled to sign the new Constitution, he staggered into her room. She and her maid, Madame Campan, had gasped, because he was so pale, his face so contorted, that he did not even look like himself. He collapsed into a chair, putting a handkerchief to his eyes.

"All is lost!" Louis blurted to her. "Oh, Madame, and you are witness to this humiliation! Why were you present at the assembly?! Why did you witness it?! What! Were you brought to France only to see me humiliated?!"

She threw her arms around him. "Oh, go, go!" she whispered to Madame Campan, who hurried from the room. Antoinette had never seen her husband lose his composure, at least not since he became King; she never saw him lose it again. But as she held him close to her, she almost felt his heart breaking within him for the Kingdom and inheritance which he had lost both for himself and his son. He blamed himself for everything—he who had dedicated his every waking moment to serving his people, who in fifteen years of reign had produced six thick volumes of new laws to ease hardship and injustice, whereas his grandfather, after sixty years, had produced only two volumes. No king had done so much for France.

In the months that followed she saw him sink into a silent stupor, as if he was withdrawing from life. It frightened her to see him so, and she summoned all her wit to help cheer and lighten his mind with humor and diversions. Eventually, with God's help, he extracted himself from such a depressed state, and with renewed courage was able to face the fresh gale of tragedy that broke upon them in the months that followed. His calm fuelled her courage; her courage enhanced his composure.

During his trial, when he was separated from her, she was unable to eat, and rapidly lost weight, so that her dresses had to be taken in. Upon her husband's execution, she had petitioned for mourning garments for herself and her children; now she wore only black, even though white was the color of mourning for a Queen of France. She devoted her days at the Temple to the education of her children, along the curriculum laid down by her husband before he was taken away. However, she never accompanied them on their daily walk in the garden, because to do so meant she would have to pass his door, which she could no longer bring herself to do.

Meanwhile, one of the municipal guards, named Toulan, had apparently fallen in love with her. She had done nothing to encourage him, other than merely treating him with kindness and basic civility. Once she showed him the locks of hair of her two children who had died. He saw her as a helpless mother, not as a licentious queen, and was transformed from a hardened Jacobin to the most devoted champion of the crown. It was a good thing, because other than faithful Cléry, the only servants they had were a certain Monsieur and Madame Tison, who were very coarse people and spies of the Committee of Public Safety. The other guards mocked them, blowing smoke in the Queen's face as she walked by. Toulan, on the other hand, was always full of plans for her escape, none of which came to anything, partly because she refused to go anywhere without her children, whom it was impossible to smuggle out of the Temple. But his good intentions touched her heart. He managed to get her husband's wedding ring and seal, which the commissaries had confiscated from Cléry. Toulan retrieved them from the Council Chamber, afterwards shouting, "Thief! Thief!" louder than anyone else. At Antoinette's request, he arranged for the ring and seal to be smuggled from the country to the Comte de Provence, her brother-in-law, whom she now referred to as the "Regent." Toulan, who also supplied her with information about the war, was eventually reported to the Committee of

Public Safety by Madame Tison, and arrested.

She should have known that something else terrible was about to happen. Then she would have been better prepared. She knew that the Committee of Public Safety wanted to kill her, and that with every Austrian victory, with every French defeat, she was coming closer to her condemnation. Even so, she had no concept of how far her enemies would go in their attempts to break her will, and destroy her before the whole world. But the Tison woman knew. She had been aware for quite some time and the knowledge had driven her mad. One day in late June she burst in upon the Queen, throwing herself at her feet.

"Madame, I ask your Majesty's pardon! How miserable I am! I have caused your death, and that of Madame Elisabeth!" Antoinette tried to raise the distracted woman from the ground, and calm her saying, "Oh, Madame Tison, you have not!"

"Yes! Yes! I have betrayed you!" she shrieked, lapsing into wild, flailing convulsions. The guards dragged her away. The next day she was incarcerated in a mental asylum.

The incident should have been a warning to Antoinette, but on July 3 she prepared for bed, completely unsuspecting. Around ten o'clock that night came a loud pounding at the door. A group of commissaries burst into the room. One began very officiously to read a long decree, announcing the decision of the Committee of Public Safety to remove "Charles Capet" from his mother's care. At first she did not understand.

"No!" she exclaimed. "Never!" She ran to her little boy, who was asleep in his bed. He woke up, crying, and clung to her. In a few seconds, Elisabeth and Thérèse joined her, and with their arms they formed a barricade around the child. For an hour, they held them off. She screamed, begged, and pleaded. Then the intruders threatened to kill both of her children before her eyes if she did not give Charles to them. Her daughter was fourteen. She did not want to think of what such men might do to a young girl. She could not keep them away forever. She decided it was better to let him go peacefully rather than be injured or killed. Trembling, she dressed him, putting on his little hat and coat. He kissed her, and Thérèse and Babette, and was still sobbing as the men led him into the darkness. The old fortress rang with his wails for hours and hours.

The next day, she felt the full horror of her mistake when she discovered he had been handed over to the crude, rough cobbler, Simon, who worked in the Temple. The realization overwhelmed her. During the two days that followed, she could hear his sobs, and occasional cries for his Maman. She thought she would go insane.

She watched for hours on end at a narrow window from which she could catch a glimpse of her child when he was brought outside. Her ears strained for his every sound and word. One day, she heard him with the guards, loudly demanding them to show him the law which commanded that he be separated from his Maman. They derided him, and told him to say. "Long live the Republic! The Republic is eternal!"

"No," said Charles. "Only God is eternal!"

Afterwards, she did not hear or see him for some days. And then, one night, when the soldiers were at their drinking, she heard, mingled with their harsh laughter, a child's voice, raised in unison with the guards in a vile, ribald song. The voice was quavering and unnaturally high, but it was Charles'. What had they done to him? Surely, they were not giving liquor to a little boy?! Her mind whirled. She was falling into a pit of blackness.

"Elisabeth!" she called. Elisabeth came to her. She grasped her sister-in-law's hand. Her own voice was lifeless, and seemed to be coming from far away, as if she was no longer a living person, but a ghost.

"Elisabeth, God has abandoned me." She could no longer pray. She could hardly even bear to think, except to reproach herself for letting them take him. Surely, it would have been better for him to have died than be corrupted.

Elisabeth clasped both her hands in her own. She looked into Antoinette's eyes, which were wells of agony. "Antoinette," she whispered, "you must pray! You must !"

"I cannot. God has abandoned me! He has abandoned me!" Her eyes were tearless. She was too numb to cry.

"Pray," commanded Elisabeth. "Come, I will pray with you." She knelt down. "*Ave Maria, gratia plena,*" she began.

"*Ave Maria,*" whispered Antoinette, but her throat was dry. She felt that she could not utter another sound. She looked at her daughter, wide-eyed and tight-lipped. Thérèse had fallen into a sort of wordless agony since her father's death, and hardly ever spoke.

"Antoinette, for Thérèse's sake, you must pray," said Elisabeth.

"Yes," she rasped out. "Oh, my God, yes."

She stumbled over to her bed and lay down. "Oh, God, help me," she called soundlessly into the darkness.

Into her mind came a distant picture of a little girl with blond hair, in a rococo chamber at Schönbrunn Palace, sitting in a big armchair, her feet dangling down. It was herself, and she was listening to Countess Brandweiss, her governess, tell a story about when the Turks had swept through the empire, up to the very gates of Vienna.

"And what did my great-grandfather Leopold do, Countess Brandweiss?" asked little Archduchess Antonia.

"He and the Polish King put the Holy Name of Mary on their banners. On September 12, there was a great battle, and the Turkish army was overcome, even though it greatly outnumbered that of the Emperor and Jan Sobieski. The Turks were driven away, Vienna rejoiced, and a glorious *Te Deum* was sung in St. Stephen's Cathedral."

The scene faded from her mind. Mary . . . the Holy Name of Mary had won the victory for her family more than a hundred years ago. The Blessed Virgin was loved by the Habsburgs, who had consecrated their dominions to her Immaculate Conception. To the Austrians, she was *Mariazell*— "Mary-Throne." Austria was Mary's Throne, and Mary herself was the Throne of God. As a child she had often gone on pilgrimage with her family to the venerable shrine of Mariazell high in the alps. At the feet of the ancient, miraculous statue of the Most Holy Virgin holding the Infant Christ, were two gold hearts, placed there by her parents after their marriage. Surely the Mother of God would not abandon her, their youngest daughter.

"*Maria, Maria, Ave Maria,*" she repeated over and over again in her mind. And the Name of Mary illumined her darkness. She mentally clung to that name, and like a gentle waterfall it eased her spirit; she sank into the forgetfulness of sleep. In a like manner she struggled through the weeks that followed, calling constantly upon Mary, and was able once again to say longer prayers with Elisabeth, and comfort her shattered young daughter as best she could.

She was calm when the soldiers came again, in the dead of an August night, and took her from the Temple to the Conciergerie, the prison which was the antechamber to the guillotine. After embracing Elisabeth, she clasped her daughter in her arms, saying, "Have courage, Mousseline, and take care of your health." Before leaving, she hurriedly gathered a few devotional and sentimental items into a large handkerchief. A glove belonging to Charles, and a lock of his hair, she slipped into her bodice, next to her heart.

The deputy had finally finished testifying against her. He had turned the banquet for the Flanders regiment at the Versailles Opera into a bacchanalian revel, in which she had presided like a harpy, stamping on the red, white and blue revolutionary cockade.

She was jolted back to the present moment by Hermann. "Have you anything to say about the testimony?" he asked.

"I have no knowledge of the majority of the incidents mentioned by the witness," she replied. "As for the bodyguards' feast, we briefly visited them while at table, but that is all."

He accused her of inciting regiments against the Revolution.

"I have nothing to say," she replied.

Next, she was blamed for encouraging the King to take a stand against the Revolution, by helping him to write one of his speeches.

"My husband had great confidence in me," she answered, "and it was for that reason that he read his speech to me before presenting it to the deputies. However, I did not make any comments, especially since my husband had his own ideas and manner of expressing them that required little alteration."

"How did you use the huge sums of money given to you by the various ministers of finance?"

"I was never given huge sums. My allowance I used to pay the people in my service."

"Why did you lavish gold upon the Polignac family and several others?"

"They had positions at court which supplied them with wealth," she replied.

The interrogation went on and on. The *tricoteuses* began shouting because they were having difficulty hearing the Queen's responses.

"Make the Widow Capet stand up!" they cried.

The Queen sighed to her lawyers. "Will the people ever grow weary of my sufferings?"

The public prosecutor Fouquier-Tinville called to the stand the procurator Hébert, publisher of the filthy gazette *Père Duchesne*. Hébert was one of the men responsible for removing Charles from her care. He began to accuse her of something so revolting her ears rejected his words. He declared that her own son, "Little Capet," had testified that she, his mother, had led him into unnatural vice in order to weaken his constitution, so she could rule France through him. Madame Elisabeth was likewise accused. Antoinette did not know why she did not die of anguish right then and there. Her mind reeled, and all she could think of was her little boy, and what might be happening to him. She wanted to scream, "Give me my child!"

What had the monsters done to a small boy to make him say such things. She was trembling. "*Ave Maria, Ave Maria*," she repeated under her breath, which kept her from wanting to kill them all.

"What reply have you to Citizen Hébert's testimony?" asked Hermann.

"I have no knowledge of the incidents he speaks of, " she said faintly.

Hébert then accused her of treating her son as if he were king.

"Did you witness it?" she calmly asked him.

"I did not, but the municipal guard will confirm it," sneered the abominable man. "You allowed your son to take precedence at table."

One of the jurors rose. "Citizen President, the accused has not fully replied concerning the incident mentioned by Citizen Hébert, regarding what allegedly happened between herself and her son."

Antoinette found herself rising to her feet. She gazed steadily at her accusers, and not a few of them squirmed. "If I did not reply, it was because nature recoils at such an accusation against a mother." She turned to the galleries; her sweet, quavering voice resounded to the ceilings. "I appeal to all the mothers who may be here!"

A stir broke out among the spectators. The *tricoteuses* all began talking at once, and a few of them cheered her, with boos and hisses at Hébert. They were generally disgusted with him. The judges and jurors whispered among themselves. Hermann had to suspend the proceedings for two hours, after which they continued again until eleven o'clock at night. The Queen was bone tired. She was led across the courtyard of the Palais de Justice to the Conciergerie and her damp, moldy cell.

Yet in that hopeless place she had received much spiritual consolation. Two of her guards were devout, and earlier in the fall had permitted the holy, non-juring priest Abbé Magnin to twice hear her confession, and once even say Mass in her cell. She had been able to receive Holy Communion for the first time in more than a year.

"Now you will have the strength to endure your torments," the Abbé said to her. The guards had assisted at Mass with her.

Two nights before her trial began, another non-juring priest secretly brought her Holy Communion. She knew it was her Viaticum. On October 12, the Abbé Emery, former superior of Saint Sulpice and himself a prisoner in the Conciergerie sent her a message, telling her he would pass by her cell door at a certain time and say the words of absolution. She knelt at her door, making an act of perfect contrition, as the priest's gentle footsteps went slowly by. How grateful she was to those brave priests.

The following day was Tuesday, October 15, the Feast of St. Teresa, her Mousseline's feast-day. The Christian calendar having been abolished in France, the new republic celebrated the day as the feast of the Amaryllis, the citizens of Heaven having been replaced with the creatures of earth. It was a rainy, windy day, and at nine o'clock there began eighteen hours of more cross-examination. She perceived that they were deliberately trying to exhaust her, to make her publicly break down and admit to being a traitor. She prayed that her self-control would stay with her to the end.

One witness went on at a great length trying to prove that she had signed vouchers in order to obtain more money from the Civil List. The Queen questioned him as to the date on the vouchers, and he replied, "August 10, 1792."

"I never signed any vouchers," asserted the Queen. "And in any case, how could I have signed anything on August 10, when we fled from the mob to the National Assembly so early in the morning, and spent the entire day in the Logographe?"

At one point, Hermann had the usher display her personal belongings, holding up each one, and demanding an explanation from her.

"A packet containing various colors of hair," he announced.

"They come from my dead and living children, and from my husband," explained Antoinette. She clenched her hand to keep it from trembling.

"A paper with numbers on it."

"It is a table for teaching my son how to count." She remembered how the Temple guards had confiscated the little arithmetic table, thinking she was teaching Charles how to send messages in secret code.

The clerk displayed her sewing kit, her hand mirror, a ring with a lock of her mother's hair. Then he held up her prayer cards. "A paper on which are two gold hearts with initials, and another paper on which is inscribed 'Prayer to the Sacred Heart of Jesus,' 'Prayer to the Immaculate Conception.'" He did not seem to want any explanation.

Finally, he held up a portrait of Princesse de Lamballe. Seeing the big eyes and delicate features of her friend staring at her from the canvas evoked the scene of horror at the Temple more than a year ago, when they had brought her Lamballe's severed head on a pike, trying to make her kiss it.

She and Louis had been quietly playing backgammon, with their children beside them. She was filled with hope because the Austrian army was coming nearer to Paris, having already captured Verdun. Suddenly there were loud shouts in the courtyard, and Madame Tison, the maid, screamed. Cléry the valet rushed in, his face drained, unable to utter a sound. Her husband looked out the window, and stared with horror. He began to pull her out of the room. The guards were laughing. "It is the head of the Lamballe woman! They want the Austrian to kiss the face of her dead harlot!" She heard and saw no more, but collapsed in a dead faint. Louis carried her upstairs to her chamber, which was farther away from the ghoulish uproar.

"Whose is that portrait?" asked Hermann.

"Madame de Lamballe," answered the Queen steadily, but her mouth felt dry.

"Two other portraits of women," announced the clerk.

"Who are they?" inquired Hermann.

"They are two ladies with whom I was raised in Vienna."

"What are their names?"

"Mesdames de Mecklembourg and de Hesse." She could not help picturing her youthful companions, as they practiced their ballet steps with her and her sisters. She also thought of her daughter's companions, Ernestine and Zoë, whom she had sent abroad to safety with some *émigrés*.

The clerk exhibited her scapular, which Fouquier-Tinville loudly denounced as being "counter-revolutionary." She was also vehemently denounced for the Sacred Heart badge that Hébert had found in her missal.

"Most of the enemies of the glorious Revolution are found with

151

this detestable symbol on their persons!" cried the public prosecutor. "Does not this prove the reactionary character of the accused!"

Eventually they came to the subject of Trianon.

"Where did you get the money to build and furnish the Little Trianon, where you gave parties at which you were always the goddess?" asked Hermann.

"There were funds especially for that purpose," replied Antoinette.

"Those funds must have been extensive," said the judge, "for Little Trianon must have cost immense sums." He was obviously not aware that she had not built Trianon; she was merely given it by her husband, keeping most of the original furnishings of the former chatelaine, Madame du Barry.

She answered with frankness: "It is possible that the Little Trianon cost immense sums, perhaps more than I would have wished. We were gradually involved in more and more expense. Besides, I am more anxious than anyone else that what went on there should be known."

"Was it not at the Little Trianon that you knew the woman called La Motte?" He was referring to the infamous thief of Boehmer's diamond necklace.

"I have never seen her."

"Was she not your victim in the infamous affair of the necklace?"

"She cannot have been, since I never met her."

"Do you persist in denying that you knew her?" asked the judge, impatiently. She looked him in the eye.

"It is the truth I have told and will persist in telling."

As the hours dragged by, they set out to prove she had been an unnatural wife. Fouquier-Tinville glowered at her and said, "Through your influence, you made the King, your husband, do whatever you wished."

"There is an immense difference," said the Queen, "between counseling that something should be done, and having it carried out."

The prosecutor pointed threateningly at her. "You made use of his weak character to make him perform many evil deeds!"

"I never knew him to have such a character as you describe," she crisply replied, seeing they were not in the least acquainted with Louis-Auguste, who could never be made to swerve from his decisions, once he made them. Again, they brought up the painful matter of her boy.

"I point out to you that your testimony is in direct opposition to

152

your son's," challenged Fouquier-Tinville.

She sniffed. "It is easy to make a child of eight say whatever one wants."

"But he was made to repeat it several times and on several occasions," claimed the black-browed lawyer, whose malevolent glare made him look more like a beast than a man. "And he always said the same thing."

In her heart she said "*Ave Maria*," as another wave of horror racked her being. How that dreadful Simon must have drummed certain hideous thoughts and words into her angel, her *chou d'amour*. "Well, I deny it." Her words cut the air like a razor.

Finally, around half-past four in the afternoon, there was a short recess, and the Queen, who had eaten nothing since morning, was given a little soup, sent to her from the prison by the young servant girl, Rosalie. If it were not for Rosalie she wondered if she would be given anything at all, but God had provided. She could not help recalling so many cheerful repasts she had had on that very day, St. Teresa's day. She envisioned herself strolling to the Belvédère through the autumn glory of Trianon, where a delightful tea awaited her. It had all happened in another world, a world that had faded and withered like fallen leaves, and she was now encompassed in one which was a living death. All too soon, the session began once more, and she heard herself accused of practically everything from forgery to treason.

"At the time of your marriage to Louis Capet, did you not conceive the project of uniting Lorraine with Austria?"

"No," she said. It would have been laughable, in the days when she used to laugh, before she became so sad and exhausted.

"You bear its name."

"Because one must bear the name of one's country." Did they not know that her father had been of the House of Lorraine?

Around midnight, Fouquier-Tinville asked her if she had anything else to say for herself. She stood up. "Yesterday, I did not know the witnesses, and I did not know what they would testify. Well, no one has uttered anything positive against me. I end by saying that I was only the wife of Louis XVI, and bound to conform to his will."

Her lawyers gave a zealous defense, begging that her life be spared, on the grounds that it was enough punishment for her to have lost her husband. Afterwards, Hermann gave a long summary of her accusation. She had aided and abetted the "last tyrant" of France, who had already been found guilty and executed. Also, a Sacred Heart badge had been found in her possession, which in itself was enough to prove her an enemy of the people, worthy of the guillotine. While the jury deliberated, she asked for a glass of water. One of the gendarmes hastened to fetch it for her. She was not surprised when the verdict "guilty" was announced, and did not display the slightest flicker of emotion. It was two o'clock in the morning of October 16, traditionally the feast of the French priest St. Gall. On the revolutionary calendar it was the feast of the Ox, an animal of the ancient Hebrew holocaust.

The same gendarme who gave her the water escorted her back to her cell, respectfully removing his hat in her presence, and putting it under his arm. He did not seem to care that the gesture was noticed by many, and would surely lead to his arrest. The *tricoteuses* were silent as the Queen wearily limped out of the Hall of Liberty. Her eyesight was worsened by fatigue and the darkness of the hour. As they came to the black entrance of the Conciergerie she said, "I cannot see."

The young soldier gently took her arm. Nevertheless, she slipped on the rough staircase. Soon she was back in her bone-chilling cell, but she did not sleep. She had to write a letter to Elisabeth. In the light of two candles, her quill began to scratch across the page.

> It is to you, my sister, that I write for the last time. I have just been condemned, not to a shameful death, for it is shameful only to criminals, but to rejoin your brother. Innocent like him, I hope to display the same firmness as he did in his last moments. I am calm, as one is when one's conscience holds no reproach. I deeply regret having to abandon my poor children. You know that I lived only for them, and for you, my good and kind sister. In what a situation do I leave you, who from your affection sacrificed everything to be with us. I learned from the pleadings at the trial that my daughter was separated from you. Alas! poor child, I dare not write to her, she would not receive it. I do not even know if this will reach you. Receive my blessing on them both. I hope that one day, when they are older, they will be able to join you again, and profit to the full from your tender care, and that they both remember what I have always tried to instill in them: that the principles and execution of their duty should be the chief

foundation of their life, that their affection, and mutual trust will make it happy.

Let my daughter remember that in view of her age she should always help her brother with the advice that her greater experience and her affection may suggest, and let them both remember that in whatever situation they may find themselves, they will never be truly happy unless united. Let them learn from our example how much consolation our affection brought us in the midst of our unhappiness and how happiness is doubled when one can share it with a friend—and where can one find a more loving and truer friend then in one's own family? Let my son never forget his father's last words, which I distinctly repeat to him, never to try to avenge our deaths.

I have to mention something which pains my heart. I know how much distress this child must have caused you. Forgive him my dear sister, remember his age and how easy it is to make a child say anything you want, even something he does not understand. The day will come, I hope, when he will be all the more conscious of the worth of your goodness and tenderness towards them both. I now have only to confide in you my last thoughts. I would have liked to write them at the beginning of the trial, but apart from the fact that I was not allowed to write, everything went so quickly that I really would not have had the time.

I die in the Catholic, Apostolic, and Roman religion, in the religion of my father, in which I was raised and which I have always professed, having no expectation of spiritual consolation, and not even knowing if there still exist priests of that religion here, and in any case the place where I am would expose them to too much danger should they enter.

She wanted to make it clear to Babette that she had not and would not receive the ministrations of a constitutional priest, nor did she want to reveal the activities of the good priests to anyone other than Babette who might read her letter.

I sincerely beg pardon of God for all the faults I have committed during my life. I ask pardon of all those I know, and of

155

you, my sister in particular, for all the distress I may, without wishing it, have caused them. I forgive all my enemies the harm they have done me. I say farewell to my aunts and to all my brothers and sisters. I had friends. The idea of being separated for ever from them and their troubles forms one of my greatest regrets in dying. Let them know, at least, that up to my last moment I was thinking of them.

Farewell, my good and loving sister. May this letter reach you! Think of me always. I embrace you with all my heart, together with those poor, dear children."

The words fell from her pen like tears.

"My God! what agony it is to leave them forever! Adieu! Adieu! I shall henceforth pay attention to nothing but my spiritual duties. As I am not free, they will perhaps bring me a priest, but I shall not say a word to him and I shall treat him as a complete stranger."

Her letter was finished. Still fully dressed, she lay down on her bed, and looked towards the high, narrow window. Soon it would be daybreak. She kissed her son's little glove, and prayed for him. She pictured him in the gardens of St. Cloud, on their last family holiday, when he had run to her with an exquisite flower called an *Immortelle*.

"Oh, Maman!" he had exclaimed. "I want you to be like this flower!" His roguish blue eyes, plump cheeks, animated form and voice full of *joie de vivre* were all so present to her in that dark moment. Soon a steady flow of tears had drenched her face and pillow. She thought all of her tears had already been wept; surely by now they would have dried up, but yet another well of sorrow had been tapped. She lay there weeping, ignoring the guard who stood in the shadows watching her, as her last morning dawned.

Chapter Eight
The White Lady

"He that shall overcome, shall thus be clothed in white garments. . . . "
—Apocalypse 3:5

Rosalie Lamorliére, morning, October 16, 1793

Rosalie wept when she heard the Queen's sentence. After a sleepless night, the young maid had finally fallen into a fitful slumber. She awoke in the faintest glimmering of dawn, with the concierge's wife shaking her.

"She is doomed!" whispered her mistress. "The execution is set for noon. Try to get her to eat—she'll need all her strength."

"Yes, Madame," Rosalie whispered back. "She hardly ate a bite all of yesterday."

The jailer's wife swaggered away. Rosalie climbed out of bed, turning up the wick in the lantern in her garret chamber. What a fortunate girl she was to have employment in such topsy-turvy times. Monsieur Richard, the former concierge of the prison, had been arrested along with Madame Richard, for being too kind to the Queen, and trying to help her to escape. They had been replaced by Monsieur and Madame Bault, who allowed Rosalie to keep her servant's position, even though Monsieur Bault was a crude man. The Conciergerie was not the most cheerful of places to live and work, but most of the inmates were good people, imprisoned for political reasons. Indeed, some were very holy people, who were not there for any crime except their faith. Many priests, nuns, and devout lay people, both peasant and noble, were housed therein. There were also many aristocrats who were there solely because of their names and lineage, such as the Duc d'Orléans, the nasty creature who had voted for the King's death.

"Philippe Egalité," as he had been calling himself, in order to be in the good graces of the new order, had nevertheless fallen out of favor with his Jacobin friends, and been thrown into the Conciergerie. There was a story abroad that the conniving Philippe had disguised himself as a one-legged man, and gone to the Temple in order to kidnap the Queen, so as to gain control of the little King. He had come upon Madame Elisabeth praying aloud for the repose of her murdered brother, Louis XVI. The sight so unmanned him that he trembled and became distraught; the commissaries recognized and arrested him. At any rate, he lived in his cell with many comforts and an elaborate wardrobe, including satin dressing-gowns, and silver plate. What a contrast to the Queen, whose shoes were dilapidated from mildew; who was so grateful when Rosalie brought her a cardboard box for her meager toiletries. Rosalie sighed as she washed her face. Yes, in these days she was blessed to have work, especially when many ladies' maids were starving in the streets. She was blessed, most of all, in having the great honor to be the last handmaid of the Queen of France. Rosalie could read and write a little, having been taught by the local abbé, before he was arrested. He had supplied her with her scanty knowledge of history, having told her stories of the saints, and of the kings and queens of France. She enjoyed hearing about Queen Blanche, Queen Marguerite of Provence, Anne of Austria and Saint Clothilde, but Rosalie knew that there had never been anyone like her Queen—Marie-Antoinette, who even when broken with sorrow was magnificent. Rosalie had never seen anyone with more serenity and resignation.

She remembered the August afternoon when they discovered the Queen was coming to stay with them at the Conciergerie. Madame Richard had been in a frenzy to get the cell properly arranged, procuring a camp bed with linen sheets. "Those coarse woolen sheets will never do for the Queen," said Madame Richard. "And make certain she has a warm blanket."

"Should I curtsey?" asked Rosalie.

"Good heavens, no, child!" exclaimed her mistress. "You will send us all to the guillotine! It is difficult, so difficult, these days. But we will do everything for her we can—cook the tastiest meals, polish our pewter 'til it shines, keep her as comfortable as possible in that hovel. I will give her a table with two cane chairs."

"I will give her my tapestry stool and hand mirror," said Rosalie, willing to sacrifice her most prized possessions. "Oh, Madame, I wish we could bring out the good silver."

"Oh, no, girl, did I not tell you that the Commune will take it away? No, we must use prudence. Remember, I have a family to feed. But you can offer to fix her hair and help her to dress."

How beautiful the Queen had been when she first arrived at the Conciergerie in her black dress and mourning veil. Her skin was like alabaster, so smooth and firm. Rosalie was awed to be so near the legendary Marie-Antoinette. She had never believed any of the ugly stories about her, and neither had Madame Richard. She hesitantly asked the Queen if she could help her to change her clothes.

"Thank you, Mademoiselle," replied the Queen, "but I am alone now, and prefer to dress myself." The poor woman's eyes were like deep pools, reflecting both patience and affliction. Rosalie's heart was wrenched with compassion. The months in the dampness of the prison soon ruined the Queen's constitution. By October, her skin was like an old woman's; even her hair was graying, dry, and brittle.

There were better cells available, but the Committee of Public Safety demanded that the Queen be put in such a miserable hole in order to break her health. After an escape attempt, in which Madame Richard was implicated in trying to help the Queen get away, the royal prisoner was transferred to a veritable dungeon, too dark for reading or sewing; she was no longer able to work on the stockings she was knitting with two quills for the little King. It was very cold, and the walls dripped with moisture. Rosalie continued to do her best for the Queen, making her a nourishing, medicinal soup every morning for breakfast. Nevertheless, the disconsolate woman continued to fail. There was always a gendarme outside her door, and another looking in the window, so she never had any privacy.

Rosalie dressed hurriedly in the chill of the October dawn. The sun had not yet risen. Over her shift and petticoat she put on a grey, linen dress, with a white fichu and apron, and a little white cap, into which she tucked her thick black curls. She was a pretty girl, with black eyes, pink cheeks, and blossom-like mouth, but being attractive was not necessarily an asset in the Conciergerie, where the real criminals were so often the guards. So she always walked modestly, eyes downcast, and so was able to keep their rude gestures and comments at a minimum.

A few nights ago, right before the trial, she had been startled to look down a lonely stretch of corridor and see a woman in white gliding along. Her back was to Rosalie, who could not see her face. In the dimness, her garments seemed faintly luminous, almost unearthly. She vanished around a corner. Rosalie, tray in her hands, followed her, but when she rounded the corner, the woman was nowhere to be seen. Rosalie hurried to the Queen's cell. The guard unbolted and opened the two, thick, nail-studded doors, as Rosalie carried in the food, arranging the dishes carefully on the table.

The Queen was looking at her. "Rosalie, are you well? You look as if you have seen a ghost."

"Oh, Madame, I saw a strange sight—perhaps it was a ghost! I always thought this old place was haunted, especially since they desecrated Sainte Chapelle next door, and took away the holy relic of the Crown of Thorns that St. Louis brought from the Holy Land." She caught her breath. Madame Richard, before being arrested, had told Rosalie not to speak to the Queen about the closing and ransacking of churches, of parodies of the Mass performed in empty sanctuaries, and especially of the desecration of the royal tombs at St. Denis, where the body of the Queen's oldest son lay in an uneasy rest. "She is distraught enough," warned Madame Richard.

"The Crown of Thorns?" inquired the Queen, thoughtfully. "The crown of France was the Crown of Thorns for my poor husband. Well, he is happy now. But what did you see, Rosalie?"

"A lady clothed in white, walking through the Conciergerie. She disappeared very mysteriously. I do not know who it could be."

"You have seen the White Lady, Rosalie. Whenever anyone in my family is to die, the White Lady always appears beforehand. I know now that my end is truly come."

A chill shot up Rosalie's spine, but she was unable to ask anymore questions, because the guard was glaring at her from outside the window. In the dim torchlight she watched the Queen carefully bless herself and pray before eating. Rosalie waited until the Queen had finished her supper, at which time she also said the grace after meals. Rosalie found little chores to do, such as straightening the Queen's cell, trying to linger

160

as long as she could, so the Queen would have some company other than those guards. Also, Rosalie loved to be near the Queen. In her slightest movements, Rosalie glimpsed another world, a world of flowers and music, of beauty and love. She became possessed by a feeling of peace and safety being near the brave, stately woman, who ate so neatly and carefully, with an economy of gesture, almost like a religious. Indeed, Rosalie always sensed an air of holiness when in the Queen's cell, as if a sacred, unseen presence hovered nearby.

Now, the trial had come and gone and the sun was rising on the "Feast of the Ox" as Rosalie entered the Queen's dungeon. The Queen lay on her bed, fully dressed and weeping, with a small yellow glove pressed to her cheek. Rosalie had frequently noticed the Queen kissing the glove which belonged to the little King. Once Madame Richard had brought her youngest son to cheer the desolate prisoner, but instead of being cheered, she burst into tears at the sight of one who so resembled her own boy. She gathered him into her arms, covering his face and hair with all the embraces she longed to lavish on her child. In those moments, Rosalie glimpsed a grief so intense such as she never imagined could exist in one woman's heart. Rosalie disliked disturbing the Queen in the midst of her agony, but she had to get her to eat something. She was herself unsuccessfully fighting back the tears. She paid no heed to the guard, whom the authorities had now ordered to stand inside the cell.

"Madame, you had no supper last night, and ate so little during the day. What shall I bring you this morning?" asked Rosalie.

"Nothing, my child, I need nothing." The Queen's eyes were bloodshot, her voice hoarse. "Everything is over for me."

"But Madame, I have been keeping some soup on the stove for you all night." Rosalie spoke like a mother to her child. The Queen only choked on tears, saying nothing. Rosalie, too, began to sob.

"Very well," the Queen said at last, "bring me some of your soup, Rosalie." Rosalie ran to fetch the soup. The Queen, with great effort, took a few spoonfuls, but it was obvious she had no appetite.

"Please, Rosalie, leave me. Return at eight to help me dress."

Rosalie took the soup and left. She wanted to find a corner in which to weep. Sobs were shaking her body, and she could not bear to break down in front of the guards. She stood in a dim niche and her tears flowed. Then she thought of something she could do for the Queen. She ran to a nearby café and bought a cup of chocolate. It was not much, but her royal mistress might be persuaded to drink some, and it would give her enough strength to make it to the guillotine without fainting. It was almost eight, and she went straight to the Queen, who was still prostrate, but much calmer. The little glove had disappeared. She sat up and drank the chocolate.

"It is time for me to dress," she said. She went into a corner by the bed and motioned to Rosalie, who came to stand between the Queen and the guard, making as much of a shield with her body as she could. But the wretched man insisted on coming over to the bed, leaning over so he could watch. Rosalie wanted to strike him. She guessed he would be high in the opinion of his drinking comrades when he laughed about it with them.

"Please, Monsieur," begged the Queen, "in the name of decency, allow me to change my linen without witnesses!"

"I am ordered to observe your every movement," replied the cad.

The Queen turned her back to him, and with the greatest delicacy possible changed her soiled linen and undergarments (she was having her monthly flux). She put on a clean chemise, and a black petticoat. Then she put on the white piqué gown that she usually used as a wrapper in the mornings. Around her neck and shoulders she wrapped a large, muslin fichu. Rosalie skillfully arranged the Queen's hair in a chignon, over which she placed a simple white cap, without the mourning veil. The authorities had forbidden her to wear black so she was to go to her death all in white.

The Queen gave Rosalie a white ribbon she had once used in her hair. "Keep it as a little remembrance of me."

Rosalie wanted to say adieu, to kneel and kiss the hem of the Queen's dress, but she could not move; there was a tightness in her throat.

The doors squealed open. It was a man in black. Rosalie could tell he was a priest, but a constitutional priest. He asked the Queen if she wished for the services of his ministry.

"I think not," said the Queen, lowering her eyes. In her mind, to do so would be like an act of apostasy.

"What will people say when they hear that you refused the consolations of religion?" He was obviously a man who worried about what others think. The Queen was sitting on her bed, shivering in the darkness of the cell. Her reputation was already damaged irreparably.

Anyway, she was beyond caring. Her voice was gentle and calm.

"You will tell anyone who inquires that God in His Mercy provided for me."

"May I accompany you to the scaffold?" asked the lapsed clergyman, trying to be heroic.

"If you wish," replied the Queen. "But do you think the people will allow me to go to the scaffold without tearing me to pieces?"

Rosalie gasped, remembering the story of the Princesse de Lamballe, who had been hideously dismembered by the enraged mob. But if the Queen rode to the scaffold in a well-guarded coach, everything should be alright. The Queen turned away from the juring priest, and kneeling by her bed, began to silently pray. The clergyman sat in a chair, looking dejected. Rosalie stood quietly in a corner, praying under her breath, "Oh, Sacred Heart of Jesus, oh, Sacred Heart of Jesus . . . !" Afterwards, she could never say how long she stood there. It seemed like centuries, as they waited for the last hour.

Several, heavy footsteps echoed down the corridor of the medieval fortress. The doors opened, and Hermann entered, attired in his black suit and black plumed hat, with two other judges, and a clerk. The Queen was still kneeling by her bed. At the sound of their entrance, she slowly rose to her feet, and faced them. Rosalie perceived the transformation. Her blue eyes, still bloodshot, shone with peace and authority. She was no longer a broken woman; she was their sovereign lady. She was the Queen.

"Attention!" announced Hermann. "Widow Capet, your sentence will be read to you!"

"It is not necessary," replied the Queen. "I know fully well what my sentence is."

"You must hear it again. It is the law."

The clerk monotonously rambled off all the gross slanders that had so tormented the Queen for the past two days. Rosalie wanted to vomit. As he finished, the big executioner strode in.

"Put out your hands," he growled to the Queen, who stepped away from him.

"Are you going to bind me?" she asked, looking horrified.

The executioner grunted in assent.

"Do your duty, man," ordered Hermann. The brawny man, the same who had displayed Louis XVI's head to the people with many indecent gestures, roughly grabbed the Queen's arms, and lashed her hands and wrists together very tightly with cords, almost up the to the elbow. She suppressed a small cry of pain. Rosalie, filled with indignation, saw the Queen's eyes flutter searchingly towards the moldy ceiling, as if pleading with some good angel to strengthen her. The executioner snatched off her little cap, and with a pair of huge shears roughly destroyed the neat, braided chignon, so that the Queen's hair resembled the ragged straw of a scarecrow. He replaced the cap, under which hung the frayed, uneven tendrils. Then he pushed her out of the cell, and she walked ahead of him as if on a leash.

Rosalie followed them to the entrance of the Conciergerie. Out of the arched, gothic portals could be seen the courtyard, and the vehicle in which Marie-Antoinette was to ride to her death. Rosalie nearly fainted when she saw that it was a rickety garbage cart. How easy it would be for violent hands to reach up and drag the Queen into the street to be bludgeoned and hacked to death. Rosalie saw the Queen blanch with fright as she, too, noticed the garbage cart. She heard the Queen beg the executioner to loosen her hands, which he did, and she ran into a dark corner of the prison office where she squatted in order to relieve herself. Rosalie winced with fear and humiliation for her royal mistress, so modest, so gentle, to be subjected to so many indignities all at once. The executioner bound her again. She straightened her back, lifted up her head, and walked towards the cart.

The defrocked cleric was hovering at her elbow. "Have courage!" Rosalie heard him say to the Queen, who looked at him fixedly in the face and replied, "It does not require courage to die; it requires courage to live."

Rosalie watched from the doorway as the Queen was helped into the garbage cart, and made to sit facing backwards in it, with the priest at her side. He had a crucifix in his hand, which he stared at with great concentration. As the cart jolted forward, the Queen lost her balance and swayed.

"Those aren't your cushions at Trianon!" shouted some bystander. Overall, Rosalie was surprised at the silence of the spectators who lined the courtyards and streets. She plunged into the crowd, and tried to follow the cart as long as she could, but the press of people was too dense. She craned her neck to see the Queen, sitting very erect, head held high, eyes downcast. In a few moments the white form faded from sight. Only a few people yelled insults like "Long live the Republic!" Most of the citizens were quiet; some were silently weeping, especially the poor. They remembered how the Queen in her happier days had supported many destitute families.

Some of those poor had banded together in a plan to rescue the Queen from the Conciergerie, but it had come to nothing. There were too many spies. As the cart turned onto the Rue de Saint Honoré, more hateful shouts could be heard. The closer she traveled to the Place de la Révolution, the worse it would be. All the fiercest revolutionaries would be waiting by the guillotine—if the Queen were fortunate enough to make it to the scaffold. Rosalie breathlessly waited in the dense crowd, for the sound of drums, and the final burst of cheers. She prayed that the Queen would not be murdered by the mob.

It was noon when the roar from the packed square resounded throughout Paris. Many around her responded with cries of "Long live the Republic!" The garbage cart had reached the guillotine. The Queen's agony was over, and she was truly free. For the first time that day, Rosalie was suddenly aware of the bright sun, blazing through the mists of the Ile-de-la-Cité.

She trudged back towards the Conciergerie. It was dinner time, and she would be needed. With her head lowered, she moved through the masses of people, all going about their business, the spectacle having ended. On the cobbles, she saw a card, and quickly stooped to pick it up. It was a holy picture of the Sacred Heart, drawn in red ink, with orange and yellow flames, and around it were inscribed in letters of gold: "Long live Louis XVII, King of France!" Rosalie quickly put the card in her apron pocket. Tears streamed down her face, as she whispered a prayer for her little King, mistreated by his jailers in the Temple. Everyone at the Conciergerie talked about it. She prayed for him, and for his sister, Madame Royale, a girl about Rosalie's own age, who like her brother was orphaned and imprisoned. "Oh God, please save them," whispered the servant girl.

Chapter Nine
The Orphan

"Daughters of Jerusalem, weep not over me; but weep for yourselves and for your children." —St. Luke 23:28

Madame Marie-Thérèse-Charlotte of France, midnight, December 18, 1795

It was a black Paris midnight. Not a single star peered through the gloom of the city, where the streets had so recently been drenched in streams of blood. No bells tolled the hours, for all of the churches and monasteries were abandoned. Paris was sleeping, with the exception of raucous carousers, who scorned the bitter night air, and a young girl, who kept vigil high in the tower of the Temple, by the light of a solitary taper. The dawn of tomorrow would bring her seventeenth birthday. By the time the sun rose, she would be far away from the medieval fortress, where she had languished for three years; far away from Paris itself, which had no connotations for her outside the destruction of her family.

She was waiting in the cold of a December night for the coach which was to take her to Austria, to her mother's kindred, whom she had never seen. She wore a black serge traveling dress, and a grey woolen cloak and hood; the latter was flung back, revealing the blond hair which had darkened into the color of wild honey. It was pulled straight back from her forehead, hanging in long ringlets around her shoulders. Maman and Tante Babette had emphasized to her that she must not neglect her appearance in prison, and become slovenly. Her deep set eyes were gray-

166

blue; her aquiline nose, from the Bourbons, as was her full mouth, but she had the determined Habsburg jaw. Her skin was very white; she would have been attractive, almost beautiful, if her expression had not been so hard, and the lines around her mouth very bitter for a girl so young. Yet one could see that if she smiled, she would be quite alluring, but Marie-Thérèse-Charlotte of France, Madame Royale, never smiled. She rarely even spoke, and when she did, her voice was husky and hoarse from lack of use. She had spent almost a year in complete solitude, except for the guards. They would burst in at any time of the day or night to search her person for secret messages, or to make certain she was still in her room and had not been spirited away. They never ceased to insult her, and say coarse and suggestive remarks to her, which in her innocence she did not fully understand except to know they were impure. Sometimes their words and looks terrified her, especially in those long nights, month after month, of being alone in the darkness. Once they threatened her with a new law that stated all women over fifteen must marry or be committed to a brothel, but Robespierre died before it could be applied to her.

She refused to cry in front of her tormentors, or show any sign of emotion whatsoever, and suppressed the tears that frequently rose to her eyes. With iron self-control, her tears dried up, but instead she suffered from a heaviness in her chest; her heart felt as if it were being squeezed, and at times she was breathless. When one of the pompous officials of the Commune visited her to see if she had any health problems, she complained of "heart-sickness."

Stifling a yawn, she glanced around the room, at the peeling blue walls, the shabby gold upholstered furniture in which her family had once sat, in that place where they had once read, sewed, and even laughed. Her father had asked them riddles and conundrums from the *Gazette de Mercure*, in the days when they were all still together. It was not an unpleasant room in itself, especially with her spaniel dozing by the stove, where the fire had burned quite low. But those walls would always echo with her mother's piercing cries when little Charles was taken away into the night. Thérèse had imprinted her own anguish on the walls by scratching with a needle the words:

> Marie-Thérèse-Charlotte is the unhappiest person in the world. She can obtain no news of her mother, nor even be reunited with her, although she asked a thousand times. Long live

my good mother whom I love much, and of whom I can obtain no news.

It was more than a year before she was finally told that her mother was dead. Even then, she could not cry for her brave Maman, with whom she had once stood on the balcony in the grim dawn of their last hours at Versailles, with the mob shouting horrible things at them. Her Maman had not flinched, even with muskets pointed in her direction. Thérèse would never forget the gruesome carriage ride to Paris, surrounded by cruel faces threatening to kill "the Austrian." Little Charles had leaned out the window, calling, "Have pity on Maman!" to the people, who shouted back, "You're not the Fat Pig's brat! We know who your real father is!" Charles had not understood the implications, but Thérèse had.

No, she could not cry for her mother. Her eyes remained dry, while her heart was bleeding. She could only weep in her dreams, when she saw her mother at Trianon in the springtime, in a white dress, surrounded by blue hyacinths, holding out her arms to her. No matter how fast she ran in the dream, she could never seem to reach her mother, who would drift farther and farther away.

The fire crackled pathetically and her dog whimpered in his sleep. Thérèse remembered the night she had said farewell to her father— how the room had swirled; she saw stars, and there was a roaring. Her shock and sorrow were so immense it was like being hit with a club. Ever since, she felt there was a cold hand clutching at her throat. Her father, who was so nearsighted he could only vaguely see what was going on around him, could always see into her heart. To lose him was like losing part of her own soul. He was such a good man—how could anyone wish him harm?

"They are the enemies of Christ," Tante Babette told her. "As the Anointed of the Lord, your father represents the Kingship of Christ, the Redeemer's authority over the temporal order as well as the spiritual order. As a righteous King, your father is especially the enemy of those who want to create a completely secular society, in which the name of God will never officially appear, and the rights of Christ the King will be publicly denied. In order to destroy Christendom, they must first destroy the King of France, leader of the nation that is eldest daughter of the Church."

Thérèse was very glad that Tante Babette had never become a

nun. To whom would she have turned when her mother was taken to the Conciergerie? How often she wept in her aunt's arms, in those days when she could still cry. They had each been brought down to the Council Chamber of the Temple for questioning. She was happy to see her little brother there, too, but the happiness quickly turned to horror. Charles was greatly altered. He was dressed in ragged clothes like a sans-culotte, with a red revolutionary cap. His eyes were bloodshot and glazed, with dark circles under them. He seemed uncertain of who or where he was. Out of his mouth came the most disgusting words and story, which he rattled off as if by rote. Most of it was incomprehensible to Thérèse, except to realize that it was a terrible lie about Maman and Tante Babette. The prosecutor questioned her about the things her brother said. He tried to persuade her to agree with it, but she said she had seen nothing. No one would ever make her say something that was not true, but poor Charles was so young. Maman had always worried that he was so high strung and impressionable.

Tante Babette, however, had gazed at Charles with horror, and cried out, "You monster!"

For a minute, he appeared to become himself again, and began to cry, "Maman! Maman!" He came up to Thérèse and slipped his hand into hers. She was so frightened and distressed; she did not know what had happened to her little brother to make him say such things. She was stunned and could barely move. Then, the guards took him away. She never saw him again.

She demanded of one of the revolutionary officials who came to see her that her brother must have a good doctor—he was obviously very ill, whatever else was wrong with him. The official had said nothing. Thérèse insisted: "Tell Robespierre my brother should have a doctor." That was after they had come for Tante Babette. She and Tante Babette had lived alone in the Temple for almost a year. Her aunt taught her many prayers, told her how to sprinkle water throughout the apartment in order to freshen the stale air; to walk briskly back and forth every morning for exercise. She taught her how to keep an orderly routine of reading, praying, chores, and knitting. They had a limited amount of wool, so after one project they would unravel it and begin another. Tante Babette was cheerful and resigned, keeping track of the liturgical calendar, ember days, Advent, Lent and the great feasts. She knew so many psalms and scripture passages by heart, and together they read aloud from spiritual books like

The Imitation of Christ.

When Tante Babette was led away, how frightened Thérèse was to be all alone, but she maintained her scheduled life. She scratched on the wall over her bed: "Oh, my father, watch over me from Heaven! Oh, my God, pardon those who have caused the death of my parents!"

Meanwhile, it had been years since Thérèse had heard Mass or received the sacraments. She remembered how she had made her first Holy Communion right after the Revolution erupted, at the Church of St. Gènevieve in Paris. Her Papa had said, "Pray for France, my child. Remember that the prayer of the innocent can turn aside the wrath of Heaven." Now she could only make spiritual communions, since she was allowed no priest. Tante Babette asked for a priest before she was put on trial, and was told: "You'll die just as well without the blessing of a Capuchin." In those days, the Reign of Terror was at its height.

The full details of her family's fate were given her by a young matron, whom the authorities sent to be her companion in the summer of 1795. Thérèse was overjoyed not to be alone. Slowly the woman began to tell her everything. After her mother was guillotined, her corpse was thrown onto the grass of the cemetery of La Madeleine, the head between the legs, without funeral services or proper Christian burial. Her Tante Babette was guillotined in May of 1794. She had been the last of a long line of aristocrats going to the scaffold, and each one knelt before her, asking her blessing, before approaching *Mère Guillotine.* When the executioner had bared her neck, he pulled her dress down so low that her shoulders and bosom were exposed, along with her medal of Our Lady.

"I beg you, Monsieur, for the love of your mother, to cover my bosom," modest Tante Babette had pleaded. As she was beheaded, the fragrance of roses filled the Place de la Révolution, confirming the general opinion that Madame Elisabeth of France was a saint. The executioners therefore took special precautions to strip the corpse and destroy it with quicklime, after throwing it into a common grave, so that relics would be difficult to find.

"In this one victim we hail the double crown of purity and devotion," Thérèse prayed the words from the breviary in her aunt's honor. "Hers the glory of virginity, hers the palm of martyrdom."

Two months after Tante Babette's death, on July 17, 1794 the Carmelite nuns of Compiègne were guillotined, singing on the way to the scaffold, and offering their lives to God. Ten days later Robespierre fell,

170

and the Terror came to an end.

With the greatest grief and agony, she heard of her brother's death, which occurred in June of 1795, and the full extent of his ordeal. As her mother had guessed, the guards had given the eight year old strong drink, making him intoxicated, exposing him to obscene pictures, teaching him filthy habits, and eventually giving him over to a lewd woman of the streets to corrupt him and infect him with disease. Simon had brutalized him, kicking him in the chest, making him learn bad words and songs. The boy lapsed into a trancelike state, occasionally regaining full consciousness, at which time he would cry for his Maman. After the Terror ended, he was left alone without care, sick, drooling like an imbecile, lying in his own filth.

When he died, his corpse was thrown into an unmarked grave. The bitterness of her brother's fate took possession of her being as she recalled the bright, lively boy he had been, who listened to her recite her lessons until he knew them better than she did, always alert, cheerful, and friendly. His personality had been so like her Maman's. What could possess people to make them want to so viciously destroy a small boy, who had done nothing except be King of France? The leaders of the Revolution had allowed it to happen. No one had pity, no one intervened to save him. They were all so in love with their liberty, with their "rights." But she knew that their glorious Republic was founded on the broken mind and body of a little child.

He had not been the only innocent to suffer. With horror Thérèse heard of the massacres of the Catholic and royalist peasants of the Vendée, of the torture and defilement of women and girls, of entire families guillotined, of mothers and children roasted alive in ovens, of the "Republican marriages," in which two people would be tied together naked and drowned. So many churches had been burnt and destroyed; her Papa's beautiful kingdom was filled with ruins and corpses. How shocked she was to hear of the desecration of Notre Dame, where an actress was enthroned on the high altar and worshipped as the "goddess of Reason." "The abomination of desolation," murmured Thérèse when she heard of it.

She did not know why she had been spared. Her inner suffering increased, as her soul discovered it is sometimes more agonizing to live than to die. Meanwhile, the citizens of Paris began to remember her. They stood on the roofs of neighboring houses so they could glimpse their princess when she went for a walk in the garden. Many wept for her, and public indignation rose against the government. It was decided to get her out of the way, by exchanging her with French prisoners of war taken by the Austrians. The Habsburg Emperor was willing to take his young cousin off the Revolution's hands. Kindly Parisians sent her a dog and a baby goat for company. It was only with them that she displayed a glimmer of a smile, as she ran through the garden with her pets, a young girl once more.

She had packed her meager belongings for the journey. She was to depart in the middle of the night, so the sight of her would not arouse royalist sympathies. It would feel so strange to be out in the world again; so strange and so frightening. The Temple was the only home she had known since she was fourteen. To leave it would be severing the last links with her family. She would be going to a distant land, a penniless orphan, to relations she did not know. She, Madame Royale, who was to have been married in the chapel of Versailles in a dress of silver was now a dowerless waif.

She pushed the thoughts from her mind. It would be odd to live in a palace again. She would be expected to make polite conversation, to be light-hearted with people her own age, who were occupied with dancing and flirting and had never seen blood spilt. She really did not know if she were up to it. But she would have to try, and God would help her.

There was a knock at the door. Thérèse drew on her gloves, and picked up her sleepy spaniel. The door opened; it was the official who was to conduct her down to her coach. Her parcel was already aboard the vehicle. She followed the man down the shadowy, narrow staircase of the tower, past the chamber where she had said adieu to her father. She trembled as they passed the rooms where her brother had been tormented. She remembered something else her companion had whispered to her: "Some say that the Little King is still alive; that he was smuggled out of France and replaced in the Temple by an idiot boy, and is now hidden away somewhere in Germany." If her brother was alive, it was her duty to find him. She would search for him, even if it took a lifetime.

The narrow door groaned open. She stepped out of the tower and turned to the minister. "I am grateful for your attentive and respectful manner," said the princess in her hoarse voice. When anyone did not mock her, it seemed as if they were being kind. "But even at the moment you are giving me liberty, how can I help thinking of those who crossed this threshold before me? It is just three years, four months, and five days since those doors were closed on my family and me; today I go out, the last and most wretched of all."

The man could not reply. Soon they reached the courtyard of the Temple, where Thérèse had not walked since that August day in 1792 when her family had crossed it together, with the guards singing a derisive song aimed especially at her mother. The official sheepishly helped her into the coach. Under her breath she recited the passage from Lamentations so loved by Tante Babette in prison, because it was used in the office of Holy Week. "All ye who pass by the way, attend and see if there be any sorrow like unto my sorrow." The horses snorted, the coach jerked forward, as the daughter of many kings drove away into the darkness.

Chapter Ten
The Pilgrim

"You shall draw waters with joy out of the Saviour's fountains." —Isaias 12:3

The Duchesse d'Angoulême, morning, May 22, 1807

The town of Mitau was bright with snow in the sunshine of a May morning, and cold winds whipped around the little palace which His Imperial Majesty the Tsar of All the Russias had generously loaned to the impoverished, exiled Bourbons. In a small, sparsely furnished room of the palace, an aged priest lay dying. In a chair beside his bed sat a young woman, not quite thirty, in a maroon, high-waisted wool dress, with a white linen apron. Under a closefitting white cap, her amber-colored hair, in a grecian knot, framed a strong, solemn face with piercing blue-gray eyes. Dipping a cloth into a basin of water, she sponged the forehead of the sick man, whose chest shuddered and heaved. At first glance, no one would guess that she was Madame Royale, daughter of Louis XVI and Marie-Antoinette, their *Mousseline la sérieuse*, now the Duchesse d'Angoulême. With closer examination, no one with her dignified, albeit rather stiff bearing could be anything but a princess. She radiated a cold majesty to those who did not know her, but in her eyes burned the fires of deep emotions; her frigid manner was from sadness, not apathy or scorn.

The priest was Abbé Henry Edgeworth de Firmont, the last confessor of Louis XVI, and he was dying of typhus. Her father's brother, the Comte de Provence, now called "Louis XVIII," had implored the Abbé to become court chaplain for himself and his threadbare band of *émigrés*. The brave Irishman did so, even though it meant he would never see Ireland or France again, or his poor parishioners in the Rue de Bac, with whom he had been so happy. The Abbé had undertaken to help Thérèse care for the French prisoners of war, for whom she operated a hospital inside the palace. Together, she and the Abbé cared for the wounded, often diseased soldiers. Her uncle, King Louis XVIII, was against the whole idea and tried to dissuade her from her project.

"But uncle, they are my people! They are our people. It is not their fault that they were sent by the Corsican upstart, that Bonaparte, to be fodder for cannon. It is my sacred duty to care for them, and nothing can swerve me from my duty!"

The exhausting toil did not make her ill. Her dear Abbé, however, had contracted typhus from the soldiers. To him she owed her peace and sanity, and barely left his side during the days of his suffering. On that May morning he showed signs of coming out of his delirium, so she had sent for a priest to administer the Sacrament of Extreme Unction. Her uncle had not thought it prudent for her to nurse her beloved Abbé, since she was exposing herself to infection. Again, she was adamant.

"I shall never forsake my more than friend, the unalterable, disinterested friend of my family, who has left kindred and his country— all! All for us! Nothing shall withhold my personal attendance on my dear Abbé. I ask no one to accompany me!" The Abbé was truly more like a father than a friend, not only to Thérèse, but to all of the *émigrés*. He had followed them all the way to the borders of the Russian empire, to the Baltic town where it seemed that spring never came except as an afterthought. The climate was alien to them all; the conditions, bleak— there is nothing colder than a drafty, poorly heated, unfurnished palace. Thérèse often recalled how once as a small girl at Versailles she had said to her father's honored guest, the Tsarevitch Paul: "Someday, I shall come and see you!" Now he was the Tsar, the mercurial, temperamental master of a vast empire, but he remembered with fondness the little princess who had sat on his lap at Trianon. He granted asylum to her motley assortment of relatives and retainers, and sent her a diamond necklace as a wedding present.

Sometimes she reflected on how she had come to live in such a far away land, in a town inhabited mostly by wealthy Jewish and Protestant merchants. It had been a long journey, with happiness eluding her wherever she went, particularly in Vienna. There, she was considered too mournful and too French. What irony! Her mother, as a girl, was too happy and Austrian to be accepted at Versailles. Not that her relatives had been unkind; they tried to divert her from her misery. Even her cousin the Emperor Francis had pushed her around the gardens of Schönbrunn in a little chair, but nothing could make her smile. Count Axel von Fersen, her parents' friend, who had organized their ill-fated escape attempt in June 1791, came to Vienna to visit her. Thérèse's relatives would not permit her to receive him; the old gossip about the Count and her mother followed her everywhere.

In his letters to Thérèse, it was obvious that he admired her mother with an undying devotion, as did many romantic and idealistic gentlemen. "My dear Princess," he wrote to her, after she had passed him one day after Mass in the Palace Chapel.

> It was an honor for me to glance, even briefly, the noble daughter of the most angelic, virtuous Queen who ever lived. Your august Mother was to me a vision of unearthly beauty, radiating joy, and a pristine delight in the art of living. With her great purity of mind and soul, with so generous a heart, she was too wonderful for this world. Never was there a Queen like her, nor will there ever be again. His Majesty, your father, was likewise a sovereign of whom the world was not worthy, who died to defend freedom of conscience from an unnatural form of government, which seeks to control men's minds and hearts. I pledge to you, their child, my undying friendship, and if ever you are in need, you have but to send for your most faithful and loyal servant,
>
> Axel von Fersen.

His chivalry heartened her, and she knew she could always rely on him, as had her mother and father.

Meanwhile, the Viennese were captivated by her tragic story, as were others. The Emperor's handsome brother, Archduke Karl von Habsburg, was enchanted by the slender princess, with her hauntingly bittersweet gaze. He had met her in the gardens of Schönbrunn, running with her spaniel. They began to go riding together, and walking, stopping in some secluded bower to read aloud and converse. Everyone whispered of a coming betrothal. Smiles began to illumine the pale princess' face, and she truly looked like the daughter of Marie-Antoinette. Thérèse's cousin, the Emperor, had other plans for Karl, however, and forbade him to enter into an engagement with a dowerless, destitute orphan. When Karl's betrothal to another princess was announced, Thérèse was driven to the brink of despair. She was saved from doing violence to herself by Cléry, her father's faithful valet, who had also come to Vienna. The presence of someone who had such a close connection with her Papa was like a ray of light to the broken girl, and she found the strength to go on.

Letters began coming from her Uncle Provence, the putative, Louis XVIII, and her cousin the Duc d'Angoulême, begging her to join them at Mitau. Her uncle the King wanted her to marry Angoulême, with whom she had played at Trianon. In the spring of 1799, she traveled from Austria to the Baltic states. She was warmly received by her corpulent uncle, whose gout was so bad he was sometimes unable to walk.

She threw herself into his arms, exclaiming, "At last, I am happy! At last, I see you again! Watch over me! Be a father to me! O, Sire, my uncle!"

He embraced her cheeks with many tears. His life's ambition had finally been fulfilled: he was the King. His only obstacle was that he had to regain his kingdom. He had wasted no time in cementing ties with the foreign powers, who could now see clearly what a threat Napoleon and the Revolution were to their own thrones. He had maintained a correspondence with Napoleon himself, before the latter decided to put the crown on his usurper's head.

Her cousin and husband-to-be, Louis-Antoine, Duc d'Angoulême, next came forward to meet her. He was short, thin, and monkey-like. She tried not to let the disappointment show on her face. He so resembled his mother, the hairy, cross-eyed, Comtesse d'Artois, but his gentle manners were the same as when he was a boy. He wept over her hand, so happy was he to see her. Her uncle's wife, the former Comtesse de Provence, now Queen Marie-Joséphine, was also present to meet her. Her nose was redder than ever; she was fat, sullen, and given to excessive drink. She was dominated by one of her ladies-in-waiting, with whom she fought like a cat, but refused to be parted. The Queen and her friend lived in a separate establishment from the King, but he commanded Marie-Josephine to be present at Thérèse's wedding. When the King refused to receive his wife's domineering friend, he and the Queen had an argument on the steps of the entrance of the palace at Mitau, the latter screaming and lapsing into hysterics in front of the entire court and passers-by.

"Madame, what will the Tsar think of us?" said the King. Thérèse knew what she thought, after hearing of the incident. Her mother would never have behaved in such a manner, especially not in public. Nothing had kept Marie-Antoinette from being at her husband's side and supporting him. Both of her Savoyard aunts had left their husbands after their world fell to pieces. The Comtesse d'Artois had gone to Germany, while her unfaithful husband Artois, lived in a castle in Scotland with his mistress. He would not be present at his son's nuptials, but sent Thérèse a bridal gown of Indian silk.

She and Angoulême were married in the Hall of Honor in the palace of Mitau in June 1799, where a makeshift altar was erected. The King gave his niece away. She wore the Tsar's necklace, and some of her mother's diamonds, which her crafty Uncle Provence had managed to acquire. The altar was decorated with palms, lilies, roses, and myrtle. Abbé Edgeworth said Mass, and Cardinal de Montmorency gave the nuptial blessing.

After the wedding, her uncle said to them: "My children, if the crown of France was of roses, I would give it to you, but as it is of thorns, I keep it for myself." Thérèse was not overly moved by her uncle's colorful gallantries, knowing that he desired the crown of France at any price, be it of thorns or of roses. But what he gave her as a wedding gift was worth more to her than all the crowns and diamonds in the world— her Papa's watch and his wedding band. Her tears flowed over the ring that a shy young prince had once slipped onto the finger of a nervous princess on a spring day in a golden chapel almost thirty-five years ago. She felt her father's blessing come upon her as she received his ring, and never ceased to kiss it as a most precious relic. The ring, with her mother's initials M.A.A.A. inscribed inside, symbolized to her a bond of fidelity that had been broken only by death.

Her own marriage was overflowing with disappointments. It was pleasant to have a companion, someone with whom to share her lonely life. But she soon discovered that Louis-Antoine could never really be more to her than a brother and, because of certain impediments, they would never be able to have children. She had not expected happiness, but she did want to be a mother. Crushed by humiliation, her husband went to Italy to fight Napoleon, where he proved himself a brave and able soldier. Thérèse was left with her sick, conniving uncle, her deranged aunt, who soon went off to Germany again with her lady friend, and a handful of discouraged, impoverished courtiers. She was compelled to sell most of her mother's jewelry in order to buy food, pay debts, and maintain the court. Had it not been for Abbé Edgeworth, she would have sunk into the mires of discouragement.

Forever engraved on her memory was her first private interview with the Abbé, when she arrived at Mitau from Vienna. She besought him to give her his account of her Papa's martyrdom, which he did with all the honesty and eloquence of his Irish nature. At the conclusion of his story, he said, "Madame, mine is the honor to have been the spiritual confidante of two great souls—your father, the King, and your aunt, Madame Elisabeth. I cannot betray my sacred ministry and reveal the details of my conversations with them, but I can tell Your Highness this: both of them had died to this world long before they were brought to the scaffold."

"And my mother, too," said Thérèse, huskily. She was haunted by the cries of her mother on the hideous night when Charles was removed from them. The Abbé's account of her father's demise caused her interior dam of emotions to shudder; all the tears she had been unable to shed in prison began to be slowly released. A trembling came over her, and an unidentifiable feeling that was too powerful to be called grief.

The Abbé was regarding her with vigilant concern, and said calmly: "It was given to your mother the Queen to emulate Our Lady of Dolors at the foot of the Cross. Our Lady was made to witness the suffering and indignities heaped upon her son, who was King, but degraded beyond recognition."

"Monsieur l'Abbé," asked Thérèse, "why, why was my life spared? Why could not I have died with my family?"

"My child," the priest quietly replied, "the Sacred Heart of Jesus has been greatly offended. The innumerable sacrileges and blasphemies, along with the shedding of an ocean of innocent blood, all cry out to Heaven for atonement. Our Lord begs faithful souls to be willing to make reparation. Your parents and aunt made reparation by dying. You, my princess, are asked to make reparation by living. Entrust yourself, your pain, your fears, your bitterness, everything to the Wound in the Sacred Heart."

"Yes, father. But my brother, my poor little brother, how he suffered! I cannot endure to think of it. And where is he now? Is he truly dead? Or is he alive and abandoned somewhere? What is happening to him? Why should an innocent suffer so? I do not know!"

"Have you meditated, my child, on the passion of the Christ Child?"

"No, father, I have not."

"Remember that the Agony of Christ did not begin in Gethsemane, in the 'olive-press'. There, the agony only reached its climax. The unspeakable anguish of the Heart of Jesus began at the moment of His Incarnation. As a babe in the womb he was atoning for the sins of mankind. As God, He was sustaining all creation. In His omniscience He saw all the sins that ever had been or ever would be. In His infinite holiness He suffered from the very presence of evil in the world. His Infant Heart endured a thousand martyrdoms. And His future sorrows were ever before Him. Mystically, He bore the marks of His Passion even while carried in the pure and gentle arms of the Virgin. In the midst of His sufferings, He remained Christ the King, begotten before all ages. Your brother was a reflection of Christ the Child-King. Like the innocent Savior's, the Lamb of God, he was called upon to endure torments beyond his age for the sake of the kingdom he represented. The boy-king descended into the olive-press of tribulation just as France sank into her own Gethsemane. Like France, he was forced to lose his identity, even as France has lost her identity as eldest daughter of the Church. Like the Holy Innocents of old, a little child was offered as an expiation for the infidelity of his elders in the most unspeakable ways. And if Louis-Charles, that is, young Louis XVII, is alive somewhere on earth, he is still making amends for France, but because he is unknown and hidden, he is not any less the King, even as the Christ Child in the squalid stable or in the carpenter's shop, was nonetheless King of the Jews. As Our Lord said to Pilate, all power is given from above, and the realm of France belongs to Louis-Charles de Bourbon, if he be yet among the living, whether or not France acknowledges him as such. All the Bonapartes in the world cannot alter the inheritance of the heirs of St. Louis, even as the Herods could not alter the Davidic lineage and inheritance of St. Joseph, who was the heir and Son of David in the midst of poverty and obscurity."

"But my father, if he lives, I must find him. It is my duty, although I fear that even if he survived his tortures, his mind might be so unbalanced, he could never shoulder the responsibilities of a sovereign." Her face was now wet.

"You will search for your brother, my princess, because it is your duty to explore this mystery. Perhaps you will find him, but perhaps you are not meant to. There is a deeper drama of atonement, a most profound immolation, being wrought in the tragedy of Louis XVII, more than what you or I can fathom or comprehend."

The dam of pain burst at last in the depths of Thérèse's soul. She sank to the ground before the priest, and buried her face in her skirts. Her body shook with the unwept sorrow of years, rising up like a deluge, as she groaned for the family she had lost. The Abbé fingered his beads, looking upon her with deep compassion, with the understanding that her salve-like tears would bring healing to her torn being.

When the flood was almost spent, he took her hand, saying, "My princess, as you have participated in the piercing of the Heart of Christ, and of His Mother's Immaculate Heart, by enduring the loss of your loved ones, I will pray with all my being that the Sacred Heart will be for you a source of peace, that you will draw waters with joy out of the fountains of the Savior and be able to say with the white-robed army of martyrs: 'the Lord if my strength, and my praise, and He is become my salvation.'"

"Monsieur l'Abbé," said Thérèse, her voice even hoarser from weeping, "I will never know true happiness again. Something in me has died, or been frozen, I do not know which."

"My child, I do not mean earthly happiness. The peace and celestial happiness that the world cannot give, but by which the saints have overcome the power of evil, these can and will be yours, if you cling to Your Saviour, and to His Mother."

Thérèse took him at his word, and as the years passed, and disappointments increased, she grew in serenity and resignation, even if the ocean of her bitterness was not entirely dried up. Under the Abbé's spiritual direction, she was able to painfully reconcile her inner conflicts by placing herself in the role of the myrrh-bearing women, going to the sepulcher in the darkness of the Paschal morn, to a tomb, a place of hopelessness, with the bitter perfume of suffering and mortification, knowing in the night of Faith that there was a dawn beyond the edge of human foresight, veiled by the purple of the horizon.

In the meantime, news came from France, drifting to Mitau like ice floes on the Baltic. Madame de Polignac, her former governess, had died shortly after Marie-Antoinette's execution. Madame Campan, the late Queen's *femme de chambre*, had opened a boarding school in France where she taught the daughters of revolutionaries how to behave like aristocratic ladies. From afar, Thérèse watched the rise of Robespierre's friend Napoléon Bonaparte, a former Jacobin, who rapidly rose to power after firing grapeshot upon a crowd of poor peasants rebelling against the Revolution. To gain respectability, he married a beautiful noblewoman, the Vicomtesse de Beauharnais, who had miraculously escaped the guillotine. He turned the war into one of conquest for France; the liberals of all the nations ran after him as after a new Prometheus. Bonaparte became in himself an embodiment of the Nation, and was worshipped as such like the pagan Caesars of antiquity. While forcing the Pope to witness his coronation of himself as Emperor of the French, he mandated that French school children memorize a catechism about their glorious new dictator. After humiliating the Pope, he tried to bring the Church to her knees, in spite of the concordat he had made with Rome. By conquering most of Europe, he spread the ideas of the Revolution, symbolized by himself, the tyrant of the tyrannical new secular order, in which the state was supreme, its dictates holding precedence over the commands of God.

In Thérèse's mind, it was all very different from the principle of traditional monarchy, in which the King held his authority from God and the Church, ruling in the name of Christ the King, Whose representative in the temporal order he was. Not that there had always been good kings; many of her ancestors had been corrupt, but the system had worked for over a thousand years. Would the new constitutional system last as long? Already the former Jacobin, now Emperor, was desperately trying to prove his royal lineage, but could do no better than trace his descent from lower nobility in the south of Italy. He created a class of *nouveau-riche* aristocrats, giving his family and friends titles and privileges to rival any of the *ancien régime*. Presently, there were whispers that he planned to divorce the Empress Joséphine, and attempt to marry into an authentic royal family, the Habsburgs perhaps. Then he would taste a full and proud victory. It only confirmed Thérèse's belief that Bonaparte and revolutionaries like him were really nothing but the most voracious social climbers. His plans for personal glory meant the deaths of thousands of young Frenchmen, sent all over Europe to fight his wars. It was those pathetic innocents, wounded and imprisoned, that Thérèse and the Abbé cared for in her little hospital at Mitau.

"Monsieur l'Abbé," she said one day, during the course of their labors. "How harshly history has judged my poor Papa, who is labeled weak and inept, although he governed France well during the fifteen years which preceded the Revolution. His reforms were extensive, to the great benefit of the people's conditions. There is documented proof of his labors on behalf of the French, unless, of course, the Jacobins burned all the records of my father's reign. Yet, he, who was a man of peace, who avoided needless strife, but was victorious when he did choose to wage war against the English for the sake of the Americans, is portrayed in an unfavorable light compared to Bonaparte, a man of strife, by whose hand thousands have already perished in useless wars of conquest. He is a tyrant and usurper, abrogating for himself authority the like of which few French kings ever aspired. Will Bonaparte rule as long and as meritoriously as my father did, before he brings upon his head the destruction he is sowing by such devastating warfare?"

"My child," said the Abbé, whose high, receding hairline showed a cold perspiration, "we must not view such happenings as the world does, but as God does. Throughout his life, your father offered everything he did and everything he suffered to God, Who is the only one able to see the supernatural merit of his deeds. Whether or not his political decisions were exteriorly successes or failures is not what matters to God, Who searches the recesses of every heart. Your father died for his Catholic faith; in doing so he won the ultimate victory, and the only true success. Even the Holy Father in Rome has proclaimed that canonically Louis XVI can be considered a martyr. Let us pray that Bonaparte, in the midst of his earthly splendor, is converted, and acquires the grandeur of soul that King Louis XVI possessed as he went to his death, amid the shadows of worldly scorn and ignominy. If he resembles your father in his last hour, then Napoleon will truly be a great man. For it is the hour of death that matters the most."

Shortly afterwards, in the spring of 1807, the Abbé fell ill and Thérèse never left his side. On Friday, May 22, Thérèse saw that the end was near, and she sent for a priest. The Abbé's eyes opened. He looked at her and smiled faintly.

"It is the end, my child?"

"Yes, my father," replied the princess. From the corridor came the ringing of a bell, heralding the approach of the Blessed Sacrament. A priest entered, carrying the pyx, accompanied by a server with the holy oils and the Ritual. A footman followed with a burning candle. Thérèse and the others left as the Abbé made his confession. Then she returned with a lighted taper, and knelt while her dying friend was anointed and received his Holy Viaticum with an expression of devotion. Thérèse was awed at the Mercy of the Good God, Who had not failed to come to His faithful servant in the hour of need, as that same servant had risked his life to come to her Papa in his hour of trial. Then the priest began the *Proficiscere*, the prayers for the dying. Thérèse followed the beautiful Latin words in the French translation in her missal.

"Go forth, O Christian soul, out of this world, in the Name of God the Father almighty, Who created you; in the Name of Jesus Christ, the Son of the living God, Who suffered for you; in the Name of the Holy Ghost, Who sanctified you, in the name of the holy and glorious Mary, Virgin and Mother of God; in the name of the angels, archangels, thrones and dominions, cherubim and seraphim; in the name of the patriarchs and prophets, of the holy apostles and evangelists, of the holy martyrs, confessors, monks and hermits, of the holy virgins, and of all the saints of God; may your place be this day in peace, and your abode in Holy Sion. Through Christ our Lord. Amen."

Thérèse offered the prayers for all of her loved ones who had gone before, from whom she had been separated at the hour of death, and a peace came over her as the sacred words drifted to Heaven.

"I commend you, dear Brother, to the almighty God, and consign you to the care of Him, whose creature you are, that, when you shall have paid the debt of all mankind by death, you may return to thy Maker, Who formed you from the dust of the earth. When, therefore, your soul shall depart from your body, may the resplendent multitude of the angels meet you: may the court of the apostles receive you: may the triumphant army of glorious martyrs come out to welcome you: may the splendid company of confessors clad in their white robes encompass you: may the choir of joyful virgins receive you: and may you meet with a blessed repose in the bosom of the patriarchs. May St. Joseph, the most sweet Patron of the dying, comfort you with a great hope. May Mary, the holy Mother of God, lovingly cast upon you her eyes of mercy. May Jesus Christ appear to you with a mild and joyful countenance, and appoint you a place among those who are to stand before Him for ever...."

As they prayed, Thérèse noticed that the death rattle in the Abbé's throat and chest was growing worse. His face had the pinched, skeletal semblance of those on the edge of eternity.

"Receive, Lord, Thy servant into the place of salvation, which he hopes to obtain through Thy mercy."

"Amen," the server responded.

"Deliver, Lord, the soul of Thy servant from all danger of Hell; and from all pain and tribulation."

"Amen."

The Abbé spoke. "My crucifix . . . !" Thérèse took his crucifix from the night stand, where she placed her candle. She sat by the Abbé's side, holding the crucifix before his eyes so he could see it. His already serene countenance reflected a deeper and profounder peace and joy. Thérèse saw he was moving closer to the possession of the reward of all his labors. He, too, had lost family, homeland, and wealth in his boyhood, for the sake of the True Faith. He had renounced even the call of his heart, working with the poor, to minister to jaded, depressed exiles. In his dying eyes fixed on the crucifix, she beheld a sublimity of the realization of the victory that was soon to be his, because it was the triumph of the Cross of Christ over this world. Her own heart filled with a light and she recaptured the supernatural joy she had experienced at Trianon, in the Temple of Love, when some celestial creature called to her from its golden dimensions, assuring her to trust always in the infinite love of the good God. For a moment, it was as if she were one with that distant ecstasy, which in some way had never ended for her, but was continuing, conquering the misery and horror of the intervening years. The priest reached the end of the litany.

"And as Thou didst deliver that blessed virgin and martyr, Saint Thecla, from three most cruel torments, so be pleased to deliver the soul of this Thy servant, and bring it to the participation of Thy Heavenly joys."

"Amen," said Thérèse. It was as if a shuttered window was opened for her, and she glimpsed a scene of springtime and enchantment. The brevity of life, the transience of the most poignant sorrows, the everlasting splendors of Heaven, truths she had always intellectually accepted, were absorbed into every fiber of her being.

"We commend to Thee, Lord, the soul of Thy servant Henri and we pray Thee, Lord Jesus Christ, the Savior of the world, that as in mercy to him Thou becamest man, so now Thou would be pleased to admit him to the bosom of Thy patriarchs....Let all the saints and elect of God, who

185

in this world have suffered torments in the name of Christ, intercede for him; that being freed from the prison of his body, he may be admitted into the glory of our Lord Jesus Christ, Who with Thee and the Holy Ghost, lives and reigns, world without end."

"Amen," sighed Thérèse. The Abbé's breathing had become more labored, but his eyes did not leave the crucifix which he weakly guided to his purple lips. Thérèse knew then that there is only one sadness in life: that of not being a saint, just as there is only one happiness: that of going to Heaven.

The priest began to chant the *Salve Regina*. "Hail Holy Queen, Mother of Mercy, our life, our sweetness, and our hope." Thérèse sang, too, in her raspy voice. At the words *"gementes et flentes"* tears trickled down her cheeks, tears of sweetness for the friend who was about to win his heavenly crown, when he left behind the valley of sorrow. The dregs of bitterness inside her were washed away. At the words *"O dulcis Virgo Maria,"* the Abbé echoed, "Jesus, Maria," and with a deep gasp breathed forth his soul. Thérèse gently closed his eyes, as she had the eyes of many a dying soldier, folding his limp fingers around his crucifix. She knelt again by the bed, as the words of the commendation for the departed encircled her.

"Come to his assistance, all you Saints of God: meet him, all you Angels of God: receiving his soul, offering it in the sight of the Most High. May Christ receive you, who hath called you, and may the Angels conduct you to Abraham's bosom. Receiving his soul and offering it in the sight of the Most High!"

Whatever further sorrow awaited her along the road of life, all things were passing, all were mere obstacles to be surmounted on the path to Heaven. As Abbé Edgeworth had often quoted for her from St. Paul: "We are pilgrims and strangers on the earth. We have not here a lasting city, but we seek one that is to come." The Abbé had followed her beloved ones to the Heavenly Jerusalem, where he was one with the others who watched over her, and would continue to do so, until her own pilgrimage had come to an end.

"Eternal rest grant unto him, O Lord, and may perpetual light shine upon him."

"Receive his soul, and present him to God the Most High."

She resolved to accept and suffer everything for the love of God. No trial was too great if it was the means by which she would win

Heaven, make reparation to the Sacred Heart, and save souls. The priest arrived at the *Oremus*.

"Let us pray. To Thee, Lord, we commend the soul of your servant Henri, that being dead to this world he may live to Thee: and whatever sins he has committed in this life through human frailty, do Thou in Thy most merciful goodness forgive. Through Christ our Lord."

"Amen." Thérèse rose to her feet. The icy winds shook the bleak, barren palace, ignoring the little room which had become an antechamber to Heaven, just as the world ignored and forgot the humble man who was now face to face with his God. As for Thérèse, she was only vaguely aware of her surroundings. In her heart, she had found her way home to Trianon, home to the garden of childhood peace and innocence. With the Abbé's help, she had finally slipped through the garden gate, the wounded Heart of the Savior. She had found an interior garden where she could live, regardless of the vicissitudes of life, and turmoil of events that swirled around her. Within her there danced again the serenity and joy she once possessed when as a little girl she had played so happily at Trianon.

Finis

14942978R00114

Made in the USA
San Bernardino, CA
18 September 2014